SHORTS FROM THE MIDLANDS

Edited by

SHEILA ASHWOOD

NEW FICTION

First published in 1992 by
NEW FICTION
4 Hythegate, Werrington
Peterborough,
PE4 7ZP

Printed in Great Britain by Forward Press.

Foreword

The advent of New Fiction signifies the expansion of what has traditionally been, a limited platform for writers of short stories. New Fiction aims to promote new short stories to the widest possible audience.

The *Shorts* collections represent the wealth of new talent in writing, and provide enjoyable, interesting and readable stories appealing to a diversity of tastes.

Intriguing and entertaining; from sharp character sketches to 'slice of life' situations, the stories have been selected because each one is *a good read*.

This collection of short stories is from the pens of the people of The Midlands. They are new stories, sweeping across the spectrums of style and subject to reflect the richness of character intrinsic to the region, today.

Sheila Ashwood
Editor.

Contents

A Roundabout Affair

by

John Kirkwood

It didn't seem right for the sun to be shining in a cemetery, not for her mood. It should have been a day of sleet with a biting wind, or snow or, at the very least, a dank, gloomy overcast day.

But it was perfect for photographing the grave, getting the headstone exactly in focus, even though she had to fight to stop her hands shaking.

She took three shots at different exposures to make sure she had it right, wound on the film, and stepped back in silent contemplation. Her overflowing memories were in contrast to the sparse words on the stone.

Marjorie June Miller. Born 1971, died 1990. Aged 19. RIP.

She crossed to her husband's grave, lying beside her daughter's, and went through the same procedure.

Robert John Miller. Born 1953, died 1990. Aged 37. RIP.

She sighed. And they *would* rest in peace, she thought. But there would be no peace for herself. Until...

She turned and strode briskly down the pathway to the gates of the cemetery, and turned right for the walk into town. What a waste. Two lives, one reaching its peak and the other hardly begun. A drunken driver, skewing her car at a traffic island and ramming two thirds of her family into oblivion. She was left with an eighteen-year-old son, memories, and bitterness.

The walk to the photographic shop took less than twenty minutes. She asked for express service, three prints of each exposure, said she would call back in an hour, and went to wait in the pub on the corner. She nibbled at a cheese sandwich without tasting it, sipped two large gins with tonic, and caressed her memories.

What a waste.

She dusted off the crumbs she had spilled, straightened her coat, and went back to the shop. The prints were ready, and she carefully extracted the best shot of each grave. 'Could you frame these for me?' she asked the assistant.

'Certainly, madam', the assistant said. 'Which frames would you like? We have a selection?'

1

'Oh, those ones there will do', she said as she pointed. 'I'll pick them up to-morrow, if that's all right.'

'Of course. If you'd just like to pay now...'

She paid and left, walked out of the shop and up the High Street to the Post Office. There she bought an envelope to fit the prints, slid in one of each grave, stuck a stamp on it, and addressed it.

Mrs Julie Browne, 31 Lime Tree Crescent.

The killing bitch.

'Is that you, mum?'

Her son, Robert junior. He was shouting from the kitchen. She sighed and shrugged off her coat, leaving her handbag on the telephone table. 'Of course it's me', she replied as she walked through. 'Since there's only you and me left in the house, and you know that you're here already, who else could it be?'

'Oh. I'll make some tea. You've been to the cemetery again, have you?'

'Yes.' She was abrupt. She knew Robert junior thought she spent too much time there, that she brooded too much. 'And I don't want tea. I'll get myself a drink.' She moved out into the living-room and poured herself a hefty gin.

Her son came in, and slumped in an armchair. 'Bit early?' he said.

She sipped her drink. 'Perhaps. Or a bit late. Depends how you look at it.'

Robert junior tensed his shoulders. 'Mum... look, I know you think I'm, well, nagging you, but...'

'Yes, Robert, you *are* nagging me. And I know you think we should forgive and forget. But that won't bring back Marjorie and your father.'

Robert sighed. 'I know it won't, Mum. But neither will you harassing Mrs Browne. Sending her photographs of Marjorie and Dad. Regularly. Standing outside her house every time she goes out in the car. Phoning her and asking sweetly if she managed to drive home safely. None of that...'

She sat bolt upright. 'Who told you I'm doing that?'

He shrugged. 'Well, they *do* live only two streets away. And Dorothy, Mrs Browne's daughter, is at college with me. It's unavoidable that we see quite a lot of each other.'

She slammed her drink on the coffee table. 'I don't want you seeing that girl!'

'Mum, I can't help it! We have the same classes, the same course. And it wasn't her fault, was it? And even the inquest said it wasn't Mrs Browne's fault, didn't it? The car's steering just went!'

'But she'd been drinking!'

'But she wasn't over the limit! It could have happened to anyone!'

2

'Perhaps, but it happened to my daughter and my husband, your sister and your father. And she got off scot free. That doesn't mean she won't suffer. Anyway, I forbid you to see that girl!'

He sighed again. 'Mum, as it happens, I'm seeing her quite a lot. We like each other quite a lot. Perhaps even more than quite a lot. And I'm seeing her tonight, at the pub. So, if you'll excuse me, I'll go and get changed.'

'Robert!' she screamed. But he was already bounding up the stairs.

It needed a few more gins for her to find the courage, but then she took a deep breath, lifted the telephone, and dialled. It seemed to take ages for it to be answered, and she almost hung up. Then: 'Hello?'

She took another deep breath. 'Mrs Browne?'

'Yes?'

'It's Mrs Miller here. You know...'

'Oh. Mrs Miller. I think I'm going to hang up now, Mrs Miller.'

'No! Wait. I mean... please. Look, I've been thinking, and I've been wrong. About many things.'

'Oh.'

'Well, maybe it's time to start again. I understand I might have taken things too far. And with your Dorothy and my Robert being friends, well...'

'Oh.'

'So I thought, maybe we could make it up. Robert and Dorothy have gone for a drink. Why don't we join them, and clear the air?'

'Well...'

'Oh, please. You don't know what it would meant to me. After all this time.'

'Well... all right. But I'll need to get changed.'

'Fine. So will I, actually. But... well, I don't like to ask, but... could you pick me up, give me a lift to the pub? Only, not having a car ourselves...'

'Well, if you don't mind, except, well, it's the same car. You know, we never changed it. That is...'

She smiled. 'That doesn't matter any more, Mrs Browne. I see your car almost every day. Let bygones be bygones, as they say.'

'Well... half an hour, then?'

'That would be lovely.' She smiled as she hung up, took the remaining shots of the graves from her handbag, and stroked them.

'Fetch us another drink, Robert', she said as she pulled a note from her handbag.

3

Mrs Browne shook her head. 'Not for me, Mrs Miller. I've already had three, and I've got to drive.'

Mrs Miller raised her hands. 'Oh, don't be a party-pooper, Mrs Browne. One more for the road. Just for *new* times' sake. We're burying more than memories tonight.'

Mrs Browne looked puzzled. 'Well... one more, Robert, then we'll leave you and Dorothy to get off to your concert.'

Robert raised his eyebrows. 'Mum?'

'Yes, fetch them in, Robert. Oh, and I'll have a word with you.'

She followed him to the bar, and clutched his shoulder. 'Robert - since it's the last round, make them large ones. We might as well enjoy ourselves.'

'Mum,? What are you up to?'

'Nothing. Burying the past. That's what you want, isn't it?'

'Yes, but...'

'Never mind. Get the drinks.'

She walked back to the table, slightly unsteadily, sat and smiled.

'Well, Mrs Browne, we'll have this one then leave these two youngsters to their own devices, I think.'

Mrs Browne looked at the drink as Robert junior put it in front of her. 'Yes, I think that would be best. I'll give you a lift home, Mrs Miller.'

Mrs Miller drained her drink in one gulp. 'Actually, I think I'd rather walk, if you don't mind. I feel a little tiddley, and the fresh air will do me good.' She stood up. 'In fact, I think I'll go now. It's been good to clear the air, Mrs Browne. I'm glad we sorted this out.'

She collected her coat and handbag, and said: 'Thanks for the lift, Mrs Browne. I hope it won't be too long before we meet again.'

It took her three minutes to walk to the roundabout where two thirds of her family had been wiped out, and she strode determinedly to the centre of it, savouring the night air and the anticipation of re-unification. She breathed deeply as she waited.

It was, she thought, a good plan and a justification. Mrs Browne had been drinking. She was driving. She had got away with it once, but not this time. And she was ready to rejoin her lost loves.

It wasn't a long wait. She saw the car, the car that had killed her husband and daughter, in plenty of time. As it approached, she gathered her courage and conviction and launched herself under its wheels as it hit the curve of the roundabout.

The car swerved madly, striking her a glancing blow on the hip before the back wheel rolled over her leg. She rolled into the opposite gutter as she watched Mrs Browne wrestle with the wheel before the car overturned and slammed sideways into a road sign.

The pain was intense, but she was amazed at being alive and didn't know whether to be grateful or disappointed. At least the killing bitch won't get away with it this time, she thought.

Then she saw Robert junior's head, bleeding and lolling from the rear window.

The Cycle

by

Catherine Lewis

It started in Spring. Some awakening that she believed he felt as strongly as she. When she touched his hand, she convinced herself that he too felt the vibes of life rushing from one to the other. Convincing herself was so easy. She had spent so much of her leisure time reading the romantic novels that appeared on the library shelves. Romantic novel after romantic novel and every word became a truth, lingering at the back of her mind and bursting to the forefront of her imagination at every opportunity. And so it was when she met him.

Spring afternoons and casual walks through the meadow, the untamed daffodils thrusting their way up through the ground, their heads exploding into clouds of yellow, and all she could see was magic.

'Just like us,' she murmured.

He did not understand. How could he? His intelligence was wrapped around scientific equations and allegorical allusions meant nothing to him. But he found her enchanting. Lightly he touched her chin and her eyes lifted up to his. They were so full of unexpected joy and he did not have the heart to tell her the truth.

'Don't you think they're just like us?,' she repeated. 'All through the Winter, lying dormant under the ground, always there, but not seen, just waiting for the right moment, and then into full bloom. Just like us.' She was content and so did not feel his premature unease. He himself was unaware of it, but it was there, lying dormant, waiting.

She was a singer, or so her mother's aspirations led her to believe. Sometimes, once she had overcome her initial shyness, she would sing to him. Her mother had insisted and he had listened. Her voice was pretty, nothing more, and yet her mother sat entranced, living every note as though it were her own. He had thought to comment. He had heard that singing was a difficult career to follow. You had to have a brilliant voice, not just a pretty voice, but he held his tongue, not wanting that cute face to dissolve into tears.

It was Summer. The daffodils had died giving way to a greater variety of flowers in the meadow and her garden was full of roses. Her mother's pride and

6

joy, which she tended with almost the same affection she tended her daughter Her husband, the family breadwinner, sat shut away, called upon only to sign the necessary cheques.

There was a stillness in the air. The heat was stifling, forcing them into a motionless embrace in the garden, alone with the overpowering scent of her mother's roses.

'Gorgeous', she whispered. 'So romantic.'

He murmured a non-committal response, thinking of paralysed physics and mathematics revision. He too had his own aspirations. University, a science course, utilising his analytical mind to the full, perhaps research afterwards. Something useful for mankind. He saw it as his purpose in life. Yet with her, he was incapable of moving. She had only to look at him and revision was left undone in preference to her.

Exams were fast approaching, but only for him. At a family conference attended only by her mother, it had been decided that she should leave school at the earliest opportunity and concentrate on her singing career. That meant no academic exams. She was delighted. No immediate work to do and she refused to let him go away and do his. In the heat of that Summer and the drugged scent of the roses, he was incapable of leaving.

The exams came. He looked at the first examination paper and could not make sense of a single question. In the middle of a whole hall full of other students, he broke down and cried.

Immediately she was there to comfort him, seeing his tears as the ultimate sacrifice to her. Of course, a failure meant another year before he could go away to university. Another year in which he could listen to her singing. They could watch the approach of Autumn together.

The same meadow, but with the Summer leaves disintegrating beneath their feet.

'My favourite season', she breathed, then let go of his hand to dance through the trees. When she returned, her cheeks were rosy and poetry was on her lips. Someone else's poetry. 'Season of mists and mellow fruitfulness...' She stopped, seeing a strange look across his face. A look of estrangement, as though he suddenly didn't recognise her, or even himself. Anxiously, she seized both his hands and pressed them to her lips. Briefly she felt his fingers quiver, then calming as she kissed them until he was himself again, drawing her close while she contemplated maturity and years into the future, her future, his future, their

7

future. As though reading her mind, the same expression of estrangement crept back across his face. Only this time it did not go away.

The gentle wind of Autumn was growing chill. He felt the cold more than she and begged that they go indoors.

'Yes, let's go inside', she said, 'and I will sing to you.'

He begged her not to sing. He wanted to be alone with his thoughts, without the intrusion of her voice. He heard her sing that evening, but it was for the last time.

The first snows began to fall, freezing the ground. He now refused to listen to the voice that had teased him away from his own purpose in life. Resitting for exams was no fun and he realised that her demands on him were a sign of her misunderstanding. And it was also his own deception. He had misunderstood himself and now he needed someone to blame.

That day, the snow seemed to muffle their responses as they trudged through the meadow. Desperately she tried to rekindle their past happiness.

'Just think of the daffodils', she was saying. 'They've gone back to being bulbs in the ground, just waiting. Do you remember last year when they were flowering?'

He could feel the chill of Winter creeping through his body. And he too was thinking of the daffodils. The seeds of discontent. They had also been waiting. Underneath the surface and he had not seen them, but now Winter's flowers were in full bloom.

Their hands were still touching, but for the first time she felt the throb of his misery. Suddenly, she pulled away from him and their eyes met. His were cold and distant. She shed a tear for him and fleetingly he lifted a finger to wipe it away. It was hot but he could feel no warmth.

Something touched her heart, another tear fell, and it was she who turned away.

Mornings at the Manor

by

Margaret Chatham

Edith had got the early bus home from work that day - so she was in time to listen to the food programme on the wireless.

The man who introduced the programme gave out a number for anyone to call with queries and Edith, feeling it was time someone listened to her, took the number - and after waiting ten minutes to make sure it was that nice-voiced food expert she enjoyed listening to - stationed herself by the telephone, hoping to get through in the next half hour.

At the third time of dialling, a voice announced, 'You are through. Tell me your name and your query. You are on the air.'

Gosh, Edith thought, this is the most famous I've ever been and went ahead. 'Sir', she said, 'I don't like this North Sea Gas - it makes everything taste salty, especially the bacon, and I'm not supposed to have salt because of my blood pressure. I don't like electric so can my stove be converted to Calor Gas.'

There came a smothered snort from the other end of the line; then the gentleman expert answered firmly that the gas might come from the sea but brought no salt with it.

'But I don't use salt on anything and I always buy sweet-cured bacon,' Edith said.

'Change your retailer', came the suggestion from the announcer, then, 'Thank you madam. Next query,' and the 'phone went dead.

Edith was very disappointed; she felt that she hadn't been taken seriously or helped at all.

All these modern methods, everything wrapped in hard-to-open packs - nothing tasted natural any more like in her childhood days. She could just remember the family keeping their own pigs. Each time one was killed half went to the government - the other half they were allowed to keep. It tasted good. Some would be bartered with neighbours for a bit of extra sugar or tea, or their home bottled fruit, when things were still on ration years after the war finished.

Well, it's no good dwelling on those days. It's all long past now, I must think up something to help myself thought Edith.

As usual next morning, which was fine and frosty, Edith arrived at Highdale Manor promptly at seven o'clock. She was their only cleaning lady and worked every day until noon, it was a very trusted job and Edith having been a widow for over ten years now, quite enjoyed her cleaning and polishing in such beautiful surroundings. The night security man, Bob, left at eight o'clock and the other one came mid-day. Afternoon staff arrived later as the Manor was open to the public from two until five daily. Being close on five hundred years old it was of great historical interest.

Bob was a decent fellow and usually had a brew-up waiting for Edith when she arrived, since it was a good steep walk from the bus stop. But it wasn't like cleaning up for ordinary people. She and Bob were devoted to the place and its past.

Tea poured, Bob said, 'I saw the grey lady again last night. Ever so plain she was, sort of sailed through the long gallery about midnight with that mantle-thing on her head.'

'Ooh how lovely', said Edith. 'I like her. She's so graceful and they say she did ever such a lot of good. Sad she went so young - only thirty-two it says in the book.'

'Yeah, I read it,' said Bob. 'I'm on to travel books and autobiographies now. I can't read murder and mystery stories at night while I'm here - it's a bit too creepy.'

'Did you get a bit of shut eye?' asked Edith.

'Not a wink - I'm going to turn in for an hour now you're here, though. I'll be able to drop off ok now I'm not alone in the place. You wouldn't like to come in half an hour earlier would you, old girl?'

Now Edith had a soft spot for Bob and his suggestion was helpful to her own newly thought-up bright idea. Now was the time for confidences.

Bob poured them a second cup of piping hot tea to which he added two spoonfuls of brandy from his every-handy pocket flask.

'If I catch the first bus, I can be here at six-fifteen every morning except Sunday', said Edith, "but in return I want you to have a bit of fire in that range, enough for us to get that griddle hot and cook us both a jolly good breakfast. I'll bring the stuff. You can pay half. I'll bet you're as sick of sandwiches as I am.'

'Hmm, who cleans the grate out and keeps the griddle clean?'

'Why you of course', said Edith. 'In return for my cooking - and mind, it'll have to be done properly every day, no traces left.'

'Right, we start on Monday. It's a deal,' said Bob.

When Edith went shopping on Saturday she felt like it was her birthday. She bought lots of groceries and treated herself to a new headscarf, a large rain-hat and some fur-lined boots which were half-price as it was the end of the season. Then she went all rash and bought Bob a half bottle of brandy. He was a good sort. She was glad not to have to come in contact much with his opposite number. A tall thin fellow who was always ultra tidy and marched about as though he owned the place. Kind of snooty he was. She would have to keep her eye on him.

Monday morning was a bit damp, but Edith's spirits were soaring and her rain-hat was a great success. The kitchen was warm and welcoming with the fire glowing in the antique grate, the griddle moved to the hearth and well washed. But where was Bob? There was no sign of him.

Edith disposed of her outer garments and put eggs, bacon, sausages and tomatoes ready. The kettle was hot. She went to look for Bob and found he wasn't in the office.

Thoughtfully she looked towards the beautiful oak staircase. It was her favourite bit of the building, long dead carvers had embellished it with horses, lions, tiger and even unicorns, which she polished regularly and lovingly. Taking herself up the stairs, Edith looked into the Blue Room, the one where Heneritta had lain waiting for Charles. Yes, there was Bob, taking his ease. He opened his eyes on hearing her exclaim.

'I'm sorry Edith,' he said yawning. 'Gosh, I'm ready for that breakfast. Is it on?'

'Yes, you old skiver, and get yourself off that bedspread. Put the dust sheet on next time', said Edith, then, 'Thank you for the fire Bob. Here, this is a thankyou present.'

A smile spread over Bob's face. He hadn't received many gifts in his life. Edith may be a bit dim at times but she was a good comfortable woman and a worker too, she had always treated him well. 'Why, thanks love,' he said 'That's mighty civil of you' and he took her arm as though she was the lady of the Manor and led her down to the kitchen, then watched happily as she coaxed their breakfast on the griddle over the glowing grate.

'I'll bring in just enough smokeless fuel with me every night', said Bob.

Breakfast was delicious; they sat back replete.

'I'm not kidding,' said Bob, 'that must be the best meal I've ever had.'

'Yes,' replied Edith, 'and it wasn't a bit salty. The old ways are the best ways. I'll bet we shall both feel more healthy and younger without all that north sea gas infiltrating into our systems.'

'What's all that about?' said Bob as he straightened up the kitchen.

'Why, old Mrs Thompson told me, her grand-daughter's a student of something or other and she said it's all the salt we are getting in this sea gas that's causing heart trouble and blood-pressure and lots of things these days.'

'Oh! Edith, you know, I think that's one of the remarks that you ought to take with a pinch of salt,' said Bob. 'Will that do now?' He looked round the tidy kitchen, all traces of the fire and their repast having been cleared away.

'Now I'm the butler and you are the housekeeper. Will you have this dance madam?' And they sedately waltzed round the kitchen table twice before they broke away. Bob to sign off and make for home which was a lonely apartment and Edith to pick up her dusters and polish.

And so the breakfasts went on, always delicious. Some mornings they were the footman and parlour-maid, and often they were the lord and lady of the Manor. The day they were Henrietta and Charles they ended up in the Blue Room and the cleaning up was done very late that morning.

Meantime visitors came and went and new ghosts left signs of being very active.

The upstairs guide said no matter how often she straightened the bedspread in the Blue Room it looked as if it was regularly used by a long gone inhabitant - even to a hollow in the mattress.

And the downstairs guide said that suddenly the place felt warmer and more lived in as though a happier ghost had come back to supervise the kitchen. How nice the cleaning lady always left the place - so spick and span. An old silver vase had appeared on the table and every day there was on fresh flower in it.

Godiva - The Bare Facts

by

Maurice Rattigan

Godiva - The Bare Facts
The News In Buff
by your ace reporter.

The whole town has been at fever pitch the past few days as rumour spread through the alley-ways and ale houses; and that rumour was confirmed this morning with a statement from the Castle by Earl Leofric.

He decreed, on pain of severe retribution, that today, all burghers should remain in their homes and away from their windows between the hours of noon and two in the afternoon.

This brief warning confirmed the story that had set the whole town agog. The Earl's wife, the Lady Godiva, Countess of Coventry and Duchess of Spon End, intended to ride naked through the cobbled streets in protest at the Earl's unjust taxation.

This proposed protest did not surprise the good burghers for Lady Godiva had always been champion of the common people for once she been quite common herself.

Fifty years ago, as a beautiful slim nineteen year old blonde, the Earl had spotted her at a public witch-dunking at the Swanswell Pool and had summoned her to his Castle.

Two months later they were wed but little did Leofric know he was marrying a female militant.

At eighteen she had become the youngest shop-steward ever employed at Baron Smithfield's pickled onion factory in Little Much Cox Street and had shed many a tear over her fellow wenches' poor working conditions.

Yes, the townspeople knew and loved Godiva, and it was whispered that at the Coventry Cross ale house where she had worked as a part time serving wench before her marriage, many customers knew and loved her a helluva lot more than the Earl would have cared to have known.

But that was over fifty years ago and time had taken it's toll on the once slim figure of that beautiful nineteen year old.

Hence the decree of the Earl who did not wish anyone to see naked, what he now called, his ton of lard and dripping.

As noon approached, from my vantage point at a first floor window of 'Ye Coventry Clarion' in Cross Cheaping, I saw the good citizens scurrying back and forth intent on being safely home indoors by the appointed hour.

I had chosen my vantage point well in order to bring to you, my readers, (and to the nationwide readers of 'Ye Daily Sun' for whom I do some occasional freelance work), a graphic account of this historical ride.

The Broad Gate of the Castle is out of my view as I look towards Ironmonger Row and to my left stretches The Burges and Bishop Street.

The position of the sun indicates it is now noon. The streets below are deserted. It is like a flag day in Aberdeen.

My quills are sharpened in anticipation of a good story. In the eerie silence I imagine I can hear horse's hoofs on the cobbled street in the direction of the Castle's Broad Gate. My hearing has not deceived me and the laboured steps of her trusty steed are getting louder and louder and suddenly I get a glimpse of the bent head of the poor white beast as it slowly appears around the corner from Ironmonger Row. As it emerged into full view I get my first sight of Lady Godiva, her long grey hair trying vainly to cover her amply proportions.

Suddenly the valiant horse stumbled and the Countess's tresses parted to expose a large, drooping, bouncy, wholesome bus...

Editor's Note

At this point, the narrative of our ace reporter, Thomas Peeping, stopped abruptly for he was suddenly and inexplicably struck blind and was unable to continue with his graphic description of the historic event.

As readers now know, thanks to his wife's momentous ride, Earl Leofric later scrapped his plan to tax lard and dripping.

Unfortunately, Neddy, the Earl's trusty steed, had to be put down.

A Twist of Fate

by

Sheila J Hodgkins

Harry Edwards trudged up the hill trying to forget his aching joints and short-ness of breath. He paused, going over in his mind the few items he needed for the day.

At seventy, he lived alone after the death of his beloved wife Mary in the house they first rented after their marriage. Things were easier then not much money but enough homes to go around and paying your rent was first on the list of priorities.

His family, a son and daughter, had stayed at home till they married but after Mary died the house was too big for him to manager and yet memories kept him there.

He believed in keeping fit and would walk up the hill to the village two or three times a week rather than catch the little bus that toured his estate. He was lucky, he thought. At least Penny came once a week to help him in the house and brought her latest grandchild Adam to see him. Adam was nearly two and Penny was his niece. His own children had emigrated years ago to Australia and though he had been asked to join them he decided to stay in England and near to his Mary, through memories.

Regaining his breath he carried on past that nice church who always seemed inviting people to come and have a cup of tea in their new centre. Harry wasn't much of a church-goer and stopped altogether when the little hut was pulled down. It was a Wesleyan church and he would go mainly to keep Mary com-pany but he sometimes missed the odd service at Christmas and Easter. How-ever when he passed this church on his way to the shops there always seemed to be people going and coming and he'd often thought of popping in just to see what went on.

He did his hopping and saw no-one he really knew to speak to except for the shop assistants and was on his way home when he slipped and fell. He was very shaken and this kind lady stopped and helped him up.

'Are you all right?' she asked.

'I will be in a moment.' said Harry, 'thank you for asking.'

'Why don't you come with me.' the lady said in broken English. 'I am going to have a cup of tea in the church hall near here.'

Harry really did feel quite poorly so he let her lead him into the hall.

Her name was Anna Palladeani an Italian. Her English was very limited but Harry learned she was alone in the world. Except for her voluntary work in the centre she had no friends. Anna made the hot drinks and sandwiches and everyone got a big smile and sometimes a hug and if she could not speak very well each person felt welcomed by her.

When he had recovered enough to walk home he thanked Anna and said perhaps he would call again.

On arriving home the house felt cold and unfriendly. He quickly turned on his gas fire and made another hot drink.

Sitting by the fire he got out his photograph album and began to live again in his memories. Mary and he loved taking photos and he always felt near to her as he turned the pages. A tear trickled down his face as she looked up at him with those big brown eyes from the photographs.

When he had finished the whole book he cried out, 'Oh Mary, how would you feel if I sought a woman's company ever again, today I have known a stranger's caring.'

Facing up to this reality and saying it out aloud was a release for Harry. He felt he wanted to live again and not to exist.

The very next day he went back to see Anna and each time he went to shop in the village he would call in at the centre.

They only ever met in the centre and he would help her when her English failed. He'd even helped her with the washing up.

In time he joined the pensioners' club and gave a talk on photography. Anna brought a new meaning into Harry's life even if she had a stormy temperament. She would fly off the handle breaking into Italian but it would be all over in two minutes and she would say with a hug, 'Sorry'.

He used to whistle now, even Penny had noticed the change in him and said so.

'Well Harry, it's nice to see you being involved in life again. You'll have to bring Anna to meet us.'

Harry had said, 'Now don't you go reading things into it that aren't there!' but really thought it was a good idea.

He had known Anna for six months now. Perhaps it was time to ask her out.

The next day he fairly ran up the hill towards the centre only to find himself very out of breath.

'Calm down, man!' he said to himself, 'you're not seventeen anymore.'

He jauntily stepped through the centre door only to find no Anna. Another lady was doing her job.

'I'm sorry, Harry,' she said, 'no-one has seen Anna today. It's not like her not to turn up and usually she rings if she's not well.'

Harry was concerned at hearing this and asked for Anna's address.

'Well Harry, I wouldn't give it to anyone but seeing it's you - she lives at 29a Pottersfield Avenue.'

'Well, really!' said Harry, 'that's only five minutes away from me.'

He took off straight away making for Pottersfield Avenue. When he arrived he saw that it was a ground floor council flat. There was a block of six, two high. He rang the bell. No reply.

He rang it twice more. Still no reply. This time he peeped through the ltter-box. There was Anna lying on the floor very still. He panicked. What should he do? He quickly rang the bell of number 29. Perhaps whoever lived there had a spare key.

A man around Harry's age came down the stairs. Harry asked him if he had a key but he said he had not. He too was upset at the thought of Anna in trouble. He said she had taken items for him from the postman but they were not friendly enough to exchange keys in times of emergency.

Harry asked the man to call the policy and ambulance which he went around the back to the kitchen and broke the glass in the back door. He soon got inside to where Anna lay. He tried to feel for a pulse by touching the side of her neck but the arthritis in the ends of his fingers made it impossible to be sure. He quickly took blankets off Anna's bed to keep her warm until the ambulance arrived.

It wasn't long in coming and Anna was alive but only just. She had fallen and knocked herself out and had a little hypothermia. Harry was very upset and travelled in the ambulance with Anna. She did not stir at all. He left the hospital only when told to and made his way back to Anna's flat. After all he would have to board up the door until the council could fix it.

When he arrived back at 29a, the other man had already started to do the job.

'Hello,' he said. 'How's Anna?'

'Nothing definite to say.' he said. 'By the way, my name's Harry,'

'And mine's Jim.'

Harry set to work beside Jim and soon the job was finished.

harry went into Jim's flat for a cup of tea. Between them they decided to do something nice for Anna for when she came home again.

Between them they started to decorate the place throughout. Harry visited the hospital almost every day but Anna was not herself. The bump on the head had left her confused. Into the bargain her English not being so good some of the nurses could not understand her. However, it was discovered that one night nurse Fabia had Italian parents and although English herself knew the language.

Harry would leave messages with Fabia and in turn Anna would send messages back.

She was in hospital for two weeks and was due to come home two days after Harry and Jim had finished the decorating. The flat looked lovely and Harry and Jim had grown quite close in working together. Jim told Harry he was a bachelor and had never had time for women looking after his elderly parents on their death he realized how lonely life was but had not the courage to do something about it.

Harry bought a large bunch of flowers. That Wednesday he had made up his mind to ask Anna out for a meal and maybe in time their relationship would grow into something more permanent. His talk with Jim had persuaded him he was not ready to stay alone without companionship anymore.

He put on his best suit and carried the flowers with pride as he entered the hospital. Anna was in a side ward so he went straight to the door and knocked on it. There was no reply. He opened the door and looked in to see an empty bed.

He did not know what to think, but Fabia came up behind him and took him on one side.

'Harry, I'm so sorry. Anna passed away during the night but not before she left this message for you.'

Harry couldn't believe her. 'But she was coming home in a day or two. She can't be dead!'

Fabia explained that she had had a relapse, the excitement of going home. Anna's message translated by Fabia said, 'My dear Harry, thank you so much for the last six months of companionship, the best time I have had since a child in Italy. I don't know why I am writing this since I feel so well and am excited to see the work you and Jim have done for me in my flat. However, I want you to know and also remember it's not always the quantity of life it's the quality. I hope you have been as happy as I, no matter what the future holds I will always be grateful to you.'

The message ended there as Fabia said she had fallen asleep never to wake up.

Harry shouted out in anguish. 'It's not bloody fair!' and let the tears fall.

He rang Jim who as also totally upset. Jim said to Harry. 'Don't go home. Come and stay with me until we are both feeling able to cope without her.'

Harry and Jim became firm friends sharing their sorrow and sorting out Anna's affairs. Jim suggested that Harry try and exchange his house for Anna's flat, after all the work they had done on it.

Harry had never wanted anything else than to live in his house of memories until now and after a time the council granted his wish.

Harry and Jim were together as friends for many years. They shared traumas and good times and always felt the presence of Anna keeping them together, until each in turn joined her in their permanent home.

Never underestimate a twist of fate.

Untamed Prejudice

by

David Massey

Leroy cast a critical glance at his reflection in the bedroom mirror, pulling himself up proudly, straightening his tie and brushing imaginary dust off his lapel. Allowing his mind to drift a little, he fought to hold back a sudden wave of anger and frustration that welled up inside as he remembered the events of the previous day. He shook his head - telling himself fiercely that today would be different, not allowing himself to be governed by thoughts of what could or should have been, but channelling his pain into a determination to be master of his own destiny...

Tomba fell to the floor, gritting his teeth, and fighting back a tear as the lash cut into the soft flesh of his back. Again and again it fell, but he refused to be cowed by the white barbarians - refused to gratify their bloodlust with a cry of submission. One month ago, he had been a prince in his own country, leader of a proud and warlike people with an oral history that plumbed the depths of time, but today he was just one more slave waiting to be sold.

'Who is he?' asked the barber-surgeon in awe.

'A bugger who's cost me two decent blokes', replied the trader breathlessly. He pulled himself straight, holding the small of his back, and gulped in the warm fetid air, out of condition and trying to catch his breath. Taking advantage of the lull in his punishment, Tomba climbed to his feet, tottering with the effort, blood tickling his back as it ran and congealed in the open wounds. 'He was a guerrilla leader who tried to stop us trading out east - curse his black hide. Set fire to some of our cottages he did, and killed a few of my associates, but we had the last laugh didn't we nigger?', the trader prodded Tomba's back with his stick causing him to gasp and stifle a cry. 'We came across him separated from his mates, and all alone. He put up one hell of a fight and killed two of my assistants...' - remembering suddenly how much his acquisition had cost him, the trader lashed out and kicked Tomba's legs from beneath him. He crashed heavily to the straw matting fighting desperately against unconsciousness, but was soon engulfed in darkness.

When he opened his eyes, at first he could not perceive any light at all and thought with rising panic that these savages had put out his eyes, but slowly, sight returned to him and his dim surroundings began to take shape. First he was hit by the heat and stench that blasted over him, and then by the raw pain of his back. He discovered that he was lying on his side and could feel the weight of a heavy iron shackle on his leg. Trying to sit up, he banged his head on a crossbeam and fell back heavily onto his arm. The indignity and injustice of Tomba's situation had not dulled his pride or anger - they merely served to hone it and give it purpose and direction. In that moment he decided to escape. The lap of water and gentle swaying indicated that he was on board some kind of boat, and from the heat and press of bodies all around him he knew that there must be hundreds in the same position.

'Brothers', he whispered loudly, '...we are more than they, who will escape with me and fling these savages into the sea?'

He was answered with groans and an overpowering sense of defeat.

'Who is with me?' he demanded again. Next to him he felt movement and a pull on his chain.

'I am with you', said his neighbour.

'And I...' a female voice. 'I have a hammer that one of the white devils lost...'

Tomba could hardly believe his luck. All they needed was leadership, and he did not doubt that wielding a weapon he could rally others to him as they saw his example - surely even death would be preferable to this? Holding the chain between them, Tomba and his neighbour crept towards the shafts of light that broke through the open hatch - left unguarded with the arrogant folly that characterised the white devils. Halfway up the steps he turned and shouted a battle cry, holding the hammer aloft.

'Now who is with me?'

Seeing his authority and bravery, the hold erupted with cries of support, but only three charged out under the open sky... Three sailors taken off their guard found themselves at the receiving end of Tomba's hammer - two died instantly, but the third raised the alarm, and from nowhere four others appeared, pinning the slaves against the guard-rail. Hampered as they were by chains, the slaves were quickly overpowered, the hammer pried too easily from Tomba's grasp and used against it's wielder.

'Keep that one', said the captain, coming up behind his men, 'he's valuable. We'll make an example of the others.'

The Bristol lay at anchor off the coast of Africa, creaking gently in the early morning silence, as captain Harding ordered the death of a nameless slave. Once the order was carried out, he had another slave eat the dead man's heart and liver. The woman was tied up by her thumbs in the sight of all, flogged and then slashed with knives until she died while Tomba, deep in the hold, vowed to himself that he would never submit - holding onto his pride as though it was a life-jacket that would save him from drowning in a sea of untamed prejudice.

Opening his front door, Leroy Tomba stepped out and breathed in the morning air, nervous now - as he was before any interview. Then, with a wry smile to himself, he glanced down at his watch and stepped out briskly in the direction of the bus-stop, hoping that this time his interviewers would see past the colour of his skin and judge him on his abilities.

Weep No More My Lady

by

Alton Douglas

Circuit Steinmayer, known to his friends for obvious reasons as Graham, drew himself up to his full height, looked the bottom drawer of the desk squarely in the keyhole and shrugged. With an air of practised nonchalance he clambered on to his chair, vaulting with ease from there on to a plank balanced across the armrests. He settled back, pausing only to remove a splinter from his sphincter. Now he made an impressive picture. Well, at least he could be seen over the blotter. He caught a glimpse of a nylon-clad leg, a whiff of expensive French perfume, and smiled. Not bad, he thought, but this is no time for vanity, let's get down to business in hand.

The story she had to tell was as old as the hills (but not as old as the one about the masseur and the crocodile). A tale of broken dinner dates, lipstick on the collar, a strange woman's name mumbled in the night - in words of one syllable - 'infidelity'. Why, oh why, he thought, would any husband want to be unfaithful to a creature as lovely as this? In comparison, Mrs Steinmayer, who was so homely she made a living out of a suitcase pleasurable, could have been the prototype for a new sex. Besides, he mused, after twenty-five years of marriage, you'd think Mrs Steinmayer would tell me her Christian name.

He watched compassionately as the distraught woman dabbed at her eyes with a piece of material torn hurriedly from his shirt-tail. It still had a knot tied in it to remind him to wear a shirt. Discreetly he looked away and taking up a rare ivory handled letter opener recently purchased from Sothebys, picked at his teeth with it. The sharp point skidded across the enamel, almost amputated his left earlobe, and finished up embedded quiveringly in the window frame behind him.

He smiled, casually, in a man-about-town fashion, as the crimson trickled into his collar. For a moment he thought of trying to seduce her, but realised that a vertical eyeball-to-kneecap confrontation was not the ideal starting point for romance. All through life he'd been held back by this close proximity to Mother Earth. He had stopped going to race meetings when jockeys christened him 'Tich', and his days as a Lothario came to an end when a potential girlfriend asked him if he had ever thought of working as a doorstop. He'd never

23

had any success with beautiful women. Witness Mrs Steinmayer. The nicest thing she had ever said to him was on their wedding night when she compared his sex appeal to that of a lamprey.

Steinmayer decided to level with the girl, knowing that most things are possible from a sitting position. 'Look', he said, his voice heavy with concern, but light on timbre, 'When a man reaches forty he often feels the need to break the mould'. Pleased with himself he repeated the line, which, aided by the shrillness of his voice, gave her the impression she was being addressed by a macaw. 'Personally I tried to defect to Russia, but I was foiled by inadequate planning. My 'A-Z' only covered as far east as Hinckley. But to re-cap. You want me to arrange to have your husband's office telephone tapped? His mail intercepted? Then you'd like me to put on a scruffy raincoat, with a cap pulled well down, and literally follow him everywhere?' She nodded miserably. He continued, 'Dodging from shop doorway, to shop doorway if necessary, making sure he doesn't see me, or suspect anything? If he goes into a building you want me to wait outside, possibly until the early hours, and then finally to report everything back to you? Who he sees - what he sees - everything?'

'Would you, Mr Steinmayer? You're my last hope. I just have to know.' Her eyes, brimming over with tears, were just too much for a man of Steinmayer's brevity.

'Of course I will', he said, making a sudden decision, 'but I want you to know, it's the oddest thing I've done in twenty years as Chairman of the Water Board.'

Spider-ee

by

Steve Roach

The air was blue with the cussing, could have made a rugby player blush. He was a lazy feller, he'd rather swear than work up a sweat, but there's only so much even a lazy feller can take. There has to come a time when even the slobs of this world get up off their butts and have to do a bit of work, mostly through the mess being piled up so high and the cigarette ash filling up every single mug in the house and all the plates being dirty and all, but work nonetheless. And he'd been stinking all week long now, he didn't mind the staleness but pretty soon his neighbours would. He'd reached his filth limit, it had come the time to have a whole day cleaning and then start afresh.

First off were the mugs, cups and glasses. Empty bottles and used t-bags littered the floors and these alone filled up a whole bin liner. Then came the plates, some covered in mould, all covered in something. In the sink they went, near as damn it pulled the sink in on itself with all the weight. Then the read-ee thingies that he liked so much, the titty books, not that he'd ever read the words in them but the titties were nice. He moved one, stuck to the carpet in something, and a spider the size of a fist bolted from underneath a wrinkled pair of 36 DD's.

He moved quick, for a fat bloke. Chucked the titty book right after it but the mean little critter was even faster, crawled right under the settee and clean vanished away. Well, there was a more cussing and a heaving of the sofa from where it had been for over ten years and the spider was there, just glaring at him like it was about to jump down his throat and eat him alive from the inside. The bloke raised his great fat foot and almost stomped it through the floorboards, but the little critter was not a slow one, he pranced out the way there and did a dance, right there in front of his eyes, like it was poking fun out of him.

He chased it around the room, panting and puffing and sweating pools of the stuff until it got bored and crawled up the wall and out of reach on the ceiling. He stood there looking at the hairy meatball for awhile, thinking about whichways to go here on in. And then it came to him, he waved his finger at it and ambled off like he was the one in control, and left the spider wondering what was coming next.

Well, the little critter nearly fell from the ceiling there when our Fatty returned with the hoover and a long pipe. And what a chase they had! Boy, he was crashing about, knocking the whole room around in an effort to catch the hairy bugger. And came the time when he had it trapped, had it so it knew there was nowhere else left to go. The hate poured out of its beady black eyes, hate aimed straight at his chubby smiling face and the contraption that sucked things inside itself. It was no good though, he was done for. He was almost too big to fit down the pipe, but the sucking pulled him right to his end, right into the hoover's guts. Fatty ceased his gloating and took the vacuum back to the pantry and sat down awhile, pondering the size of the skanky little beast.

Then came the cleaning up, so much work that he almost killed himself through sweating so much. He was so tired by the end of it that he could keep his eyes open no longer. Bed called him and he lay on the sheets and they soaked up his staleness and sleep engulfed him. Until a knocking noise was heard from the pantry.

He supposed it was a burglar at first, he woke up with a start and sat there shaking like a fat leaf. Burglar must have gotten trapped in the pantry in the poor light and was crashing around in there, trying to beat his way out by the sound of it. He jumped as he heard the door splinter into a hundred pieces and then sat in morbid fear as he heard the whatever-it-was clank from room to room looking for something. And then it came knocking on his bedroom door.

Door was slightly open of course, he couldn't get used to his own smell when he was cooped up with it for a whole night. He sat there with his heart in his mouth as the door creaked open and something dragged itself into the room.

He could see the silhouette of it in the darkness and he almost swallowed his heart back down again. For it was the hoover, and the hoover had grown legs, eight hairy, thick, alive legs! The hoover crawled into his room on those legs and the thing stood at the end of his bed like it was just staring at him, gloating almost. And when it had done with that, it raised the long pipe and proceeded to beat our Fatty bloke to death, not stopping till he was long since mashed to a pulp.

And then when it had done it's business, it calm as you like clanked back to the pantry and stayed quiet. Taint moved since. Nor our Fatty bloke.

The Brightest and the Best

by

Richard Harris

'Turn that torch off before the batteries go altogether'. Larry demanded to his younger brother.

'But I don't like the dark!' Simon sniffed sullenly.

'Well you've picked the wrong hobby then!' he said, throwing the final bits of paper on an already diminishing fire.

'Nothing like this has ever happened to us before has it Laz!'

'It did to me last June, remember that search party dad called out!'

Simon gave a realizing smile and Larry began to tell of his adventure in the Dover caverns.

'It happened in just the same way as today. The two of us, me and Mo exploring the caves at Dover ridge. And we lost our way in exactly the same way.'

Simon's head lowered. It was his fault the map had dropped down the crevasse and it was he who'd panicked and made Larry take that bad fall.

'Tell you what', Larry said noticing Simon's gloom return, 'we'll play the game me and Mo thought up while we were waiting for help. It's called 'what is!'

'What?' Simon frowned screwing up his nose.

'I ask a question I know the answer to and you've three chances to guess. First one to ten.'

Simon sighed, not at all keen to co-operate even though he normally loved a game.

'Okay', he huffed, 'you start.'

'Right. What is,... Cody Adams middle name?'

'God knows!' Simon shrugged.

'Well come on! Guess, it begins with 'M'.'

'Mary?'

'No.'

'Melissa?'

'No.'

'Marjorie?'

'No, you've had three, it's Marie.'

Simon tutted and hugged his mackintosh tightly, signifying that the cold was once again beginning to beat the puny heat of the fire.

'What is... a Griffin?' Larry continued.

They played for almost an hour until Simon was yet again stumped by Larry's 'what is the brightest thing known to man' question.

'I don't care'. Simon snapped, 'this is a rubbish game and I don't want to play any more.'

A tear overflowed his right eye and Larry knew some brotherly love was called for.

'Don't worry', he said placing an arm around Simon's trembling shoulders. 'They'll find us soon.'

Hours passed and Simon finally slept, quietly huddled beside Larry. Above, condensation had formed on several large stalactites and now the rhythmic dripping tapped the seconds away.

Looking at his watch through the fading torch light, Larry noted that they'd been trapped for almost fourteen hours. It was now three in the morning and he too was becoming more and more fatigued.

Larry didn't know how long he'd been asleep when Simon knocked him back to consciousness. All he could hear was the frantic hysteria of his brother and at first thought something terrible had happened.

'*What*? What is it?' he blurted hobbling to his feet. His trousers were soaked and his bottom was numb through sitting on the hard rock floor.

'Look up there!' Simon squealed almost falling over his eagerness.

A laser fine thread of light was streaming through a crack only visible now the morning had dawned.

'A way out!' Simon said peddling up the ragged rocks.

'No you don't!' said Larry grabbing at Simon's climbing harness. 'I'll check it out,... you stay put.'

After snatching up a rope and hammer axe, he began to ascend towards the light with Simon's hopeful gaze following all the way.

The crack was about two feet long and only inches wide. It was far too narrow for a body to pass through, but with luck, and a sharp piton hammer, Larry felt he could widen the opening sufficient enough to squeeze out.

It took ages before the first chunk of granite thudded to the floor, splintering on impact into dozens of sharp slithers.

'Move away stupid!' Larry shouted, 'and get your helmet on.'

Eventually, the crack was wide enough for Larry to attempt the squeeze to beat all squeezes. Simon looked on wide-eyed and helpless as his brother's legs dangled precariously from the crack.

After minutes of grunting and heaving his whole body disappeared from view and Simon waited in yearning silence.

Then, from the crack fell the orange rope, followed by Larry's ecstatic call.

'I'm out.'

All their worry and panic evaporated as they gleefully hugged the sun soaked cliff top, laughing and whooping with utter relief.

'The sun!' Simon suddenly exclaimed, through frowning closed eyes.

'What about it?' Larry said with a wry smile.

'It's the answer to your 'what is' question,... what is the brightest thing known to man!' he said rhythmically, 'the *sun's* the brightest thing known to man.' They both laughed once again and as the reality of their situation sunk in, Simon added gratefully,

'The brightest,... and the best.

Pilkington House, Private Concern

by

Frank Richards

The advert read:- 'DIY handyman instructor required, some driving of mini-bus involved, transporting personnel.'

I had recently returned from working abroad, this looked promising. The location was Pilkington House on the edge of town. No one seemed to know if it was a rehabilitation centre for ex-prisoners, or released people who had been mentally disturbed.

It turned out to be a large house without walls or bars. I stopped in the car-park looking for a space, when a young man appeared wearing a blissful smile but with rather vacant eyes, shouting 'come on guvnor' and tried to guide me into a three foot gap between two cars. Now we know what sort of people are here, I thought.

After parking the car I noticed a door marked office, opening this led you into a large, long corridor with several more doors, I paused at the nearest one marked 'recreation room' quietly easing myself through into what was obviously an office.

Across the room was a young female. 'Hello can you tell me where the manager is please?' I said speaking in what I hoped was a pleasant cheerful tone.

She leaped as though suddenly touched with something hot, looked at me with wild eyes, shaking with rage and shouted:- 'You can't come in here, all private now you're not supposed to come in here, very private concern.'

This chastened person retreated back into the corridor thoroughly subdued. The next door was marked 'games room'. I opened it with trepidation, what kind of games? I thought.

This was obviously the kitchen and a motherly looking lady smiled, saying 'you can have a cup of tea but mind my eyes.' I was beginning to know how 'Alice in wonderland' must have felt, everyone I had met so far seemed so much percent crazy, or suspect.

My instinct was to flee, but the tea was just right. After a few minutes through the far door came one of the tallest men I have ever seen, muttering something to the kitchen lady and gesticulating wildly. 'Well it's not my fault if he's not here to play you at bowls', she suddenly shouted, banging pots and other utensils around, as if to emphasise her words, 'why don't you ask him over there to give you a game?'

'Where is the games room then?' I asked him. 'Is it the room marked kitchen?' He beamed at me and said 'come on pal!' We went right down to the end of the corridor through a door marked 'toilet', there was a large room with table tennis, and a pool table.

My companion whose frame from head to toe must have been over seven foot swung one leg right over the middle of the pool table, straddling it and shrieked, 'have you ever played under a bridge? You can't watch all the balls you know.'

I persuaded him to take first shot in the proper manner.

The game was progressing normally except my tall opponent, who insisted his name was 'poison dwarf' kept striding and leaping around excitedly and yelling 'my shot' frequently. I decided to let him win and at the end, he was over the moon.

Nevertheless I was relieved when another man with a rather lugubrious expression came in saying 'you for interview? Come on follow me.'

Along the corridor again and, as if by magic, out stepped the young lady who had previously bawled me out of the office. She stared, intently and accusingly. 'How nice to see you again.' I stammered 'and you looking so pretty.' I expected her to shout 'off with his head!' but was rewarded by seeing her eyes soften, as she followed us both into a big office.

Seated in a row were four young people, two men and two ladies, gazing at me as if I was under a microscope. They all looked more unbalanced than the people I had previously met. 'Oh Lord, these are the staff.' I thought.

'Why do you want to work here?' snapped one female.

'He must be mad' giggled poison dwarf. I mumbled something about good rate of pay, reasonable hours etc.

'What would you do if attacked?' the question was flung at me from a man whose face in the shaded corner made me think of a gnarled old oak tree. 'If someone throws at tantrum?' he went on. By now I was passed caring and countered with, 'I don't think I will be attacked, as anyone can see I'm already fighting.' I paused and then muttered, 'for breath.'

The burst of laughter from everyone was spontaneous and uninhibited. 'Okay', said someone, I was handed some more documentation as I staggered out of the building to my car.

The next week I received a cheque for expenses and an invitation to come to a second interview.

This time the atmosphere was more orderly, the doors seemed to be marked correctly. The very tall man introduced himself calmly as the team-leader and explained to me:- for the interview day everything was meant to confuse a newcomer. Some patients still under treatment swopped places with staff and the latter pretended to be irrational.

This was to test a persons patience and tolerance, which were the main characteristics for the job, 'you passed' said the team leader 'the job is yours if you want it.'

I still sometimes have difficulty in remembering who is what. But where is the borderline between normality and needing help?

Crossroads

by

Raymond K Avery

That very morning, as the sun wearily found its way above the dark grey-skinned hills that stood in the distance, my woman stopped banging her head against the low brick wall just long enough to ask me to go to the soul supermarket. She had heard there was a special offer on Siamese, perhaps we could afford a twin-pack. They would certainly make a change from the halfpound of broken promises we usually had for breakfast.

I agreed the trip might be beneficial as I seemed to be spending too much time lately working on the mathematics of innocence with my good friend the Arabian mind doctor who lived within my inner ear, tormenting me with useless equations that only made sense if you lived in a sixty watt electric light bulb.

Putting on my cloak of complete indifference, I left my partner quoting words of Omar Khayyam to an audience of interested greenfly who had turned up unexpectedly. She was happy, it wasn't often anyone listened to her.

I made my way across the steaming highway to the abode of my secret lover, a crippled Indian flute player who spends her days in fruitless searches in the back streets of Abyssinia looking for a wreath of blue roses with which to make her own thorny crown. She really loved all the pomp and ceremony of fancy dress parties. She once won first prize as the left eyeball of Bob Dylan.

I knocked, using an illuminated crucifix that they gave away with every two gallons of petrol. While waiting for her to answer, I drew my own version of the last supper on her doorstep, juxtaposing several Disney characters for the Apostles. Donald duck was about to dip his bread in the chalice when my lover appeared.

'Come in', she said 'but please do not tread upon my carpet of dreams that is undulating across the golden floor.'

Grinning inanely I jumped into her room, my feet never touched the Fata Morgana of my Icarus with the broken wing.

'Would you like to take a trip with me?' I asked my low caste paramour. She nodded her assent, she couldn't speak, her mouth was full of ashes from the fires of many crematoriums.

We take the scenic route along the coast where we watched Neptune's hand-maidens collecting green strands from the loom of St Catherine to make new coats for sea horses.

Leaning forward, I kiss my love. I taste sea side rock, it reminds me of my childhood, now no longer a child I decide I do not crave childish pleasures, now my tastes are different.

After making love, we continue on our way toward the crossroads where we are to board the bus. We hurry now, knowing there will be a queue, there always is.

Soon we arrive and take our place in the ever increasing line of circus performers. Midgets and tumbling acrobats now surround us while grotesque clowns try to steal our minds. The woman next to us is gently combing the head of John the Baptist which is screaming obscenities about James Dean. It wasn't loaded, the gun wasn't loaded. What we have here is a failure of communication.

Hearing the sounds of hooves upon the highway, I turned to see a knight seated on a black mare rein in next to me. Removing his visor he speared me with his eyes and handed to me a bag of bluest leather containing the sins of all mankind. Trembling, I took this offered gift. The weight of nearly drove me to my knees. My messenger drew circles in the air that only served to bring psalms from the Poor Sisters of St Clare who happened to be passing in a pink cadillac bopping to old Elvis Presley songs.

Someone happened along and handed to me a silver plate they were polishing with the skins of new born babies for the better protection of inner reflections. I placed the bag on the tray, it didn't make it any lighter. Then I had a brain-wave, opening the bag I plunged my hand inside and withdrew a few thousand transgressions. I popped then into my mouth, they didn't taste too bad.

'What are you doing?' asked my lover, frightened at the change in me.

'It's alright, I guess I'm just another Jesus looking for a Calvary.'

34

The Wheels of Borrowed Time

by

David Shepherd

Horace strolled along at his own leisurely pace and his dog, Silas, wandered from side to side of the path in his wake.

The dog, a bull terrier, had a wandering streak which Horace envied and admired, because he never had the chance himself. Silas had been a faithful companion for the last ten years and was remarkably frisky for his age. He could smell field mice and was anxious to get at them, but the voice of command stopped him in his tracks with a skid.

'Silas! Come here', Horace shouted. 'You don't want to ruin a crop, do you?'

Silas looked up at his master's face, searching, but saw no severe anger, so he continued sniffing the hedgerows.

Horace walked on along the old disused railway track, under the warm comfort of the Autumn evening. The twin hedgerows stretching into the distance until they met at the focal point, forming a spiky green avenue. The rails and sleepers had long been removed and sold for scrap and firewood.

This line was now just an overgrown bank of earth and a convenient exercise yard for retired old men and their dogs, and anyone else with nothing better to do than wander along it. Horace had known the time when the coal trains had shunted along here, creating a line of artificial cloud between the main line and the pit.

He started to daydream about the old days on the railways - it was nearly every boy's wish to become an engine driver, and Horace was one of the very few whose boyhood dreams had come true.

He remembered the heat, sweat and dirt of the footplate which made a man of him. His work was hard and honest. He was one of the best in the business.

His pride and joy was an express passenger steam locomotive, and together they had covered many thousands of miles of steel tracks. The rhythmic hissing of her powerful cylinders dragging the 300 tons of train through ever changing landscapes were an indelible part of his way of life.

But as the years progressed, all these things slid into memories.

Horace switched his attention back to Silas, who kept catching the scent of mice from the fields and longed to get after them.

'Easy, boy', Horace grunted. He lit a cigarette and took a deep relaxing pull. Expelling the smoke slowly and watching it drift aimlessly upwards, he reflected on its similarity to the chimney of a shunter idling in a marshalling yard. He had worked in those yards as an apprentice, and was reminded of a terrible memory. A memory which was still fresh in his mind even after the fifty year interval.

He recalled the lunch-break hooter sounding and his workmates, in high spirits, making their way across the lines to the canteen.

'Com'on, Hosha!' his mate shouted. 'I'll race you.'

'You're on!' Horace snapped, and started to sprint across the steel rails like an Olympic hurdler. Just as he reached top gear, a set of points changed without warning, biting his foot like a man-eating animal. He crashed to the ground with a scream of agony as the bone snapped, almost fainting with the pain as he lay among the ribbons of glistening steel. Lifting his face, he saw the column of smoke belching toward the sky from an approaching engine and realised his terrible predicament.

'Help me!' he yelled. 'Anybody, please!'

But the engine kept coming. He writhed to escape the path of those steel wheels that would cut, crush and mangle. The oncoming black monster seemed to tower over him, and he panicked. Then excepting the inevitability of his fate he passed out, gushing cold sweat.

He never knew until recovering in hospital that his workmate had operated the handpoints diverting the train to another line.

Horace stubbed out the remains of the cigarette and stretched. He had spent many weeks in hospital recovering from that smashed ankle, and considered it little short of a miracle to have recovered with no permanent deformity. Almost a year passed before he was able to walk properly, and he still felt a twinge today, particularly during damp weather.

Worse than his physical injury were the weeks of whimpering in his sleep and the necessity to dose himself with drugs to kill the constant image of those bright silvery wheels towering above him, rolling ceasingly forward, crushing the life from his body and leaving only a pile of cold meat.

Horace had looked death in the face that day in the marshalling yards and still to this day he dreamed of those shining steel wheels.

'Come on, Silas,' he called. 'That's enough for today, boy. Let's go home.' The dog emerged from the hedge.

They resumed their walk a little faster than before, approaching a crumbling canal bridge. Once more Horace called out to his best friend.

'Here, Silas.' The dog obeyed.

'You stay close boy. No wandering near the water. I only bathed you yesterday and we both know what you're like when you're near water. Can't resist jumping in, can you?'

They crossed the bridge slowly and continued for another hundred yards. Home was only about half a mile further. Horace thought about his home, his wife and three children who all had their own families.

He suddenly sensed the absence of his friend and turned.

'Silas, come out of it!' He started to run back down the line.

'Come, Silas. Here, boy. No, don't go in the water!'

Splash.

'Oh! Too late, you bad dog!' he yelled.

As he ran his toe crunched against an unseen projection, and, arms flailing, he crashed to the ground. His forehead smashed against the sun-baked earth and beads of blood leaked through the reddened skin.

As Horace raised his head, his dazed eyes saw the image of an approaching train with great billowing clouds of smoke towering upward and huge silver wheels flashing towards him.

He lay trembling, watching it bearing down on him. The imaginary smoke filled his mouth and nostrils, stifling his screams, then came the final agony.

The dog arrived home alone several hours later, caked with slime and mud, and Horace's wife went to the police.

Next day a policeman, searching the old railway line for Horace, found his body, dead from a heart attack. He lay peacefully on earth which had once lain between the steel rails. Never again would he be tormented by a fate which had almost been his fifty years before and had, at last, caught up with him.

The Photograph

by

John W B Barklam

Photographs are harmless enough you may think. They can't possibly do you any harm can they? Though it may be comforting to think that is so, you may be wrong. Let me tell you what happened to Dave.

The holiday snapshots had come out very well thought Dave, smiling at several of the scenes portrayed before him. They were a welcome reminder of the enjoyable time he had spent there. He was amazed at the clarity of the pictures. Finally he came to the last photograph in the pack. He was puzzled and his brow creased to a frown as he looked on it in amazement. He had not taken this shot and he could not remember anyone else doing so either. It was not even a holiday snap.

It was a picture of him coming out of the house - not something anyone would normally bother to photograph. For some reason the picture held his attention, his eyes staring unwaveringly at it. He put it on the mantelpiece to think about it later when he had more time.

Later that day he had chance to look once more at the picture of himself. His mind registered strong anxiety as he studied the photograph. The scene was somehow different, there was something else there, but what? Then he saw it! At his side he could just make out a small figure. He was sure it had not been there before. And who was it? Try as he may he could not make out who the figure was. It was most strange. Replacing the picture on the mantelpiece he went about his work.

The next day Dave's attention was again drawn to the photograph. As he looked he could not believe his eyes. He stepped back in amazement at what he saw. It was just not possible. The photograph had changed again, of that he was absolutely sure, but how?

He could see that the small figure he had seen at his side had moved! He knew it had moved, even though he knew it was impossible. His mouth was suddenly dry and blood pounded noisily in his head as he gazed in silence upon the small picture before him. Perhaps he had been mistaken and the small figure had not really moved after all? Yes, that was the only logical explanation.

For days after Dave would not look at the photograph, afraid of what he might see. He knew it was illogical but the thought of losing his mind filled him with an unnatural horror. Finally, he could resist it no longer. He had to look. He had to find out.

He recoiled in horror at what he saw. It was true, he really was going mad, the picture had changed again! The figure was now not so small. It appeared to have been walking out of the picture, out towards him! He still could not make out a clear face, but he did not care. It had moved and that was what frightened him. Beads of perspiration trickled down the side of his face as he stood, rooted to the spot with fear, staring wide eyed at the picture, his mouth frozen open with terror.

Each day things got worse; the figure grew larger and larger as it moved slowly out of the photograph, until one day....

Dave looked at the picture, unable to move. Icy fingers of terror crept up his spine, tearing at his nerves and chilling the blood pounding furiously through his veins. His heart struggled to regain a steady rhythm as his breathing became more rapid.

It was the most sinister thing he had ever seen. The small, child-like figure was larger than ever and in its raised hand was a gun, and it was pointing directly at him from out of the picture! He could stand it no longer, and he ran from the room, his heart pounding vigourously against his chest and his ears ringing with the build up of blood pressure.

Dave slumped in a chair his breaths coming in short sobbing gasps, his body shaking with fear. He had not told anyone about the photograph in case they had thought he really was mad, but he wished now that he had confided in someone. There was no rational explation for what was happening to him. After he had calmed down a little he went back to look at the picture.

The small figure was still pointing the gun at him, but it was now dressed completely in black. But that was not all. As Dave looked at the picture, beads of sweat trickling down his face, he saw the most unbelievable thing. A bullet seemed to be coming out of the picture towards him. It travelled slowly as if in slow motion, but it was definitely coming towards him. He could see it clearly...there was no mistake...the figure was shooting at him from the photograph. He felt cold, very cold, his body shook with fear. He had to get away, and get away now. He ran for the door, but, as he opened it, he stopped, terror gripping his heart and soul. How could such a thing be happening, and why? He could not believe what he was seeing!

A short distance away he saw a small figure coming towards him, a figure dressed in black. It was like the figure in the photograph! He could not escape the ghastly sight before him. He could not move and his mouth hung open in disbelief. The gun was pointing towards him. It was too much...it could not be real.

He remembered nothing after that. The scene faded from his consciousness and he felt himself falling. A strange sort of pain seared through his chest and...nothing.

The neighbours could not believe it. To have had a heart attack like that, and to die so young, and on his own doorstep too. It was such a shame. And little Jamie had had such a shock. He had run out of the house in his black cowboy suit and pretended to shoot Dave with his toy gun. He had such a surprise when Dave keeled over...dead! It was something he would never forget. He remembered how his parents had told him never to point a gun at anyone. He had only forgotten this once. Surely his neighbour wouldn't have died just because of that. But then again, strange things do happen in that mysterious world between life and death...

Mirror Images?

by

B J Dove

'What on earth is the point of it? Life is just a succession of problems, once you've solved one you come up against the next.' I spoke aloud in frustration and didn't get much of a response from the only living thing in the room. Sam, the retriever cocked an ear, looked bored and returned to his contented slumber in the bean bag. How wonderful to be able to just sleep on, I had tossed and turned all last night and I suppose I must have slept a bit, but it certainly didn't refresh me for today. Here I was in my pyjamas still, at 10am, gazing out at the rain and wind thrashing down on the first spring daffodils.

'Oh sod the weather! Sod everything! I hate living like this and most of all I hate him!'

As I said the words of anger so I felt my muscles tighten, my heart race and I wanted so much to hit something, to lash out in fury, to give full unrestricted freedom to my feelings. I wanted to, but somehow I couldn't, something stopped me and I jumped up out of the chair and marched towards the kitchen instead! The breakfast things were still spread about the work tops, crumbs, milk bottles, mucky plates, the dog's lead and someone's keys in the middle of it all. The Daily Telegraph regally opened up over a jar of marmalade and the sugar bowl, abandoned at the political cartoon page as if the reader had suddenly been called away on a matter of life or death. The news of yesterday and the clutter of even a few minutes ago forgotten in an instant with the surge for the challenges of the new day.

As I stood and surveyed the battlefield of breakfast I felt so angry at my husband for being able to abandon it, leaving me with it - alone with it! It - the left overs of living - the mess - the monster that just sits there refusing to be ignored, never disappearing, always growing that little bit larger and more demanding.

'Why should I have to be a slave to you,' I shouted at the congealed egg and greasy bacon rind.

'And you needn't sit there smirking at me!' I thrust the newspaper aside and it took along the sugar bowl for company. What a deliciously satisfying sight - to see a thousand grains of golden granulated sugar rise up into the air, as if in

41

slow motion, and after hovering for a second, cascading to the floor like the storm thrashing outside the kitchen window and the battle deep inside me.

'That is me on the floor, that is me spread about the work tops - I am the mess! If I am a slave to it, I become it, how dare it have that control over me!'

Sam had decided that even a dog couldn't sleep through the present rather noisy conditions and having poked his head around the doorway realised he was in for some good pickings if he could lick his way across the kitchen floor. I watched him in a detached sort of way and felt very calm. As I watched I thought that normally I would have pushed him to one side, viewing him as another problem to be controlled by me - everything had to be done by me!

In that instant of detachment when the sugar grains and my 'self' were the same I suddenly realised that the only person making me a slave was my own 'self'. I felt responsible and so I was trying to control everything and yet really everything in the world was controlling me. The mess, the dog, even my husband could not have any control over me as long as I controlled myself. But how could I do that when I quite obviously wasn't in control of anything, least of all myself.

'I can't, I just can't, God help me, I can't cope anymore, I give up, let the dog take his sweet spoils.' I sobbed as I ran from the room, feeling a failure, feeling empty, feeling a no one.

I splashed the cold water over my face. It was so soothing, cooling down the red puffiness which had resulted from sobbing. It felt like a life time of tears and I scarcely recognised myself as I looked up into the bathroom mirror.

'Who are you?' I asked, 'Please show me what to do, how to live.'
I felt myself becoming light headed and the image in the mirror blurred and became very bright until I could see nothing at all except bright, white, light. It was so warm and I felt elated, as if I was needed and worthy, I was drawn towards it as if by a magnet. The peculiar sensation of being pulled came over me. I felt encouraged and confident to step into the light. I moved towards it and as I did so I remembered for an instant that it was the mirror that I was moving towards. However, all I could see was white light and all I could feel was the warmth beckoning me.

I did it an instant of abandon! I dived into the light. I felt it was an action I could live with forever. I felt confidence, trust, freedom and elation drawing me up and up, feeling as if I was flying. I heard a loud crack and could hear a rushing sound, the feel of wind on my face, moving through space and time, pulled through a tunnel of hope, on and on, flying, yes I was definitely flying. It was marvellous, I was free, I was myself, unrestrained and alive.

'This is life!' I called out, 'Thank-you, I love you, you are wonderful, you are everything.'

I could see myself clearly now that I was above myself and flying on I could see my family and those I love, I could see their lives and mine interwoven and entangled in places. On and on I flew, up and up, drawing out the tangles as I shot past! One minute feeling I was going back into the past and the next moment feeling I was going towards the future. I had flown so high that I could see the whole world below me - it was so very, very beautiful. A beautiful, serene globe which I was viewing from a distance and wanting to be part of.

I was suddenly still, absolutely still and calm and certain of who I was. I was out here in space and this was where I belonged, this was my home. I had arrived at last.

'I'm home, darling!'

'I'm back, where are you, have you had a good day?'

'What on earth is going on, what is all this mess, where are you?'

'Come on Clair, you've had your little joke, I know you are there somewhere. You wouldn't leave the house unlocked, you are hiding upstairs, I'm coming to get you.'

The beautiful globe moved slightly in my vision to allow me to see my husband running up the stairs, running into the bedroom and finally the bathroom.

It was strange to see the expression on his face as he entered the bathroom, it was an expression of shock, absolute shock and disbelief. He just stood there staring at the mirror and looking paler and paler by the minute.

From my detached perspective I hardly felt he was my husband at all and I was very curious to see what it was that was having such an impact on him. I tried to look where he was looking and could just make out the edge of the mirror. As my field of vision increased I suddenly saw the huge gaping wound where the mirror had cracked and there in the gap was the distorted face of my husband. He was mesmerized by this grotesque image of himself and, as I stared the image full in the face, I saw the features distort even more and change before me into my features.

I was now staring out of the mirror straight at my husband's shocked face and as I locked my eyes on his I knew I loved him, I didn't hate him at all, I wanted to care for him and share my life with him. Was it too late, I could see him shrinking before me and very slowly collapse to the floor and I was so sorry for him, I needed to help him but I couldn't get to him.

'Hi, I'm home!'
I could hear his voice and feel myself gripping something, what was it? The wash basin? Where was I? In the bathroom? I looked up and the image in the mirror smiled back at me serenly, knowingly, absolutely timeless - I turned and called out,
'I'm here in the kitchen cleaning up spilt sugar.'

The Great Ride

by

Elizabeth Hillman

It was a hot, slow December day in the village high in the Andes, and after the noon meal, people gathered in the cool church hall.

'Don Juan, please tell us about the Great Ride,' begged young Manuel.

There was a universal sigh of pleasure. Old Juan coughed impressively, and smilingly began the familiar story.

'This, though true, is like a fairy-tale, full of magic,' he said, and the older people nodded their heads profoundly in agreement.

'Some years ago - before quite a few of you young ones were born - something marvellous happened. It was on a hot day like this - it was a Wednesday, I seem to remember - and the men were working in the fields. The women were starting to think about supper, spinning, sewing, or perhaps even gossiping.' He looked slyly at the murmured protests of the women.

'The air hung heavy and still, as if an enchanter had put a spell on the land and nothing would change here for a hundred years - much as it is now.' Juan looked out at the quiet square, the cobblestones shimmered in the heat reflected from dazzling white walls, and the crimson and purple Bougainvillaea hung motionless in thick, heavy clusters around deep-sunk dark windows and doorways.

'Nothing moved in the silent heat, and then -'

Juan paused to roll a cigarette, his eyes twinkling at the expectant audience. Carefully he licked the paper, smoothed it, and finally lit it, slowly savouring the first deep inhalation of the pungent smoke.

'Then came the noise - quiet at first, like a bee's lazy buzzing in the marigold fields. Gradually it grew louder and closer, more like a dragon's snorting. No-one had ever heard anything like it, and I think that some of us wondered whether the old tales were coming true and that monsters were walking and coming from the caves over the mountains.'

A few young men smiled indulgently at such credulity, but many glanced up at the distant white peaks where no human had ever ventured.

'The men stopped working and watched the hill above the village, wondering what was approaching, and the old folk and the women, being of a curious nature, came out of the houses.

'Closer and louder came the noise. At last, at the top of the hill appeared a cloud of dust surrounding a great silver and scarlet monster. The sun's glitter on its sides blinded us at first, but as it came slowly down to the village, we could see its glory - a beast whose gleaming shell was half hidden by huge gasps of steam. We gathered around it as a safe distance, and some children cried and hid behind their mothers' skirts.'

Pausing for another deep puff at the cigarette, Juan looked at Raoul, a noted bully, who blushed and kicked the bench with his boots, while his victims laughed.

'What happened then, Don Juan?' clamoured the children, though they knew every word well.

Juan carefully stubbed out his cigarette. 'The doors of the odd thing slid open with a mechanical sigh, and out stepped a crowd of creatures such as we had never seen before. Their clothes were like a rainbow that had been stirred with a giant ladle. There were blues like the sky, like birds' eggs, like ink, there were pinks like fruit blossoms and watermelon centres, and purples like orchids and irises. There were yellows like butter and cheese and mustard - even the men's shirts were of cheerful colours and patterns. They put us to shame, like peacocks among crows.'

Some of the young men sighed enviously, looking down at their dark home-spun clothes. The girls proudly glanced at their own full skirts of blue or green, surmounted by brightly striped scarlet shawls.

'They talked with quiet voices in a strange flowing language. Fortunately the strangers had a guide, a young lady from the city who wore a smart uniform, like Sergeant Julio on a feast-day.'

Everyone laughed, for the unfortunate sergeant had expanded with the years, and his tight old uniform was worn with great care on special occasions only.

'The guide said that the Thing needed water, like a thirsty beast, but had to cool down first, and could the strangers rest in a shady place and perhaps have some refreshments. They were unused to the altitude and heat, being from a cool, low country. Of course, our men ran to fetch umbrellas to shade the guests, and Father Bernardo opened this hall. Chairs, food and drink were set out and the guests made comfortable.' Juan drew himself up proudly.

'We were able to offer good wine, fruit, nuts, fresh cheeses and bread, crusty and crisp from the ovens. The guests ate well, and then bowls of warm water were brought for them to wash their hands. To our surprise, they were delighted with the towels, calling them works of art.'

Juan paused for the usual groans from the girls who spent many painful, laborious hours learning the exquisite embroidery techniques with which they decorated the small hand-towels which were sold in the city or, if especially well-made, were carefully laid away as family heirlooms.

'Then came a throbbing noise from the Thing, like a refreshed creature eager to be away. Someone asked if we could look inside, and the guests suggested that we should go for a ride in it.

'Some of the older people stayed to entertain the guests, but most of us eagerly climbed into the Thing. The men stayed near the front to watch the driver working all the knobs and switches, and Antonio worked the lights and horn.'

The village mechanic, used only to repairing old, small equipment, smiled proudly.

'The women and children examined the marvels of the Thing thoroughly. There were wide, thick seats with head-rests, a carpet on the floor, many lights in the roof - even a real outhouse in the back, with a porcelain bowl and running water just to wash in, and a mirror. Oh, the Thing was bigger and finer than our houses, and as for comparing it to the market bus - well, it would be unthinkable to take baskets of vegetables or hoes or chickens on such a magnificent Thing! We were worried about our heavy muddy boots spoiling the carpet.

'Off we went, purring along the road at a tremendous speed, looking out of the great windows. We soared up the hills and swooped down to the valleys, and it was like being on an eagle's back, flying effortlessly.

'It was hot, so the driver turned a knob and instantly, with a soft hum, cool air swirled everywhere, like magic. We stopped on Bus Hill to look at the view, and we got there in only a quarter of an hour.'

The children murmured in amazement and disbelief, for it took their aged weekly market bus over an hour to struggle that far, and Paulo, the driver, always had to stop at the top of the highest hill to let the bus cool down - hence the hill's name.

'Paulo always gets us there somehow, and we don't have to worry about spoiling his bus,' remarked Alfonso loyally.

'We drove back here,' Juan continued. 'We waved to everybody we passed, and how they stared at us as we swirled by. It was an incredible ride.'

Those who had been there agreed, and Fernando, who had been on the ride but had been too young to remember it, looked both proud and sad.

'We thanked the guests for our wonderful treat,' Juan said.

'We gave each one a small towel as a souvenir of that day, since they liked them so much, and they left us all kinds of strange, marvellous things - business cards, magazines, newspapers, cigarettes, pens, sweets - in fact, Alfonso still has the lighter he was given.'

Alfonso, grinning, held up a blue plastic disposable one, long since empty, but still precious. Most of the houses had walls decorated with rather faded pictures cut from the glossy magazines, of large houses, flower-filled gardens, of fashion models, advertisements, and elegant kitchens and bathrooms.

'It was a time we'll always remember,' said old Juan, and he felt in his pocket for the now battered business card that was always with him. Though he could not read them, he loved to feel the thick, glossy letters as he gently rubbed them with rough work-worn fingers.

Far away in Wolverhampton, Susan Hall was tidying her linen closet, wishing that the winter was over. Turning over some pillow-cases, she found two small embroidered hand towels. Smiling, she lightly ran her smooth fingers over the delicate stitches.

'John,' she called, 'let's get out the slides from our South American trip, we haven't looked at them for ages. Do you remember that tiny village we stopped in when the bus broke down? Really, I'm glad the driver got lost and took us off the main road. The people were so kind, and I'm sure they gave us just about all the food they had. They seemed so poor, yet they gave us these lovely towels. My goodness, didn't they enjoy that ride in our bus! I wonder if they ever think of us at all?'

Jim Doesn't Live Here Anymore

by

Malcolm Storer

'I hate you' Sandra shrieked as Jim came into the house, quietly closing the front door behind him.

'How could you? How could you ditch me for a barmaid?' He didn't reply and tears pouring down her cheeks, she continued the tirade.

'My mother warned me about you and your family. She said that none of you were any good. I wish I'd listened to her.'

'So do I' he muttered, making to brush past her into the living room. She remained firmly anchored in the doorway, barring his path.

'And just where do you think you're going now?' she choked 'This is typical of you; Whenever we have a problem you run away.'

A look of deep resignation crossed Jim's face.

'I suppose' he replied as calmly as he could that we've had so many problems over the past couple of years, I've stopped noticing, Now, if you'll excuse me, I'll just get a few things together and leave; It's over, Sandra. Let's, at least, try to part as civilised human beings'.

'Civilised!' she screamed. 'What do you mean, civilised human beings? You walk out of here and I'll see that you and your fancy woman regret it. How could you? I've been a good wife to you for the last ten years and all I get is tossed aside for some painted floozy from the Rose and Crown.'

The tears flowed with renewed vigour and, for Jim, composure went out of the window.

'Good wife!' he yelled. 'You talk about being a good wife after that exhibition you made of yourself with Pedro in Benidorm last year.' He spat out the name of the Spanish barman, treating her to a look of total contempt.

'You wouldn't know how to start being a good wife. You were always more inclined to listen to that interfering old bitch of a mother of yours then to me. I'll bet she's breaking into a song and dance routine at the thought of us breaking up.'

'At least Pedro was sober.' she raged bitterly 'He wasn't sleeping off one drinking session after another.'

'Probably because he was selling me most of the booze', he replied coldly.

'I knew what kind of a holiday it was going to be when you insisted on your mother coming too.'

'I only wish I'd listened to her before we got married.' Sandra cried amid fresh floods of tears. 'It might have prevented all this'. She warned me about you.'

'I'll bet she did', he countered. 'The old bat must have broken the four minute mile getting round here to tell you she'd seen me with Barbara'

'At least my mother shows some interest.' she sobbed. 'That's more than your mother's ever done. She hasn't been here since last Christmas, when your precious brother got drunk and flattened the Policeman.'

'And whose fault was that?' he roared. 'If your mother hadn't lost her pension book and accused him of stealing it and then called the Police....' his voice shook with rage as he recalled the incident....'and then when she found it down the back of the settee, accused Joe of putting it there. Anyway my mum stays away because yours is always in residence. That's why I spend so much time in the pub. I prefer the company.'

'Like Father, like son.' she crowed, her tears temporarily ceased.

'Your old man drank himself to death and left your mother to bring up six kids, didn't he?'

With an effort he restrained his impulse to hit her.

'My Father died of cancer', he replied his voice icy, 'caused by thirty years in the pit. And contrary to what your mother has no doubt told you, he was a good Father. I would imagine that yours couldn't wait to die after putting up with rent a mouth all those years.'

'How dare you?' she screeched, her voice breaking as the tears began to flow again.

'Get out, you pig! Get back to your tart from the pub'.
He made a move towards her and she hastily stepped back. With a supreme effort he checked himself.

'I suppose your mother has given you an assassination of Barbara's character? he shouted. 'I'll tell you this though. When I'm with her I, at least feel like a human being. I'm happy for the first time in years. She's warm and kind.....'

'Warm! kind!' she exploded. 'You make me sick. You're like a big schoolkid with a crush on the teacher'.

'Better that than some Spanish barman', he replied. 'At least Barbara speaks English. As it happens, she's got a degree in it.'

'My! You have come up in the world' she said sarcastically. 'What does she see in you then? You can't spell any word with more than four letters. Are you her little bit of rough?' she paused before adding, almost as an afterthought. 'Pedro had a degree too'

'What in, mixing cocktails?' he laughed harshly, 'They must give degrees away with lottery tickets in Spain.'

'At least he made an effort. He was someone I could talk to,' she cried.

'You weren't doing much talking when I found you' Jim snarled, the bitter memory of that afternoon returning. 'How did you manage to talk anyway if he didn't speak English and you don't speak Spanish?' His hand reached for the doorlatch,

'I'm going now'. He was calmer now 'I'll be back for my things tomorrow. I'd be happier in the morgue than I've been here. Are you getting a coffin in the cellar for Dracula's daughter to live in when she moves in? Before she could reply the door slammed and he was gone.

'Jim! Come back!' she screamed, rushing for the door 'Oh, come back, please. I love you!'

'Let him go and good riddance', came the voice of her mother from the kitchen.

51

Day of Departure

by

Alan N Marshall

Number 53 was the only inhabitable house left standing in Trafalgar Road.

The last in a row of terraced dwellings, it stood narrow and forlorn in a sea of rubble, whilst all about its erstwhile neighbours were being shovelled away piecemeal.

That 53 should have survived this long was due entirely to eighty-two year old Albert Cutler, its stooped and stubborn tenant for some sixty-two years.

Now, on this fateful day, his resistance to eviction was to end, for even he could foresee that the spot where he laid his head would shortly become the check-out point in the latest of a very long line of supermarkets.

However, Albert was not one of those unfortunates whom no-one wants, on the contrary he had been offered accommodation by his sister, his daughter and grandson, even a nice little flat by the council, but, truth to tell, he had always hoped that he would see his days out at number 53, where his history lay.

What on earth would he do under someone else's feet all day?

Now he stood in the cocooned surroundings of his snug sitting room, with its stained, spring busted chintz sofa, plain wooden table, and the dusty china ornaments, and awaited the arrival of 'the movers'.

At ten o'clock, as a final gesture before moving to another part of the site, the driver of crane number four swings his heavy iron ball on the end of its chain, at one of the two surviving walls of number 47, a mere fifty yards from Albert's house. It is a fluke blow causing the entire spread of bricks to fall wholesale, the vibration re-activating the timing mechanism of the one thousand pound bomb, which has lain dormant under the foundations of 53 since 1940.

The timing clock will tick on for exactly two hours before detonating the explosives which surround it... that is, unless some other heavy vibration accelerates the process. Now, all that remains standing of number 47 is the chimney structure, which has miraculously survived the onslaught of ball and chain, and stands tall and alone, like a shaky monument.

Alec, Albert's pampered tabby cat, rubs past the old man's leg, fat face wreathed in an ecstatic smile, tail acquiver like an aspen leaf.

Albert lowers himself onto the twangy settee, and abstractedly rubs the cat behind his left ear. Alec closes his eyes and purrs throaty contentment.

Albert looks at the grimy faced clock on the mantleshelf, vaguely aware that someone should, by now, have arrived to start moving his belongings, but not concerned enough about the delay to worry about it.

10.38. A stiff breeze springs up suddenly and sweeps across the site. It flattens the smoke from the large bonfire of burning timber and, together with dust and refuse, snakes across the area at ground level, hugging the contours of rubble heaps and depressions, and fanning the flames so that pockets of resin gas in the timber explode like pistol shots.

The chimney of number 47 trembles slightly but remains erect.

10.44. With a squeal of rusty brakes, a dilapidated van of the 'sit up and beg' variety, stops at Albert's door, followed closely by a dusty blue mini.

Painted on the sides of the van is the legend;

'K. Farique. Dealer in Fruit, Vegetables, Fish & Poultry of Quality.'

A young man of Asian origin steps down from the van, closely followed by Albert's grandson, Terry.

From the mini emerge Flossie, Albert's sprightly seventy-five year old sister, and Jenny, Terry's wife.

All four make for the front door of 53, and rap smartly.

After some delay the old man appears and ushers them inside.

10.53. They are all temporarily installed on sofa or chairs. Flossie says;

'What we all need is a nice cuppa.'

She looks around.

'Where's the teapot?'

Albert points tremulously to a brown, chipped enamelled pot on the side-board, and a primus stove on the corner stand. All main services have been disconnected, now it is catch as catch can. The teapot needs emptying.

Flossie hands it to Jenny.

'Nip out to the stand pipe across the way, and fill it with water, will you dear.'

Jenny takes the pot and steps outside.

The breeze has freshened, and as she picks her way carefully across the site, she squints her eyes against the dust.

As she passes the odd looking chimney, she thinks she sees it move slightly, but puts it down to a trick of the light.

Some labourers treat her to wolf whistles as she swills out the pot. She grins back, secure in the knowledge that husband and family are at hand, and carries the water back to the house.

11.00. Terry has pumped and lit the primus stove, and as he waits for the water to boil he asks;

'Have you decided where you're going Gramp?'

'With me of course.' Flossie snaps.

The old man nods.

'Right.' Terry replies, relieved.

'What's going and what's staying?'

11.03. The timing clock on the bomb beneath the house has now ticked more than half its life away, and the chimney outside is now leaning at an acute angle, against the opening of the ground floor fireplace.

At number 53 the tea has been made and poured.

'We'll have to get moving after this.' Terry says. 'Krish has a load of produce to collect at twelve o'clock.'

'Well there's nothing to stop you two getting on with it.' Flossie replies. 'We'll pack up the small things later and bring them with us in the car.'

Terry nods his assent, and the two men go out to open up the back of the van.

Alec, the cat, sensing disruption, disappears from sight.

11.10. Albert gets to his feet, crosses to the sideboard and extracts a photograph album from one of the drawers.

Jenny looks alarmed and starts to protest, but Flossie whispers;

'It's all right. We've plenty of time while the others are moving the furniture. It will take his mind off the move.'

Albert sits between the two women on the settee, and reverently opens the album.

11.15. The chimney of number 47 finally collapses harmlessly in upon itself with a dull thump and a clatter of bricks, but the clock in the foundations of number 53 ticks relentlessly on.

11.30. Albert closes the album abruptly.

'Honest Floss, I don't want to leave here, start up again somewhere else at my age. It's a pity that Betty and me didn't go together.'

Flossie dons her stern look.

'Now you know that's silly talk. It's not as if you're going to strangers.' She squeezes his hand.

'There'll be lots of fun, just wait and see.'

11.35. The removal of furniture has now been completed, all that remains is the final packing of small items.

11.45. The two tea chests have been taken out to the car and stowed away.

11.50. A final look around to see that nothing useful has been left behind. All is well.

11.52. Albert stands for a moment in the doorway for a final soaking up of old memories.

Jenny toots the car horn, and he reluctantly closes the door behind him.

11.54. They start off, turn twice right, and pause opposite number 53, only fifty yards distant, across open ground.

Albert, to his surprise and horror, suddenly realises that they have forgotten the cat.

He snatches the door open, and begins to hobble across the rubble strewn ground towards his old house, shouting'

'We've forgotten Alec.'

A hoot of laughter from behind causes him to jerk round, Alec has emerged from the back of the furniture van and is following close on Albert's heels, delighted to be going back to his old abode.

'You cunning old devil'. Albert laughs, scooping the cat up in his arms and hurrying back to the car, and as they move off the dashboard clock registers 11.58... two minutes to detonation.

It takes another minute to reach, and pass the first row of houses not yet demolished, they are all talking and laughing now, so they pay no heed to a low, rumbling vibration, but if they had chosen to glance round they would see a great plume of dust and debris rising high into the sky, which was all that remained of number 53, Trafalgar Road.

Shades of Night and Day

by

Mary Well

The abnormal coldness and darkness hit me as I stepped through the front door. I told myself it was due to coming in out of the Spring sunshine, but as the day wore on my sense of unease increased.

There was something not quite right about the house. Yet it was a redbrick semi detached built in the late 1930's, and recently modernised to include every possible convenience and labour-saving device. The flowery wallpapers, white paint, light carpets and curtains, meant to add brightness failed lamentably. The flowers on the wallpaper seemed to droop and the curtains hung limp.

I felt a wild urge to run home, but I couldn't. I'd promised my friend, Charlotte, to help nurse her aunt dying of cancer.

Charlotte and Sophie, her sister, had turned the big living room into a sickroom. All the furniture had been removed except a well-preserved chesterfield and an easy chair.

We planned I would sit up all night with Aunt Emily. Charlotte and Sophie would take it in turn to sleep one night on the chesterfield, one night in bed. I would rest during the day. I am one of those fortunate people who do nicely on a couple of hours sleep.

Before her illness Aunt Emily had the look of a Rubens woman - all wonderful curves and glorious colour. Now she reminded me of an emaciated daddy-longlegs. Only her beautiful green eyes remained alive. They didn't miss a trick. As Charlotte and I made her comfortable for what we hoped might be a few hours of sleep, she raised her hand.

'What's that?' she asked, pointing the dividing wall. 'Is it a ghost?'

I felt my arms goose-pimpling. I gaped at Charlotte who looked as if she had been turned to stone.

'No, it's nothing.' Aunt Emily dropped her hand and closed her eyes.

I wondered if she had reached a stage in her illness where everybody and everything looks unreal. I hoped so. I could do without ghosts.

Charlotte kept her thought to herself.

Charlotte fell asleep quickly. Aunt Emily drowsed contentedly. I sat by her bedside trying to make something of The Times crossword.

Only gradually did I become conscious of something forming out of the dividing wall. A dense hulk, roughly man-shaped. My pulse and breathing were suspended. Stark fear had me by the throat. Then Aunt Emily spoke.

'Water, please.'

The hulk vanished. On jellied legs I attended to Aunt Emily's needs. She settled quickly after a few sips of water.

Feeling in need of strong coffee I made my way to the kitchen where the cold was so intense my skin felt seared. Waiting for the kettle to boil I felt I was under strict surveillance. Abandoning all thought of coffee I fled the kitchen on trembling legs.

Apart from intensification of the darkness and coldness the remaining hours passed without further ghostly manifestations.

The second night came. With every light blazing the darkness grew deeper. The heating, turned up to maximum, had no effect on the searing cold.

Charlotte went to bed. Aunt Emily appeared to be sleeping. Sophie was restless.

'Would you like a warm drink?' I asked.

'I'd like some Horlicks.'

It - She - was waiting for me in the kitchen. A black and white woman sitting on a chair where the refrigerator normally stands. Her hands lay relaxed on her lap. Her hollow eyes assessed me from head to toe. Her smile was evil.

I don't remember how I got our of the kitchen. Probably on my hands and knees, I was mindless with terror.

It was a relief to find Sophie had fallen asleep without her Horlicks. Nothing would have induced me to return to that kitchen alone.

I honestly believe Sophies's stentorian snoring saved me from further haunting. Because, by now, I was convinced there was either some unfinished business troubling the house - like a violent death - or I was going nastily around the bend.

As we ate a breakfast of underdone toast and too strong tea, I decided to ask a few leading questions.

'Who lived here before your Aunt?' I asked Sophie.

'I have no idea. Aunt Emily bought the house about twenty years ago.'

'Why do you want to know?' Charlotte asked.

'Curiosity.'

'You think the house is haunted, don't you?' She accused.

'Yes. Do you?'

'There's something evil in the house.'

'Have you seem something, Charlotte?' I asked.

'No, but before Aunt Emily had her operation I heard an infernal din in the kitchen. As if murder was being committed.'

'Really, Charlotte, you're the end. I've stayed here scores of times and never heard anything.' Sophie was frankly sceptical.

'I asked Aunt Emily if she'd ever heard anything. She said no, although the original owner's wife had died tragically. Apparently she was a sleep-walker. She fell down the stairs and broke her neck.'

'No reason to haunt the place,' Sophie said.

'Unless she was murdered,' I replied.

'From the evidence, the Coroner concluded she'd either tripped or missed a step. The verdict was death by misadventure.'

'How very convenient,' I muttered.

'You think the husband murdered the wife?' Sophie asked.

'Yes.'

'What have you seen?' Charlotte asked.

'At first it was the abnormal coldness and darkness that got to me.'

Charlotte shivered. 'I noticed the cold, but put it down to one of Aunt Emily's economy drives. I paid no attention to the light.'

'A house with as many windows as this shouldn't need lights blazing twenty four hours daily.'

'I see what you mean, but a cold, dark house is not indisputable proof of a murder committed some fifty odd years ago,' Sophie argued.

'I agree, but I've seen things.'

'What things?' Sophie demanded.

'A hulk of a man forming out of the dividing wall. Here, in the kitchen, where the cold is most enervating, I saw a woman sitting where the refrigerator stands'

'I'm afraid.' Charlotte looked calm enough.

'You're lucky to feel just afraid. I'm plain yellow with fear. Last night I thought I'd go out of my mind.'

'One of us must stay up with you tonight. The other sleep on the chesterfield,' Charlotte said.

'I don't think Aunt Emily will last the day out,' I told them.

Aunt Emily died before midnight. A serene death. If ever a soul went straight to it's God, it was hers. We opted to spend the rest of the night sitting around the breakfast-room table, drinking coffee laced with brandy. I was gut-terrified of sleeping alone in any part of the house. Charlotte felt even worse. The charged atmosphere didn't trouble Sophie. That worried me. Was Charlotte the focus of all the evil?

When daylight came Sophie made for the bathroom. Charlotte and I repaired to the kitchen to make tea and toast. Charlotte was still crying. The brandy hadn't helped.

'I know I shouldn't cry.' She blew her nose. 'Aunt Emily would tell me off if she could see me.'

'She can see you. She's closer to you now than your own skin so make her proud - stop crying.' I turned to rescue three slices of toast before they were black beyond eating.

No-o-o-o.' It was a long-drawn-out cry of sheer terror and protest.

I swung to Charlotte and *Saw It* - a woman dressed in black and white gingham - pressing herself into Charlotte.

'No', I shrieked. 'Get back to hell, whatever you are.' I grabbed Charlotte as she folded in a dead faint.

Sophie, hearing my shriek, came running. 'What's wrong?' she asked.

'Charlotte's fainted', was all I said as I cradled her head on my knees and lifted one eyelid.

Charlotte gave a shuddering sigh and a big sob. Her green eyes were awash with tears. 'What happened?' she asked.

'You fainted', I told her. 'You need food.' I helped her to her feet and onto a chair.

'I'm sorry. It all seemed too much. I suddenly felt I couldn't go on, didn't want to go on. I'm sorry. I'll be all right now.' She took a healthy bite of richly buttered toast and marmalade.

'We'll feel better away from this house', I said. 'I don't think we should spend another night here.'

'I want only to go home', Charlotte said.

'We'll leave just as soon as the undertakers have been and gone', I promised.

'If we stay here long enough you'll have *me* seeing things.' Sophie poured fresh tea.

'No way, Sophie. You're a born devils advocate', I told her.

Charlotte gave a weak giggle.

Hearing it, I thought, thank God she has no knowledge of the excrable vision I witnessed. I'll remember it to my dying day. An evil ghost-woman trying to take possession of Charlotte's body. The hulk, presumably her husband and killer, taking on the form of a man. Oddly he looked more a victim than a murderer. Nevertheless he killed her once more.

Perhaps in saving Charlotte he has expiated his sin and hers.
I didn't linger to verify the possibility.

Mathilda

by

Isobel Ray

It was dark in the cupboard and it smelled of tallow and chalk. Stacked shelves rose up away from her and disappeared into the gloom above. Somewhere, unseen water dripped onto tin. Mattie listened to the dripping of it, trying not to remember that she was alone.

A sudden scurry in the darkness made her squeal but her own voice, echoing, only frightened her more. Mattie pressed herself into the corner of the cupboard and thought of her home. Her mama would come for her. 'Mama will come', she whispered into the darkness.

It seemed like a long time since she had heard Miss Laker ring the bell in the classroom beyond. She had listened to the clatter and laughter of the children as they hurried off towards home. Mattie suddenly wondered if Miss Laker would keep her locked up all night.

'Mama won't let her', she said aloud but sharp little tears of dread moved behind her eyes.

Mattie was five years old.

'Dear Lord, where can she be!'

Grace Beeson turned from the darkening window and glanced again at the clock on the mantle. Five to seven! It would be dark now, along by the canal. The woman went over the feverish search of the past three hours in her mind. She had found no trace of her child. Just empty streets and people walking; people talking; people laughing; people whose own children were safe at home.

What if she'd gone in the canal! She was so little. She could have tripped and fallen

Grace Beeson turned roughly to the ten year old boy who was watching her from the stool by the fire.

'Why didn't you wait! You were supposed to bring her home. She is your sister!'

The boy began to cry again and she turned away from him in despair. Her eye caught the cap and coat hanging on a nail behind the door. She plucked them down and threw them towards the boy.

'Go fetch your father', she said 'run to the factory and tell him he must come. Tell him I said. Tell him Mattie's not come home.'

The darkness was thicker now. Mattie tried to think about when it had been light. She remembered the sun on the cobweb by the gate in the garden at home. She had stood, watching the heavy cold dew which was caught in the web like a million tiny silver fishes, and Toby had been cross with her for dawdling. Toby was her big brother. She wondered, now, what he had thought when she was not by the gate at home time.

Her feet were cold and her legs ached. She wanted to sit down but the floor in the cupboard was chalky. Mama would be cross if she spoiled her dress.

Not as cross as Miss Laker, though. She had such fat mauve cheeks and eyes that went big and round. She smacked the boys with the stick from her desk but she put the girls in the cupboard.

Mattie had never been in the cupboard before. The place on her arm still hurt where Miss Laker had dragged her from her seat. Mattie rubbed at her arm and began to sob quietly. She wished she hadn't have talked when Miss Laker said silence!

Harold Beeson was a big rough man. He wasn't used to these sort of dealings and he didn't like it.

'She'll be lost I expect', he said. An attempt to steady his wife and stop her crying.

'And what were you at, leaving your sister and coming home!' He leaned over, as if on an afterthought, and cuffed Toby's head.

The boy had been snivelling but now he shot round in anger. 'It ain't fair!' he said 'I waited but she never come. I didn't know what to do but come home.'

Harold Beeson stood a moment, deciding what to do. Suddenly he made for the door. 'I'll go for the police. You stop here until they come.'

His wife's voice came out in a thin wail. 'The police? Oh father!'

Harold Beeson looked back at her from the door. 'She's got to be found.' he said 'I'll not be long.'

Mattie longed for a drink of water. She had felt hungry for a while but now she could think only of water. She wondered how long it took before you died.

She didn't think about Toby or her mama much anymore. Even Miss Laker seemed part of something that was no longer of her world. Now she had the darkness and the silence and the thirst.

She chewed her tongue again. It had helped at first but now it was only sore.

Once more she ran her outstretched hands along the bumpy backs of the row of books on the shelf before her and was comforted. She could not see the books in the darkness but they were always there, dependable, when she reached out for them.

The policeman hurried along the road with Grace and Harold Beeson. They were going to the teacher's house - Miss Laker - at the top of the hill.

'Makes sense to ask her if she saw the child leave with anyone', the policeman panted as they turned in at the white wicket gate.

It was several minutes before the heavy door was drawn back and the warm smell of lavender polish wafted out onto the chill night air. The face of the small plump woman at the door clouded with concern at the sight of the policeman.

'Good gracious, yes!' she said when all had been explained, 'I'm afraid it's me that has caused you all this trouble, officer. I had to punish Mathilda for talking in class and I rather think I may have forgotten all about her.'

Grace Beeson knew her place but she had been worried half out of her mind. 'What have you done with her?' she cried, and then shrank back as the schoolteacher turned to look at her directly.

'Why, I locked her in the store cupboard', she said, and waited for a response. When it didn't come, she went on more gently. 'She can't come to any harm. Come along, I'll let her out immediately.'

'Well, all's well that ends well', said the policeman as they marched towards the school house. 'I was beginning to fear the worst, I can tell you. And I expect Mr and Mrs Beeson, here, must be more than a mite relieved to have her found safe.'

Harold Beeson grunted for both of them. He knew his wife felt the rage, same as he did, but what could you do? He hated the way these people could make him feel less than a man.

Mattie sat by the fire with the bowl of soup. The basin was burning her legs through the thin material of her dress but she didn't mind it. All she could see was her mama's face saying 'thank you' and Miss Laker saying 'that's all right.'

The policeman had told her not to get into trouble again now she knew how it felt to be locked up and he'd laughed with Miss Laker but she didn't mind that.

She minded her mama not being cross with Miss Laker.

She minded her father saying 'sorry' to the policeman.

She thought again of the row of bumpy-backed books and they made her feel strong. She smiled a secret little smile that was safe and dependable because it was inside and within. Mattie knew that she would never be alone again.

Before she was strong she had cried about going to school and her mama had said, 'you must go. You will learn things.' And now she had learned to live in her own secret world where no one could reach in to hurt her.

Mathilda lived to be ninety eight years old. She was my grandmother. Like everyone else, I never really knew her.

Lakeside Conquest

by

D L Bromwich

Because it was such a beautiful Summer's day Hayley Newcombe decided to spend her lunch-hour by the side of the lake in the Regency gardens. Her plan was to eat her lunch and then drape herself decorously along a bench and bask in the admiration of the other al-fresco lunchers. (Well, the male ones, at least).

As she strolled along the crowded paths between the flower beds she pretended not to notice the many heads that turned in her direction.

She was, as usual, dressed for maximum impact. Her coffee-coloured skirt, figure-hugging and ending at mid-thigh level, not only displayed her long shapely legs but also emphasised the fullness of her upper thighs and the firm roundness of her buttocks. She walked with her right hand resting carelessly on her soft leather shoulder-bag. Her head was held high and her shoulders were pulled well back. Her breasts strained proudly against the white crepe-de-chine of her blouse. Nature's gifts of high cheekbones and long-lashed, limpid brown eyes were accentuated by skillfully applied make-up. Her coral-coloured lips were in gentle harmony with the auburn hair that cascaded over her shoulders.

She looked stunning, and she knew it.

Hayley worked in the perfumery department of an up-market multiple store, but her real ambition was to become a model. She cherished a dream that one day a famous photographer would discover her and whisk her away to a life of glamour and riches. She was in fact frequently chatted-up by strangers, but they were the wrong sort of men with the wrong sort of offers. Outwardly distainful, Hayley secretly enjoyed these encounters. She revelled in the power that she had over men.

The lake was surrounded with trees. Beneath the trees were benches. Seated alone on one of the benches was a young man reading a newspaper.

He was wearing horn-rimmed spectacles and had thick mousey hair that flopped down over one eye. His rumpled T-shirt, disreputable jeans and scuffed trainers all contributed to his somewhat dishevelled appearance.

By his side was a leather hold-all on the top of which rested a very expensive-looking camera.

Hayley had a vague notion that all the best photographers were scruffy. She felt a flutter of excitement, could this be her lucky day? All she had to do was attract his attention, he was bound to want to photograph her.

She sat down exactly opposite the photographer, just a few feet away from him, and waited for him to notice her.

Nothing happened.

Hayley sighed loudly and shuffled herself about on the bench.

He continued to read his newspaper.

Hayley leaned back and spread her arms along the back of the bench. Then she slowly crossed her legs, rasping one nylon-covered thigh against the other.

The photographer turned over a page and continued to read.

Feeling rather annoyed, Hayley reached down and pulled up the hem of her skirt a few inches. Then she uncrossed and re-crossed her legs; slowly, as before.

Still no response.

Angrily, and completely forgetting where she was, Hayley yanked her skirt up round her waist and stretched her legs out in front of her. She glared across at the photographer and willed him to look at her.

'Nice pair of legs you've got there, darlin'.'

Hayley's attention had been focused so hard on the photographer that she had not noticed the approach of the three unpleasant-looking characters who now stood leering down at her.

They were identically dressed in dirty jeans and black zip-up jackets. The one who had spoken was tall and burly, with a huge beer-gut. He sported a black moustache which grew down on either side of his mouth to his chin. His black shoulder-length hair was lank and greasy. One of his companions was hunched and rat-faced. The third and youngest member of the unlovely trio was still in his late teens. His florid complexion was embellished by clusters of yellow-headed pimples on his chin and forehead.

'Don't worry about covering it up' said Beer-gut as Hayley hastily rearranged her skirt. 'We've all had a good eyeful. We've been watching you flashing those green knickers at his lordship here.' He jerked his thumb in the direction of the photographer; who, at long last, looked up from his newspaper.

'We could see that you're fairly panting for it' went on beer-gut, 'so we decided to offer you our services. Between us we can give you as much as you want. Let's go somewhere quiet where we can all have a good time.'

Rat-face stared hungrily at Hayley and moistened his top lip with his tongue.

'I don't know what you're talking about' said Hayley. 'Go away and leave me alone, you disgusting creatures.'

'Don't come that with us' said Beer-gut. 'We know what you want, and we're the boys to give it to you. You come with us, we'll see you all right.'

He grabbed Hayley by the arm and pulled her to her feet. Pimples took her by the other arm. Their combined breaths stank of stale alcohol and curry.

'Get away from her.' The photographer had risen to his feet. Hayley noticed absently that he wasn't very much taller than she was.

'Who rattled your cage? said Beer-gut. 'You had your chance. Go back to sleep and leave the men's' work to us.'

'I said get away from her.' The photographer took a step forward. 'I won't tell you a third time.'

'Oh, ho' said Beer-gut. 'We've got to sort you out first, have we? Right lads...'

The three yobbos advanced towards the photographer and then hurled themselves upon him, fists swinging.

The photographer moved as gracefully as any dancer. His three assailants seemed to be getting in each others way. Then, one after the other, three bodies were flipped into the air and came crashing down on to the grass.

Rat-face and Pimples lay groaning where they had fallen, but Beer-gut hauled himself to his feet, and, sobbing with rage, pulled a short length of heavy chain out of his pocket.

The photographer took a few steps backward and waited.

Shouting obscenities and whirling the chain round his head, Beer-gut rushed into the attack for the second time.

Again the photographer danced. A turn of the body, a flick of the hips, and Beer-gut had dropped the chain and was flying; straight into the shallow waters of the lake. Ducks and geese scattered, squawking indignantly.

The photographer picked up the chain and turned to face Pimples and Rat-face who by this time were back to their feet.

'It's all right said Rat-face, holding up his hands and backing away. 'We're out of it, we're going.'

'Then take him with you, now that he's had his bath' said the photographer pointing to Beer-gut who was crawling out of the lake.

He watched the three yobbos slink away and then dropped the chain into a rubbish bin.

There was a ripple of applause and a murmured 'Bravo' from the small knot of spectators that had gathered.

The photographer gave an ironic bow.

'Are you okay?' he asked Hayley.

Yes I think so, thanks to you. You're very good at karate.'

'Actually it was aikido.' He began to gather up his camera gear. 'It's time I got back to work.'

'Me too' said Hayley, looking at her watch.

'Are you a professional photographer?' asked Hayley as they made their way towards the exit from the gardens.

'No, just an amateur. I like photographing birds, so I sometimes come in here at lunchtimes to photograph the ducks and geese.'

'Oh, I see' said Hayley.

'I've seen you in here before' he said. 'And I've seen you working in the perfume counter in Markhams. I even know your name, I read it on that name-badge that you all wear.'

'It almost sounds as though you've been spying on me' said Hayley.

'Now really. It's just that you're a girl that it's difficult not to notice.'

The slightest suggestion of a blush tinged Hayley's cheeks.

'Look' he said as they reached the main road, 'my name's Percival Knightly. Could we meet by the lake tomorrow lunchtime? I'd really like a chance to get to know you.'

Did she want to get to know someone whose name was Percy? Hayley asked herself. She was surprised to find that she did. He wasn't much to look at, but the way he'd dealt with those three yobbos...'

'Yes' she said. 'That would be nice.'

'Great, I might even take a photograph of you. You're much more photogenic than the ducks.'

'Let's hope that you don't have to defend me again' said Hayley.

'Oh, I don't think we'll have any more trouble. By the way, I think that chap who I chucked in the lake must be colour blind, don't you agree? Your knickers aren't green, they're blue.'

Printout

by

Stephen Fellows

Male, forty-two, five-foot eight, not bad looking, everything in life but a
partner, wishes to meet blonde, attractive girl for permanent relationship.

Well, back in the nineteen-nineties, that was one of the ways single people
found their soul-mate. There was of course the 'disco', or you might even have
joined a dating agency.

But in the year two-thousand and fifty-one, people have another option: 'Future centre'.

After paying your money, you are 'wired' up to a computer, and your future is
foretold. A sort of micro-chip palm-reading if you like, only this 'reading' is
deadly accurate.

Besides giving a printout of your future, it also charts your mind and brain
patterns so precisely, it can match you perfectly with a member of the opposite
sex.

These computers also give printouts of major happenings in your future year.
(Its limit in foretelling happenings is one year).

You may, for instance sometime in the coming year rob a bank, or defraud
millions of dollars. Such events would appear on your printout. Minor events,
such as running over your neighbours' cat, or cheating on your wife wouldn't
show up.

If, for example, your printout revealed that in July two-thousand and fifty-
two you will defraud a company of millions, the police would be notified of
that. You, of course would be duly arrested and put in jail the month before the
foretold felony. The printout permissible as evidence against you in a court of
law.

The police in fact, wanted these 'readouts' to be compulsory once a year for
every citizen. That way, they argued, they would be aware, well in advance of
serious crime, thereby eradicating it. But amid cries of 'big brother', the government vetoed the request.

Needless to say, the operators of these centres could only divulge pertinent
information (that being about a suggested partner) to the client. These 'Future
centres' were franchised by the government, and they were strictly controlled.

69

Every week they were inspected by government officials who had the power to close down any centre and lock up its operator should any of the strict guide-lines be transgressed.

One such operator was Sally Green. She'd ran her centre for two years now, and just lately, business wasn't very good. She wasn't making the money the glossy advertising brochure said she would when she bought the franchise.

It was Wednesday the tenth of August when Joe Lyons walked into Sally Green's 'Future centre' for his first 'readout'.

It was easy to see why Joe would seek the help of Sally's computer.

He was short, fat, with greasy, untidy hair. He had a permanent leer across his 'not much to look at' face. Sally took an instant dislike to him.

Joe was quietly spoken, and seemingly shy. He found it hard to attract women. The few he did, soon left him. No, Joe wasn't good at relationships. Fact is, he didn't really like women.

Could Sally's computer find him his perfect partner? He hoped it would.

Sally, being reluctant to touch him, carefully attached the electrodes to Joe's head as he sat relaxed in the reclining chair.

'Let's get this over with quickly, and get him and his smell out of here', Sally thought to herself.

She switched everything on and sat down near the printer, not bothering to pay much attention to it, preferring instead to file her nails.

'What could the future possibly hold of any interest for him?', she said under her breath, giving him a 'what have I just stepped in?' look.

Casually glancing at the printer, Sally caught sight of a word that made her eyes widen. The word was, 'priceless'.

Sally, captivated by that word, prematurely stopped the printer, ripped off what was printed, and held it closer: her jaw dropped. It read: Mr Joe Lyons, 67, Sunset Blvd., Los Angeles. Priceless diamond taken from wall-safe..... September..... armed gang.....

'This disgusting person has a priceless diamond?' she uttered to herself incredulously.

As Joe reposed in his chair, oblivious to all around; Sally was cooking up a plan.

Satisfied she'd read enough, she put her 'find' through the shredder, smiling as she did so.

Sally then walked over to Joe, 'unhooked' him from the computer and pro-ceeded to give him a load of hog-wash about everything being fine; and how

70

she'd found 'just the girl for him' from her computer files. Joe, of course was pleased to hear this.

Sally had indeed 'found' a girl for Joe: her devious little sister, Jane. Jane was, how shall we say; a 'lady of the night', and would agree to any plan that paid this well.

And the plan was simple. Get themselves invited to the house. Pull a gun on the creep; force him to open the safe, grab the diamond; then shoot the creep. Cold-blooded, yes. But these two girls weren't sentimental where money was concerned.

Joe left Sally's centre quite happy. Sally had told him that she would contact the girl she had in mind, and phone him tomorrow with a view to meeting at his house on Friday.

As Joe disappeared, Sally put the 'closed' sign in the window, locked up, and left.

The next day, Sally phoned.

'Hello Mr Lyons, it's Sally Green here, how are you? Fine! Oh good. Now I've spoken to the lady concerned and she'd love to meet you. Can we come to your house Friday evening?'

Joe, sprawled out on his sofa was delighted.

'Yes, of course', he said. 'Be here at 8.00 we'll have dinner together.'

'That would be nice Mr Lyons. We'll see you tomorrow then, bye.'

Sally replaced the handset, looked excitedly at Jane who was next to her and laughed. They both laughed. At last, they'd hooked the 'big one'. They'd booked their flight reservations; this was their last job.

Jane crawled out of her bed. The time was 11.55 am; it was Friday, 12th August.

Bleary eyed, she walked into the kitchen looking for a drink, alcohol would do nicely.

She looked in the mirror, and, not liking what she saw, screwed up her face. 'How much did you have to drink last night?' she asked her reflection.

The phone rang. It was Sally.

'Hi Jane.'

'Yeah.'

'You okay?' Sally enquired, anxiously.

'Yeah, I'm okay', Jane mumbled. 'Just had too much to drink that's all.'

'I don't believe it!' said Sally, obviously annoyed. 'Our big night, and you're hung-over!'

'Quit the sermon will you', Jane protested. 'I'll be fine later.'

'Well you'd better be! I don't want you screwing up tonight... I'll pick you up at 7.30, be ready!'

Sally slammed the phone down:

The girls reached Joe's house on time. He welcomed them into his home; and Jane sensed his staring eyes boring into her; that leer, ever present.

She felt reassured by her handbag, and as her hand dropped to it she felt the gun inside and thought to herself 'this is for you, creep'.

Sally and Jane were eager to get their well manicured hands on the diamond, and scarper, but they were prepared to wait. They figured that by biding their time and getting some drink down him, he would be easier to handle.

Dinner was delicious, Joe was most concerned that it was to their liking. He was very polite, nothing it seemed, too much trouble for him. Conversation was sometimes a little strained, Joe wasn't really comfortable with women.

He did of course ask Jane to stay the night, and Jane, knowing of his coming fate said that she would: but of course, she wouldn't be!

After a few more drinks, they all, especially Joe, seemed more relaxed: an air of expectancy filled the room.

What a night it was going to be!

It was Saturday, 13th August.

The maitre d' looked anxiously at his watch, it was 1.20 pm and Mr Lyons wasn't at his usual table. Where was he?

He'd had his 1.00 pm reservation for eight years now. And if he couldn't make it, he always phoned.

The government inspectors had arrived at Sally's centre at their usual time, 4.00 pm. They were most concerned to see the 'closed' sign in the window.

The door was forced open, and the officials hurriedly entered and began searching; a look og disquiet on each of their faces.

Where on earth could Sally Green be? One official noticed that the computer was 'flashing' *print*, and that strangely, the printer was switched off.

Click; and official finger released the type-head from its untimely pause. He watched as it continued to dance across the paper.

The other silently gathered round, their stern faces transfixed on the print-out.

Would they soon have the answer to Sally Greens whereabouts?

The officials stared at the printout as it finished a report on a diamond robbery: it continued printing; they had their answered: it read: 'Diamond dealer murders two sisters!'

Christmas Present

by

Peter Bailey

Forrest told himself that the terrible cold might dull the raging pain of his injuries and the mind-blowing pounding in his head. It didn't. Savaged by vicious sleet and the unrelenting wind which turned any protection from his worn and torn denim jacket and jeans into a joke, he knew that coherent movement would soon be beyond him.

Still he stumbled blindly through the black loneliness of this back lane a thousand miles from warmth and sanity. In more than two hours just two cars had swept carelessly past him. He'd wearily hung out his good arm, thumb extended, to be rewarded by their wheels spraying him with freezing filth.

It was now almost midnight on this nightmare Christmas Eve as Forrest staggered on through unending agony. His mind drifted into rare and bitter reflection of his pitiful forty three years. His brief disastrous marriage. The string of women during and after it. The odd menial job, always unfulfilling.
'Unfulfilling. Yea, that's what it's been.' Did he speak aloud? It seemed somehow important.
Unfulfilled. Except; ah, except. There was one shining beacon in his nondescript existence: his deep passion for rock'n'roll music and for the cars from its period. He nursed a dream of cruising lazily in a big late-fifties American 'tank', for preference a Chrysler LeBaron, rock'n'roll blaring from the chrome-faced radio, a gorgeous fifties 'chick' by his side.
As ever, of course, he'd compromised. His 'cruiser' was a '62 Ford Anglia and his women were usually too tarty even for Forrest's taste, deadbeats like himself.
Nevertheless, his little blue Anglia had provided a niche, a certain flair which he perceived as sadly lacking in most people in the nineties.
But now even his little car had failed him. Or perhaps it had simply grown weary, like his women, of his shabby treatment and decided to call it a day.
Forrest had long known that the brakes were dodgy. Predictably, he'd put off investigating the problems before leaving his scruffy Midlands flat today to

73

spend Christmas in Cornwall with the faded but still sexy forty-odd-year old widow who had served his expresso in a seedy Truro cafe back in the summer. Anticipating delights greater even than frothy coffee, and with Anglia's tape-deck pumping good old rock'n'roll, he'd pushed the tired old car too hard into a muddy bend on a narrow lane some local had recommended as a short-cut at the pub he'd paused at.

As he panic-braked and fought the sliding and swaying car, a front brake cylinder had finally let go. The car shot broadside, headlights crazily dancing across deserted waterlogged fields, hurling itself with agile abandon into a deep West Country drainage ditch.

It sat, totalled beyond hope, in the black water and stinking weeds. But, as it died, it had taken its revenge, dealing Forrest a stunning blow to the temple with some part of its anatomy. It further contrived to smash his left knee and dislocate his shoulder. Coming round and painfully crawling from the mess, Forrest was violently sick. But his terrible nausea did not lessen and, as he sagged against the steeply-angled rear bumper, the pounding exploding in his head rapidly increased.

Surely another vehicle would appear. Forty minutes later one hadn't and he decided he must make it back to the pub. Otherwise he could freeze here and he cursed himself for bringing only the clothes he stood in. Shuddering and heaving, he started back along the lane with no backward glance at the little car that had meant so much to him.

Peering groggily now into the enveloping night, he realized he should have come upon the light of the pub before this. Blindly staggering, pain and fear his only companions, he'd obviously blundered down a wrong fork. Even Forrest's numbed senses could detect that this lane was decidedly narrower than that which he'd followed in the car.

There was no light, no trace of human or animal habitation, and Forrest now faced the fact that he was totally lost, very ill and desolately afraid. A violent spasm shook him, causing his injuries to flare in thought-blocking agony. He whimpered softly, a tiny cornered animal sound. He shook uncontrollably and knew that he could go no further. Unless help came now, this was the bottom line, the end of the road.

Swamped by pain and utter hopelessness, he huddled on a soaking drift of leaves, his back to the rough trunk of a tree beside the lane. At first he was oblivious to the approaching headlights. It was only as the car stood idling before him that the soft burble of its big V-8 engine penetrated his numbed senses to strike some chord deep within him.

Straining to focus, he didn't believe his aching eyes, though even through the murk the sleek shape was unmistakable. This was his dream, a fabulous '57 Chrysler LeBaron. The sleet, fast turning to snow drove and swirled in its head-lamp beams and in the blood-red glare of the huge tail lamps. His over-stressed mind had conjured a vision. But no vision could so perfectly reproduce those superb lines and elegant trim.

His excitement dissipated nausea and pain. This of all cars to come to his res-cue! 'Oh thank you, thank you,' he croaked. He didn't even notice the blood sluggishly erupting from his mouth.

The front passenger door swung open and the interior light blinked on. At the wheel, amidst acres of soft vynide and glorious chrome was the most beautiful girl Forrest had ever seen. Her smile was magical in the green glow of the dash lights.

As Forrest approached the girl started with concern. 'Heavens, whatever's happened to you? Her voice was low and soft. Forrest began to mumble but she quickly interrupted. 'Never mind, just get in. We'll soon put things right'.

He sank into the plush seat, closed the door, and was transported into a per-sonal heaven as the girl accelerated the car in a superb power-surge.

'I live quite near,' she told him, 'We'll soon have you fixed up'.

'No hurry,' Forrest whispered, 'no hurry at all now.'

The big LeBaron gliding through the night, its heater purring healing warmth, soft upholstery cosseting him, the snow racing in the headlamps was a million miles away through the huge curved windscreen. The girl's skirt had ridden up her thighs as she drove and, between her and the car, Forrest thought he had never seen so many gorgeous curves at one time.

The radio wafted some smoochy Fifties ballad and the total effect on Forrest after his ordeal was too soporific. He drifted, lulled by the warmth and the car's soft hum into dreamy contentment. 'Wow', he murmured, 'oh wow...'

Driving nearer, the girl saw that what she had taken for a bundle of rubbish beneath the tree was a man. 'Oh God, it's some poor tramp. He must be nearly frozen to death'.

Leaving the car's engine idling, she scrambled through the muddy under-growth, ignoring the damage to her elegant clothes, towards the huddled figure. She wondered frantically how she was to get the poor fellow to the car but, bending over him, she realized with a sick lurch that he was quite dead. The light powdering of snow on his devastated face was just beginning to melt in the wintry morning sun.

His passing could hardly have been pleasant, but the girl was surprised by the gentle smile on white but blood-spattered lips.

She decided there was little point in driving the ten miles or so back to her parents' country home. Better to continue the couple of miles to the country pub and report her unpleasant discovery there. She'd been headed there anyway for a Christmas morning drink with friends and to show off her father's new car which she'd been allowed to use for the first time today.

Obviously, her finding the body would now take precedence but, upset and saddened though she was, the brief unbidden thought came that this was a bit of a shame. She'd been looking forward to her friends' reactions to the car. After all, a brand new Chrysler LeBaron was something of a rarity in rural England in 1957.

Immortality

by

Robert Edward Pee

My name is Richard Caswell; Doctor Caswell to the people I work with. I am a scientist.

I look out of the lab windows, and reflect on what has happened to change the world of 2050 so much, so irreparably in these past few hours. I can hear screams, and see a little group of people running in search of safety across the street. They won't find it, there are no safe places anymore. The sky appears to be on fire, although perhaps that is just the effect given by all the collapsed, burning buildings.

Most of the complicated, intricate machines which formerly filled the lab are smashed; some appear to the burning.

Jelt is on his stretcher, still connected to his mind-boggling complicated life-support machines, exactly where we left him when it began. Jelt's black-uniformed 'attendants' - bodyguards would be a better term - stand either side of him, occasionally glancing at me accusingly.

Doctor Benedict is crouching on the floor, quivering in terror. I don't care, its all his fault. Although, to be fair, I must shoulder part of the blame myself. To think that the people of the twentieth century used to fret about nuclear weapons! If only they'd known about the menace posed by time-travel.

My mind drifts back to this morning, when everything seemed so normal....

I arrived at the Institute at about 9 a.m., dressed in a pinstripe suit. I breezed into the lobby, taking scant notice of the chairs and potted plants, and walked over to the reception desk.

'Any messages for me?' I asked curtly.

'Yes, Doctor Caswell. Doctor Benedict is waiting for you in the Project Lab, along with Mr Jelt.'

'Mr Jelt?' I repeated disapprovingly, and set off towards the lab.

Mr Jelt. Another rich client, no doubt. If only I'd known how my research would be used, I might have stopped before the big breakthrough. Or perhaps not. Out of the world scientific community, only Doctor Benedict and I had managed to discover an effective method of time-travel. At the moment it was still very primitive, but objects could be sent into the past.. or brought back.

As you know, for the last fifty years or so, the human race has been getting genetically weaker; by this I mean that our life-spans are growing shorter, we are more susceptible to diseases, each baby that is born is smaller and weaker than its forefathers. And there are people in our world who have money and power, and who don't want to die young. Not at all.

It was a simple matter to bring people out of the past, bodies for these people to inhabit when their own pass away. Carried on indefinitely, this would confer upon them immortality. But there were many dangers inherent in this process...

I changed into my lab coat and a few minutes later I arrived in the lab. Lying on a stretcher on a table near to the door was Jelt. He was not an old man, but his hair was falling out, his skin wrinkling, his sight failing. He lay silent, occasionally gesturing to one of his three 'attendants', who had positioned themselves around the stretcher. To me he looked like a short, shrivelled gargoyle. Would this happen to me in a few years time?

Monitoring the machinery, a pencil tucked behind his ear, was Doctor Benedict. I glanced over the time-travel machinery before going over to him; it even awed me, its co-creator.

The machinery consisted of a group of computer consoles, studded with buttons and screens and winking lights, arranged around a raised, circular dais in the centre of the room. Positioned over it was a glass tube, which could be lowered onto the dais by the huge robotic arm which was gripping it at the top. This shielding device was necessary, as time-travel products harmful radiation which can be fatal.

I went over to Benedict. He is a short man, and very ambitious, as short men often are. His eyes seemed to sparkle, as if reflected the one hundred plans and schemes filtering through the brain behind them.

He spotted me. 'You're late!' he said irritably. 'Jelt's 'attendants' have been giving me funny looks for the last five minutes! They probably think we're trying to back out on the deal. Get working. It needs two people to work the machine properly.'

'Do you think we should do this?' I asked quietly.

'Do I think... Do I think...?' Benedict stuttered uncomprehendingly. 'Of course. We got five million riding on this!'

'Look!' I said with unaccustomed self-assertion. 'The Time-scoop was constructed to transport people - observers - into the past, not to take things out of it! The process is far too dangerous. Sure, there have been millions of insignificant people in the past who you can kidnap, but what if once, just once, we snag a Stalin, an Ivan the Terrible? What would happen?'

'I don't know, what?' Benedict asked shortly.

'We'd create a paradox which would shatter the Web of Time. Human history would never have taken the course we know it did. Heavens, we might all be suddenly struck dead. The universe might collapse in on itself. The consequences would be incalculable.'

'Yes, but ...'

'Have you thought that we may be causing the wakening of our race? The time-travel process releases huge amounts of radiation into the past you know!'

'Have you thought that we might be responsible for the evolution of the human species?' Benedict retorted.

'My master wishes you to hurry up,' one of the 'attendants' said, glaring at us. There was a pistol in a holster by his side.

'Look we have to do it this time, we've taken the money' Benedict said. 'But I'll think about you've said.'

I knew he was lying, but it would have taken more courage than I possess to back out at that stage. We began the process. The glass tube was lowered down by the robotic arm until it fitted snugly over the dais. A sort of fog began to appear in the tube, with little jolts of electricity passing through it, creating an amorphous bluish glow. Then, a body began to appear. We could only see a black shape first, like a shadow, then details began to appear, little by little. And it became clear to me that we'd snagged an important one.

The man was tall, and dressed in some kind of white toga, in the Roman fashion. He was tall, and had blue eyes. He wore a diadem on his head, a circlet of gold and jewels. A Roman Emperor. I knew a bit about history. We'd got Constantine, or Diocletian, or one of that crew. Benedict knew too - I could tell from the horror on his face.

'Shut it off!' I shouted. The lab was suddenly filled with a howling wind, and I struggled through it towards him. 'Shut the damn machine off!'

But he couldn't, or wouldn't. He just stayed there, hand hovering over the set of controls that would end this nightmare, staring into the tube.

The man inside was looking about himself in surprise. Perhaps he thought he was in heaven or hell or somewhere. Then the tube exploded, raining glass all over the lab. I shielded my face with my hands. I didn't see what happened to the time-traveller; I just dragged Benedict away from the computer console, which was begin to vibrate and spark alarmingly. I suppose it was more than he deserved.

A great gout of flame shot out of a bank of computers, singeing my lab coat. Most of the computers and machines were in flames now, or exploding. It seemed that the whole world was made of fire, and I think this extended far beyond the lab; I could dimly hear people screaming outside.

One of the 'attendants' advance ed towards us, pistol raised.

'You have failed to carry out the contract, as we agreed', he said. 'Therefore, you will both die.'

'That's crazy!' Benedict said. 'I made sure your Mr Jelt knew the risks before we fixed the payment. He knew what he was getting into.' Fresh inspiration. 'And how are you going to explain away the presence of two corpses in this lab. Jelt may be rich, but he doesn't rule the world.'

'I listened to Doctor Caswell's little speech,' the 'attendant' said. 'In the chaos that is to follow, I don't think anyone will notice'.

In the corner of the room, Jelt was croaking and waving his hand. One of the 'attendants' leaned closer to try and make out what he was saying. Our prospective killer turned around to hear the verdict. The 'attendant made frantic 'stop' signals with his hands.

'Well, it seems your lives are to be spared', the 'attendant' said, and retreated into the corner of the room sulkily.

Since then, Armageddon has been gathering speed. When the process finally stops. I don't think humanity, or the Earth, will exist. Perhaps the universe will be gone. We thought we were Gods. We took it upon ourselves to meddle with the mysteries of life and death, the future and the past. The ancient Greeks called overweening pride hubris, and believed whoever was afflicted would be laid low by the Gods. So it has happened here. Because of our overweening pride, we have destroyed our race.

Untitled (A Dream)

by

Neil Thorley

A dream. The first real day of Spring, sunshine, still air, and an almost forgotten warmth waiting beyond the spiteful cool of shadows. Striding out in t-shirt and jeans, walking for the sake of it, to exult in escape from the suffocating embrace of winter clothing. Deep breaths down by the park, people suddenly lighter, buoyant, intoxicated by the welcome infusion of Vitamin D.

Looking around, I notice life and activity non-existent last week, when I took the same route; that time motivated by the desire for a little gentle exercise and isolation, grey mood matching the grey day and quiet empty expanses awaiting. Today, squirrels, birds, dogs, scampering children, transform the previously monochrome park, enticing an unconscious smile to my face. Life's not so bad, after all.

Following a pause, I carry on, leaving behind the hubbub centred on swings, slide, roundabouts and a still empty paddling pool. What a marvel this park is, slap bang in the heart of the large industrial town I grew up in, an oasis of green calm in a maelstrom of traffic, fumes, noise and hassle. Living close, I've enjoyed its patient seclusion many times for refuge, a soothing antidote to the stress of urban circumstance.

A breath of wind stirs the leaves above as I head for the largest open space in the park, aiming at the middle, to sit and ease the tension produced on an individual in a cramped life of co-existence.

The ground is dry, well drained here, shrugging off the memory of not so long gone rain. Might as well lie back for a while, and close my eyes thankfully. The heat close to the earth is delicious, my mind wanders off, prey to the stimuli of small sounds - insects, birds and distant shouts. Marvellous.

Close to dozing off, I suddenly realise the white light that burned through my closed eyelids has gone, replaced by a much diminished hue, and a sense of solitude defiled. I crack open one eye irritably, squinting yet at the assault of light beyond the figure standing over me.

My perusal garners no response, so I sit up, opening the other eye to see better what I'm presented with. Female, and pretty, but dressed heavily for the day, and somehow dishevelled, lacking the smoothness of habitual personal grooming. She stands there unspeaking, yet I am aware that since we occupy a small space in a large area, she must have approached deliberately. After a while she sits too, sinking cross legged to the ground, her long dark skirt silently concealing any awkwardness. The large canvas bag she carries is kept close, not cast aside, a thing of importance.

Ill at ease, I search for something to say, eventually arriving at the brilliant, 'Hello'.

'Hello', is the witty riposte, her voice small and child-like. I examine her more closely, the shabby winter coat she wears shields her frame from appraisal, but her face is soft and unlined, putting forward an age anything from 15 to 25, but I suspect the lower value to be closest.

She's too small for her silent regard to be threatening, but it's not exactly comfortable either.

'Can I help you?' I ask her.

Hesitatingly, 'Well yes, actually.' Her accent's not local, lacking any immediately identifiable inflections. I have to wait for her to continue, seemingly unsure, managing to convey an air of vulnerability that suddenly makes me want to warn her about approaching strangers, but not knowing how to do so without the warning itself carrying tones of menace.

'This isn't easy, I don't know what to say'.

'Just relax, it's a nice day, what's your name?' I say.

'Helen'.

'Well Helen, let me help. I'm not so devastatingly handsome that you just had to come and speak to me, am I?'

'No'.

'Oh, thank you very much indeed, I wouldn't have minded if you'd said yes, you know.' A slight smile lifted her serious expression.

'Ah, getting better, you almost smiled then. Well maybe you've lost a contact lens and need my help to find it.' Feeble.

'No, my eyesight's perfect'.

'As is the rest of you, in my estimation.' Flattery, the old weapon, slips out before I can stop it, inappropriate I feel with hindsight. And ineffective anyway, she breaks her previously locked gaze, casting her eyes down, one hand grasping at an errant stalk poking above the short grass.

'Sorry, old habit, automatically engaged when my brain registers a pretty girl.' Oops, I'm at it again, but she doesn't respond to the charm.

'It's money, I need some money.' She drags out the words unwillingly, not able to look at me.

82

'Oh,' is all I can say, somehow affronted, my perception of the situation galvanised into a harsh un-cooperative stance. Ready to demur, mumble a few platitudes of refusal and put some distance between myself and such an offensive request.

The way she sits there, awaiting pronouncement of my judgement, stays my tongue. A sense of shame creeps up on me, and with it the blush of embarrassment. Call yourself a humanitarian, I think. You can easily afford to give her some money. Why so mean, why did I instinctively want to refuse? And not only that, but to refuse with condescension and ill-humour.

'Look, I'm sorry, I haven't got much money on me'. I finally announce. She starts to rise immediately, still unable to look at me.

'That's OK, don't worry, it doesn't matter.' Her voice quavers, humiliated.

'Wait a minute, don't rush off, you can have whatever I've got, I don't need any before I get back home.'

She stops, turning back slowly, unspeaking.

'Please, won't you sit down again, perhaps I can help in some other way.'

'What do you mean, I don't need that sort of help.' she rattles out, a strain of alarm in her voice, taking me aback.

'Please, sit down, I didn't mean to imply anything. Just tell me a bit more about yourself, are you living rough?' Her defiance crumbles swiftly and she wearily returns to her previous seat.

'I guess you can call it that.'

'Why?' A naive question, provoking a bitter laugh.

'Why? Why not. Don't tell me you want a complete breakdown of my motives and circumstances.'

'No, but you sound educated and intelligent, surely you don't think you can doss indefinitely.'

'What choice do I have, it's easy to drop out, not so easy to get back in.'

'But you can't be very old, what about your parents, your home. Can't you go back?'

'Oh sure, they'd be more than happy to see me, especially him, but I stuck it as long as I could, he'll never get his hands on me again,' Her voice carries an overwhelming tone of deep horrors lurking beneath.

'I'm sorry to hear that. What about the social services, can't they find somewhere for you to stay?'

'Oh they have, a couple of times, but it always ends with someone like you.'

'Like me, what do you mean, like me?'

'Pretty. I heard you, I know what you were thinking, you're all the same, disgusting, filthy. Forget it, I'm leaving.'

'No don't', I say quickly. 'Look, you need some help, don't just rush off. I don't know you very well, but I'm worried, you're too young, too small and too vulnerable for life on the road.'

'What do you suggest.'

'I don't know, but you can come with me if you like. I live alone, you can have a meal, clean up a bit, and we'll see what's available here for you.' I say without thinking, losing control of the situation. Jesus, what a reversal from a few minutes ago, when I wouldn't even give her the change in my pocket.

Her energy has returned, the weariness banished by an almost visible preparation for fight or flight, she stands quickly, supply, her youthful bones re-awakened.

'Too young I may be, but I'm learning, I knew it when I saw you, knew what you'd want from me in exchange. Maybe one day I'll sink that low, but not yet.'

'You're off again, you really have got a problem. I most definitely didn't mean anything except a desire to help. If someone doesn't reach out a hand, how will you ever escape from your trap?' She starts to cry.

'I don't know.' Utter despair, she grabs at the bag, which had momentarily been forgotten on the ground, and suddenly runs.

'Stop, wait, the money'. I shout, fumbling in my pocket. She sprints away, her loose clothing making her gait inelegant and difficult. Doesn't look back, doesn't slow, disappears from sight into a row of trees, beyond which waits a park exit and the harsh streets.

I look down at my hand, four pound odd, and feel a wave of my own despair.

A dream did I say, or a nightmare?

The Creature Within

by

Stuart Gentry

The creatures only just made it out of the house in time. As they emerged, coughing and choking from the pyre, the roof of their shack, tortured beyond endurance by the greedy, licking flames, subsided first with a tired groan and then with a rending crash. Only half-alive and clutching pathetically at sacks and toys, they melted from the lurid scene into the grey netherworld of a small-town dawn. Behind them the agitated mob were drawn to the burning shack like satellites being sucked into an ancient, imploding star at the furthest, most Godless edges of the Galaxy.

Ed McCrarey carefully detached himself from the mob and, unobserved, made it to his car. He couldn't repress a satisfied half-smile as he slammed into gear and roared out into the dust-bowl. 'This is *my* territory', he thought, 'Where a man can make a living out of hate.'

Watching the indistinguishable miles being eaten up, he let his mind catalogue the events of the last three weeks.

This last project had been almost too easy for him - a small, isolated community only too ready to have their unvoiced suspicion of an immigrant family ignited into a smouldering hatred and then into violent action. He had identified the Canowski family with their unfamiliar appearance, dress and customs as his target on his second day in the town and he had set to work at once. With his immaculate suit and expensive car Ed had been welcomed by the town's bar-tender (who recognised a real gentleman when he saw one) and Ed was assured from the start of a rapt audience amongst the clientele.

Acting the part of concerned by-stander to perfection, he began by asking rather too many questions about the Canowskis. He had said nothing explicit but took care to retire to his room upstairs just as he saw puzzled glances bounce around the room. The seeds had been planted and during the next days he constantly wheedled away at the townsfolk.

It was a week later when the bullying began. Small, petty acts at first:-the store-keeper kept Mr Canowski waiting until last before he served him; the children were shunned by schoolmates; people in the street started to gossip and stare when Mrs Canowski came down to town. Soon after this Ed judged that the time was right to use his special word.

Letting the bar-tender press more drinks on him than usual, he pretended that a former reticence had been overcome and he made his play.

'I'm surprised that such God-fearing, upright men as yourselves should let such *creatures* as these live amongst your wives and children!', he had exclaimed with much passion.

The atmosphere of the bar began to glow with emotion as the faces around him set into undisguisable masks of hatred and they would have driven the 'creatures' out then and there if Ed had not stopped them. Leaping on to a table he stilled the mass with an appeal to their patriotism.

'This is not the way we do things in *our* country', he had preached, 'We must have a proper campaign, a petition...'

Of course they had agreed and who else to organise it but their friend Ed McCrarey. Of course there should be a campaign fund, they would do everything by the law of the land.

This fund now sat snugly in the wallet which kept Ed company on the passenger seat as he hauled his car down an unexplored road which wound like a gunpowder trail towards the distant grey foothills, emissaries of the translucent mountains beyond.

It was early evening before he sighted any dwelling - a ramshackle farm half matchwood, half kindling but his hunger was such that he pulled off the road in any case in the hope of finding a bite to eat. His map showed that the town he was making for was at least three miles further on and he could not wait any longer.

He pushed open the ancient gate and walked warily up to the house. Rounding an old hay barn he saw something which froze him to the spot with amazement.

In the farmyard a decrepit old man was bathing at a pump and on his naked back were strange green markings which resembled symbols of some kind.

'Here indeed is a creature!' he chuckled to himself, withdrawing silently.

Once in the town he immediately set about his work and was surprised how quickly the townspeople responded to his hints. The hermit, Old Wilson had always been viewed with extreme suspicion and Ed's declaration that he was some kind of creature was lapped up readily. With the fund well established and feelings at fever pitch he led the townspeople along the road to the farm to show them the final proof.

The old man could only stare in dumb comprehension at the smouldering mass of people in front of him. Striding confidently up to him, Ed took hold of the old man by the shoulders, pulled him round and in the same motion ripped the shirt from his back.

'Here's your proof!' he shouted at the sheriff. 'Here's your creature for you!'

Rather than advancing and licking around him, the wall of fiery rage in front of Ed suddenly became a wall of stone as the now silent townspeople stared coldly into his eyes. Then, without a word, the men grimly removed their shirts to reveal identical strange, unworldly markings on their backs.

Ed McCrarey's mind crawled with fear and he felt in a flash his own house burning, burning...

In agonising slow-motion the sea of faces broke and covered him, dowsing the fire and drowning the creature within.

Out of the Shadows

by

Kay Smith

Gerry Porter drove too fast across the darkened garage forecourt in his brand new Porsche feeling mighty pleased with himself.

His ritual Saturday evening check of the week's takings showed he was well on the way towards making his first million. Not bad for a bloke who'd started out with absolutely nothing except a burning ambition to better himself.

His was a real Rags to Riches story. The less said about his poverty stricken and abused childhood the better. But for a kindly childless couple who had taken him under their wing he dreaded to think how he'd have ended up. The man, a skilled mechanic, had taught him all there was to know about anything with an engine and four wheels.

When Gerry left school his benefactor found him a job in a garage. By saving hard he was able to rent a derelict warehouse before he was twenty, and set up business on his own account.

He often remembered that old place, a far cry from the thriving garage and petrol station on the town's ring road, with his name on the illuminated fascia sign.

Now nearly forty he'd got it made. A luxury home, a thriving business and a promising career in local government. What more could any man wish for?

The girl who stepped out of the shadows into the path of his car jolted him back to reality. He practically stood on the brakes, gripping the steering wheel as the car juddered to a halt. He closed his eyes, hardly daring to believe he hadn't mowed her down.

His heart thudded and the blood pounded in his head until he was sure he'd pass out.

Eventually he risked opening his eyes. The girl was watching him, apparently unscathed and not a bit bothered that she'd scared the living daylights out of him. It wouldn't do his standing as a magistrate any good, to be charged with manslaughter due to careless driving.

He took stock of the girl. A skinny plain eighteen-year old who looked as if a few nourishing meals wouldn't come amiss. Her skimpy leather waistcoat, faded polo neck jumper and briefest of brief mini skirts did nothing to enhance her non-existant charm.

Her sandy colouring, pale blue eyes and sprinkling of freckles across the bridge of her nose reminded him of himself at the same age. He'd never been much to look at then, either.

He pressed the automatic control that wound the window down.

'What the hell do you think you're playing at?' he snarled, 'You're lucky my brakes are good'.

'You Gerry Porter?' she asked.

He nodded, her cheeky familiarity angering him further.

'About time you showed up. I've been waiting ages,' she said.

'Nobody asked you to hang around. Why didn't you come to the office during working hours,' he snapped. If she was after a job she was going the wrong way about it.

'Wanted to see you on your own. It's a private matter.'

'Hurry up then. What's the mystery?'

'No mystery. Just thought it was about time we met..dad.'

'Eh? Whassat? Wotcher say?' He lapsed into the Black Country dialect he'd spent years trying to lose. Then, re-asserting himself he told her in no uncertain terms to go back home to her mum and stop playing games.

She didn't move.

'Haven't got a mum. She's dead. Buried her yesterday. That's why I'm here. When she knew how ill she was she told me not to worry. 'Your dad will look after you' she used to say.'

So that was her game was it? Wanted an easy handout and was trading on their superficial likeness to get it.

She'd had him worried for a minute, though. He'd sown his wild oats in his youth, but always made sure to take proper precautions. He'd no intention of being trapped in marriage like most of his pals.

Curiosity made him ask, 'What's your mum's name?'

He prided himself on his excellent memory. Never forgot a name or a face.

'Phyllis Hicks,' the girl answered, 'I'm Paula'.

'Name doesn't ring a bell,'

'It wouldn't. She hated her name. Everyone called her Blondie on account of her hair. Lovely corn coloured hair she used to have, till her illness took it all off. You both met up at a party, ended up getting sloshed. You never got past the Christian name stage. She only knew you as Gerry. I was the result'.

'Why didn't she get in touch before, then?'

'Apparently it was quite a large party. She did ask around, but never managed to track you down. Then you began getting your piccie in the papers. She recognised you. Used to cut out every news item about you and paste it in a scrap book. The family album, she used to call it.'

Silently he cursed the power of the press.

'Why pick on me?' he growled, 'I can't be the only sandy haired bloke called Gerry. Everyone has a double.'

'But not everyone has a port wine birthmark covering his...'

At the mention of a very private part of his anatomy he blushed like he'd never blushed before. Only someone with intimate knowledge of him could have furnished her with that information.

He longed to wipe the triumphant smirk off her face.

Pushing open the car door he got out and stood towering over her.

'OK, what's your price? A luxury apartment in the best part of town? An annuity for life? A one-way ticket to Australia?' he added hopefully.

Her look was wide eyed surprise.

'I don't want anything like that. Mum was an only child and so was I. She never married. Now she's gone I'm completely alone in the world. Or would be, but for you. I want to come and live with you, be your family. I am your daughter, after all.'

This was worse than anything he'd imagined. Money he could deal with. Everyone has his or her price. But acknowledging this plain slip of a kid as his offspring was unthinkable. He'd be the laughing stock. His reputation as a caring pillar of society would drop to rock bottom if it came out that some poor woman had reared his love child single handed with no financial help from him.

He suddenly wondered what he was panicking about. Here she stood, a tiny sparrow like creature who barely came as high as his belly button, daring to challenge him with this harebrained scheme of hers. Why, he could crush her with a single blow any time he wanted. And why not? He could hide the body and no-one would be any the wiser, if what he remembered her saying was correct.

Just to confirm, he asked,

'You're all alone in the world, are you Paula?'

'That's right,' she nodded, 'I lost touch with all my mates while I was nursing mum. There's not a soul who'd mourn me if I died tonight.'

He shivered. Had she read his thoughts? Not that it mattered. There was only one way out of this predicament, and he intended carrying it through.

Inside the garage the inspection pit was conveniently open. Just too bad if she fell into it, with a little help from himself. He'd make sure she was dead, shove her into the boot of one of the old cars due for the scrap yard, and the jaws of the compressor would do the rest. Even if anyone did miss her, well, youngsters went missing every day, didn't they? He'd make sure there was nothing to link her with him.

Trustingly she agreed to step into his office while he phoned his housekeeper to lay an extra place for the evening meal.

'Ooh, isn't it dark in here!' she sounded nervous as he unlocked the garage doors and ushered her inside. She probably never noticed the open pit until the hearty push he gave her sent her sprawling into the dark chasm.

Closing the garage doors and switching on the light, he guessed from the awkward angle of her neck that she must be dead, but he clambered down just to make sure. There was no pulse and the gaping wound in her temple where her head must have struck a girder made him feel sick and ill. It was all he could do to climb out of the pit and stagger into his office.

Collapsing into the leather chair in front of his desk he lay his head back and closed his eyes as waves of nausea washed over him. If only he could wake up and find it was all a ghastly dream.

The telephone began ringing and he considered ignoring it. But the caller could be his housekeeper. She took her role seriously and worried about him. He wouldn't put it past her to alert the police if he was later home than promised.

He daren't risk the cops nosing around until he'd disposed of the body.

He lifted the receiver, fighting to compose himself and invent some plausible reason for his lateness.

An unknown voice, mature, female, said,

'Am I speaking to Mr Gerald Porter? You don't know me, but I wondered if Paula Hicks is still with you. I'm a neighbour. She's been staying with me since her mum died. She mentioned coming to see you and promised not to be too late back. She's been gone for hours. I'm worried. You hear of such dreadful things happening nowadays, don't you? Mr Porter, are you there?'

No-one answered. The telephone swung like a pendulum beside the desk. Gerry Porter lay slumped in his chair, his face a startled mask in death.

Coming to The Bridge

by

Christopher Fewtrell

From beneath the imposing arches it was a wonder to behold, conjuring vague sepia images of 'Progress', clean cut, idealised Stakhanovites toiling beneath the imperious gaze and fob watch of some Brunel or Telford. So much vision, so much endeavour, so many bricks to lift the commuter crossword above so little. A tiny fire and some huddles of rags which, on this coldest of evenings, served as little purpose as the might and arrogance of the viaduct that strutted across the wasteground.

Mulraney was sprawled across the powdery earth with the glorious unconcern of a man who was dirty and knew it. Bryant, however, still clung to a vestige of that absurd stiffness his forebears rightly reserved for 'Sunday best', precariously perched on an oildrum that, for its part, had had the good sense to see that its usefulness was past and had toppled over long ago. Chick? Chick had not considered his position, scarcely to the point that he even knew he was there. It only mattered that his papers were safe beneath his tousled head, that was enough. His moist eyes were fixed upon a point deep within the meagre fire that struggled to illuminate their corner of the archway.

'Bloody cold.' said Bryant, nudging a recalcitrant chip paper towards the flames. Chick was unmoved by this intelligence, not a flicker of awareness disturbing his stare. Mulraney simply smiled, warmed by his own, well oiled, central heating. Eventually he ventured,

'Ach, it'll be a sight colder than this before the winter's out, right enough. Tis a bloody good job you're not living in your Russia or your Iceland, now dere's cold for you.'

'Cobblers! Tonight'd freeze the brass monkeys off an Eskimo....unless he'd got three parts of a bottle of Johnnie Walker inside of him. 'Bryant shot an accusing glance at the empty bottle that had rolled from Mulraney's grasp. Yet he was oblivious to such criticism, his thoughts having meandered down a diverting by-way.

'Tis a positively balmy evening by your Russian standards, if it were like dis in Moscow, I'd be strolling 'cross Red Square nice as you please, shorts, shirt sleeves, a Panama, the whole ensembleee!'

Bryant attempted to exchange glances with Chick, but he appeared content with the blank expression he already had. Nonetheless, Bryant remained unconvinced of the relative luxury of their situation, as outlined by Mulraney. Still, the Irishman (or was he a Scot?) felt satisfied with his reflections, and nodded vigorously for an unnecessarily long period in order to lend emphasis to his point. The younger man's thoughts turned to his toes, or at least that area of his anatomy experience suggested they might be found. Sighing, Bryant gingerly prised off his raddled boots and removed the stringy socks that offered token coverage of his feet. They hurt like hell earlier in the day, the result of a fruitless slog to secure a flop house berth. Gradually, however, the sensate area of the feet had diminished, the probing cold mercilessly chilling their extremities. He manoeuvred the toes closer to the fire, they were as hard as his luck and dirty, but even through the crusted filth their redness was apparent.

The silence was only punctuated by the fitful crackling of the flames, though Bryant was forced to withdraw his feet when a peculiar aroma suggested they were slowly roasting.

'I'm hungry.' the words fell from Chick's mouth like drool, their very fact the cause of considerable surprise. Bryant hastily pulled on his boots, as he did so he glanced at Chick, whose focus had still to shift.

'We're all hungry mate, I've had sod all today,' he turned to Mulraney,

'Has the van been 'round tonight?'

'Does it look as if I've been feasting upon your hautee cuisine, does it look like I've delighted in devouring game bird, washed down with a cheeky little claret?' Bryant remained deadpan in the face of the Irishman's (?) sledgehammer sarcasm.

'No, but has the van been around?'

'The van', as it was known to all those who were interested in it, was operated by some local church group, no-one was sure of the denomination and no-one particularly cared. What mattered was that it doled out food. Admittedly, it was food deemed too corrupt to be pedalled to the general population, but grub was grub however old. As it happened 'the van' had not been around as yet, so hope of sustenance remained.

'I'm hungry.' Chick repeated his earlier complaint with a chilling lack of emotion, it was frighteningly detached, paying no regard to the conversation that had gone before. Slightly unnerved, Bryant blurted,

'Is that all he can bloody say?'

'Oi!' Mulraney's face darkened,

93

'Just leave it be, he's not himself. As for saying summat, well, I tell you, when he's got summat to say it'll be worth hearing. He's not the likes of you or me Bryant, we know why we're 'ere, 'cos we liked the piss too much,' he gestured toward the spent bottle, 'but our friend 'ere, oh no, I bet there's a story to him, not excuses. He was, is a scholar.'

'And a gentleman?' was Bryant's snide intervention.

'Perhaps, who can say? But what I do know is that there's a lot goin' on in that nut of his, a sight more than we know. He used to...'

'I'm hungry.' again Chick spoke with no attention to the conversation. Mulraney shook his head,

'He's been in this state two days and more. Won't say a thing, 'cept I'm hungry, I'm thirsty, I'm cold. Don't get me wrong, 'e was never one to rabbit but, well, there used to be more than this.'

Poorly disguising his curiosity with a veneer of contempt, Bryant extended a fag brown finger towards the grubby bundle that supported Chicks head.

'What's in that lot then?

Mulraney pursed his stale lips,'Sweet Jesus alone knows, he's never loosed 'em from his grasp so far as I know. I reckon they'd say a few things right enough. Lot of learning in there, why he used to spend all day in your bloody library,'

Mulraney stretched a consoling hand to Chick shoulder,

'Till they chucked the poor old so and so out. Those snobby bastards are to blame for the way he's gone, said they'd 'ad complaints. I bet, just jealous 'cos he's read more than they ever will, the whole lot, from your Dostoyevsky to your Dr. Doolittle, why if......' the distant sound of a car horn echoed across the void. It was 'the van', parked in its usual spot at the far corner of the wasteground. It never came to the bridge, for the hard baked clay frequently erupted into housebricks, impossible for the vehicle to negotiate. For this the volunteers were eternally, if secretly grateful. Those who wanted food were thus forced to trudge the rubble strewn field in order to reach their 'benefactors'. There were supermarket sandwiches, crisps, biscuits, a little fruit, all beyond their sell-by dates, but gratefully accepted by the careworn cognoscenti nonetheless. Bryant and Mulraney scrambled to their feet, but Chick remained supine.

'Come on mate, grubs up.' Bryant's words fell on deaf ears. Mulraney shrugged,

'It's no use, he won't move now. I'll pick summat up for him. Come on.'

The two men disappeared into the blackness, their steps bent towards the bright discs that flickered in the distance. They were soon there and, following a desultory conversation with the earnest individual dishing out the grub, were soon returning to their fire. Mulraney was talking animatedly,

'I'm telling you old son, bible bashing skirt is all the same, play your cards right and the promised land is yours for the taking!' he smirked and let out an obscene, throaty laugh which rasped across the open expanse. Bryant was also amused, but their thoughts soon turned to the food as the gaping mouth of the archway loomed. Chick was as they had left him, the two men greeted him as they bundled themselves down.

'Here you go mate.' Bryant waved a tuna sandwich in Chick's face. He did not react.

'Come on, I thought you were hungry?' There was still no response. Mulraney's mood was transformed in an instant, he stared at Chick before gently nudging him. Chick's head slipped from its paper pillow and sagged into a tussock of grass. It came as no surprise. Down, down here, death had not the same currency as elsewhere. It was as much a feature of life as the trains which frequently roared overhead, or the rains which teemed like a curtain at the tunnel entrance. It was Bryant who spoke first, between mouthfuls of the tuna sandwich he had proffered,

'Bloody shame. Still, he was never right was he?' Mulraney was silent for a second, and then said, calmly,

'Oh yes, yes I think he was...he was.' with that, he struggled up from the earth and stopped to roughly gather his late friend's papers.

'What you doing with them?' asked Bryant, puzzled, 'are we gonna have a look what he had to say?'

'This is what they say.' without another word Mulraney cast the tattered bundle into the flames so that they might have warmth.

Red Rapunzerella

by

Kiranjit Dhillon

'Take me down to the paradise city, where the grass is green and the girls are pretty, Whoaaa won't you please -'.

'Margurita! Margurita! Get down here Nooow!'

'Zppggynnzzpypp'

'What'

'Get down now!'

Margurita, well Margurita Tracey Elizabeth Royal was christened Margurita Tracey Elizabeth Royal because her parents, one being the executive of a company - her dad, and her mother being a housewife, wanted their only daughter to appear to live up to the standards that her surname set. She did until the of eleven - when she first heard of heavy metal.

Her life drastically changed from then on. It was Guns 'n Roses, Iron Maiden etc., heavy metal magazines, posters, leather jackets - everything she lived for had something to do with heavy metal. Everything that is except her parents. But what could they do? They tried to move away from the hustle and bustle of the city - into a wood, living in a cottage, but it didn't change her a bit.

Margurita stamped down the stairs which creaked badly - well they would after the amount of times she'd danced down them (that is if you'd call it dancing because the noise was a combination between thunder and - well something worse than thunder, whatever that could be).

'Okay what is it?

'Go to your grandmother's and -'

'Uh-uh no way, every time I go down she treats me like her personal slave, and she rabbits on about the war and her Jack who fought and killed Hitler personally. What she doesn't realise is Hitler committed suicide rather than face the music, oh yeah that reminds me I need some dosh to get a new album.'

'No you're already advanced on your pocket money by eight months and three weeks to get that dreadful - whatever.'

'An electric guitar mom.'

'Anyway you're to go to your gran's - and did Hitler really commit suicide?'

'Mom come on, anyway Pistol is picking me at five so I can't go.

96

'You can if you leave now, so go.'

'Parents' Who needs them? And grandparents who've got more than a screw loose.' Margurita ran up the stairs which creaked, picked up her personal stereo with an INXS cassette in it, grabbed her leather with all its metallic bits and bobs, slammed the door shut, after picking up the quiche for her gran, and was on her way.

Before long she was freaking out, bipping and bopping along the path, trampling all the flowers, making the owls think they were having a nightmare, scaring the birds so that they jumped out of their feathers. All the animals hid away and locked their doors, that is if they had any.

At this point, a gross kid in Margurita's form happened to be there. He was nuts about her, or was it bananas - well it was some sort of food. Anyway he just couldn't take her hints, her subtle hints, her very subtle hints like

'p*** off Jacob.'

He still reckoned she was crazy over him. His plan was to jump in front of her, pin her to a tree and kiss her, well try to as his specs always had a tendency to fall off his nose at the wrong moments - but he wasn't about to let anything get in the way of his undying love for Margurita. He was all ready and here was Margurita.

'Yahhhh!'

'You're one of my kind! screamed Margurita, shooting a pose for this line of one of her most loved songs. This pose included having her left arm thrust out in front of her, and her hand clenched in a fist. Jacob was in front of her and this quick pose just, well knocked him out cold. Margurita somehow didn't realise and just bopped over him as the next song had started.

Eventually, after causing enough unknown damage, she stopped and changed the cassette over. Suddenly she heard some music in the background. She decided to investigate as it was useless going to her gran's - she'd totally given the quiche a new image, so she chucked it.

'ACIIDD'

'An acid house party!' she screamed. She loved any sort of party and so invited herself in.

'Wow! she never knew such life existed in the wood. All of a sudden she was whisked over to a room - shut in with this thing whose face was unknown to anyone as its ('its' because she couldn't tell if it was a man or a woman). 'It' moved its hair out of its face. 'It' was a man, a nice trendy man. The man spoke.

'Hi I'm Dave.'

'I'm Marg - well I'm known as 'Hot Toots'.' Which of course was a load of bull but she had to play it cool.

'Yeah well', continued Dave. 'This is sort of a private party, no-one's supposed to know about it'.

'That'd be a bit hard, the music was blasting!' Answered Margurita grinning like a cheshire cat.

'That's why we're having it in the woods, out of earshot. So I hope you don't mind but I'm gonna' have to lock you in here. We 'ain't taking no risks you see'.

'What?'

'Look I'm sorry but if the old Bill catches us we're in the slammer, and life 'ain't easy in the slammer, we should know, we've just come from there'. And with that Dave locked the door, and so she was all alone in a room high above the ground.

'The puny git' thought Margurita. 'I knew I shouldn't have come. I just knew something was going to happen to me today. And I'm gonner miss my date with Pistol, oh great'.

Well time flew (well literally dragged itself) by and here was poor Margurita locked in a room high above the ground with nothing but a window to keep her occupied.

'Vroom! Vroom! Vroom ketchicum.'

'That sound sounds familiar.' She looked out the window.

'PISTOL!!! PISTOOOOLLLL!'

'And what may I ask are you doing here? I came down to yer house, yer mom tells me ya wozz at ya gran's, but I thought nah not her, but I came along anyway, when I hears this music blarin' out, so I says to meself 'Fred Pistol me old friend, old brother, old pal, old buddy, old - anyway I says to meself 'Pistol think logically. Your babe don't like going to her gran's, there's music in the other direction, what does that tell ya? It tells me that my babe is at a bleedin' acid house party, probably in a bedroom with someone, so who's tryin' to pull the wool over me eyes eh? Come on speak up!'.

'Pistol shut up, there 'ain't no-one just me, and I wanna' get down!'.

'Go use the bloody stairs, that's what they were invented for, to go up and -'

'I do know what they're used for I just can't get out of the room, I'm locked in!'.

'What? I'm comin' up'.

'No don't! They'll lock you in as well, then we'll both be stuck!'

'Ah yeah! Didn't think o' that'.

'Nah you wouldn't, you thick twit!

'Well you could let down yer hair like they did in that story Goldilocks, or woz it Rumplestilskin, it could've been the three pigs-.'

'You nit! Does my hair look long enough? Eh tell me does it?'

'Just a suggestion.'

'Yeah a stupid one too!'

'Well you think of a better one'.

'Shut up I'm concentrating' said Margurita 'which is more than I can say for you, you're supposed to be my boyfriend and all you can think about is Rapunzel, and how she got down from that high tower!'

'That's it!' screamed Margurita.

'What?'

'You climb up this ladder that just happens to be here, funny I didn't see it before, anyway then you save me.'

'What's wrong with you just climbing down.'

'Cos' I'm afraid I might fall.'

'Oh alright. The things I do for you.'

Well Pistol (funny name Pistol, what's wrong with Fred?) climbed up to the window, awkwardly picked up Margurita (lucky he was well built) and climbed down.

'I love you' whispered Margurita once her feet touched the ground.

'Well how could you resist?' And with that they had a rocker's smooch - believe me it wasn't any normal smooch.

'Come on let's zoom else we'll be late.' They were going to a party, but now Margurita wasn't so sure about going after this little fiasco.

They drove off into the evening, with the sun setting, a beautiful view it was and to top it off the soothing sound of....Iron Maiden!

Well the party was the type of party you'd only enjoy if you were into heavy metal, but for some reason Margurita didn't feel like head banging to Def Leopard, or rocking to Faster Pussy-cat. She felt, well she felt like taking a breather, so she went out.

She went to the car and...the car wasn't there! She thought maybe she'd forgotten where they'd parked it...no it was definitely that same dent in the lamp post that she'd made earlier (she was having a look to see how far they were from the pavement when WHAM!! She forgot to notice the lamp post!)

So she just sat on the pavement, when she felt something nibbling at her boot, it was a mouse. She didn't scream, she loved mice, as they were the motto of one of her favourite rock bands and anything they liked she liked. Instead Margurita picked it up, jumped up and began walking. 'It's just like Cinderella' she thought to herself 'only' instead of losing a slipper...or a boot in my case, I've lost my boyfriend. And instead of falling for the prince I've fallen for the mouse that was one of the horses to my carriage, or a wheel to that crampified Mini.'

And they both walked away and lived happily ever after, that is after the 'once upon a time' at the beginning because these sort of incidents don't happen nowadays. I wonder why not........

The Bill

by

Julia Barrett

Shirine looked at the bill in her hand. The paper was flimsy, light, with the eagle heading on the top of the page, the writing in faded black ink. At the foot of the page was the square official stamp in blue ink with the date and signature of the relevant authority and in the middle, the list of charges and the total amount of money owed.

Her hand trembled and her wedding ring glinted in the morning sun. Over the years, increasing weight had changed her body from the slim young girl she had once been to a comfortable, plump cottage-loaf shape and the ring no longer fitted the finger on which it had first been placed by an ardent groom nearly thirty years before, so now she wore it on the little finger of her right hand. Successive diets had only had a temporary effect on her figure so now she joked that she was practising to be a grandmother and had given up dieting in favour of providing a warm, comforting lap for future grandchildren.

It was a beautiful day. The temperature would not rise over 100 hundred degrees Fahrenheit until the afternoon and a fresh breeze rustled the leaves of the banana trees at the side of the gate. The orange trees were still covered with white blossom and quite a few oranges that were beyond her reach. It never failed to surprise her, how the orange trees could carry both fruit and blossom at the same time. Yet again, she made a mental note to get someone to pull the remaining oranges down off the trees. She could always squeeze them and store the juice in the freezer for the searing heat of the summer months when there would be no citrus fruits in the shops.

In the road, a group of lads were playing football. Bricks were the goalposts and their shouts almost drowned out the cooing of the doves in the nearby orchards. They were the neighbours' sons and friends since birth, most of them, of her own son. Not so long ago, he too would have been playing with them, his black labrador dog running beside him, determined to join in firmly believing that she was a boy. When she got hold of the ball, she would grip it firmly in her jaws, refusing to yield it up to either side. Sometimes her sharp teeth would puncture the ball so then she would be banished to the garden behind the locked gate where she would sulk and whine.

The bill had not been delivered by the postman but in person, by the party representative of the district. He still stood in front of her, eager to drive away in his shiny new white Super Saloon with its air-conditioning and four antennae, shuffling from one foot to another and refusing to look her straight in the eyes but equally determined not to leave before being paid.

Shirine wished her son was there. Oh God, how she wished he was there beside her! The last time she had seen him was almost six months ago when he had been on leave from the north. He had told them such terrible tales of the fighting against the enemy, of the atrocities both sides were inflicting on each other. They had tried so hard to delay his conscription into the army; he had studied day and night to get the grades needed for university. Once there, he like all his friends, had carefully calculated how many exams they could deliberately fail so that they would be able to repeat the year but not to be sent down and therefore lose their exemption from the army.

By such means, he had been able to spin out the four year engineering course into six years but eventually all possible delaying tactics had been exhausted and he had graduated. Shirine had the studio photograph of him wearing his cap and gown, diploma in hand, pride of place on the wall. Whenever she looked at it, the unbearable conflicting emotions rose up in her again: the natural pride of a mother in her son's manhood and achievements, the dread of the implications of that manhood and its possible awful consequences.

'Hurry up! I can't stand here all day,. you know! I've work to do, much more important than this bill. Once you have paid, I will give you the receipt so that you can make your own arrangements for collection and disposal.'

Shirine winced at the harshness of his voice, blinked and forced her swimming eyes to focus once more on the wording of the bill:

In the name of God, The Bountiful and the Merciful.

By order of His Excellency, The President of the Republic of Iraq, Saddam Hussain (May God grant him Long Life!) and the Council of Ministers.

For the execution of the deserter and traitor *Sami Ilyias Masri* in refusing to obey orders and carry out the necessary duties required by his commanding officers:

5 Bullets 762 Lead tipped	ID 5
5 Members of Firing Squad armed with Kalashnikof rifles	ID 10
Total cost	ID 15

With shaking fingers , Shirine reached into her pocket for her purse.

The Birchills Bridge

By

Jo Harrington

Gina shivered as she stood looking at the bridge from the footpath of Green Lane. Behind her traffic streamed past and a couple of raindrops fell too close for comfort. But she wasn't going for shelter now, not now she'd actually found the bridge.

She was sure this was it - scene of a family scandal. Nan's diary, recently inherited, had started that it was black bricked and carried a canal. A later entry claimed you had to approach Birchills from Bloxwich to find it. Well, she's found it...

Beneath the bridge was wasteground, far below her feet, but in her nan's youth the wasteground had been a railway line.

The story had been simple enough. Her nan, Sarah Mary, and her lover, known only through the diary as J., were prevented from marrying as Sarah's father, William Littlejohn, had thought the leather-worker below his daughter. Sarah had fallen pregnant, so the highly strung J. had suggested a romantic suicide pact, the impressionable Sarah agreed.

The bridge had been chosen for maximum effect, or so Sarah presumed, she left the arrangements to J., they met there one night, climbed onto the thick bridge wall, J., leapt to eternity... Sarah bottled out and went on to give birth to Gina's mum.

The scandal had rocked the community and ruined the family. She eventually married and the father didn't object.

Gina knew all this as she turned towards Stephenson Avenue, to gain access to the canal walk and the bridge. She merely wanted to see it, as she had every building or monument to her family history since she had begun tracing it five years ago. Nothing morbid, more like fascinating duty.

The wind whipped her hair against her reddening face, but the threatened rain didn't fall past a couple more fat drops. For the dryness, at least, she was grateful. She had found her way to the near side of the canal walk, the wrong side it seemed - while both had pathways trodden along them, the one on the opposite side was wider and obviously the better used. On her side the track was about a metre wide and mainly grass.

103

She had meant to sit on the wall but found it taller than expected, the top wa
level with her forehead and she dared not jump up at least she fell backward
into the dark canal. The best she could do was perch herself at the end of the
bridge wall, were it sloped conveniently nearer her height.

'Having trouble?' A male voice startled her out of her thoughts.

'What?' She spluttered feeling inexplicably embarrassed.

'Oh! I was just going to see over.'

'It's a long way down ... you'd probably break your neck if you slipped ...' he
glanced behind himself, 'Or drown.'

Her face blazing, she nodded and proceeded to look away. She caught him
smiling and opened her mouth to speak, but he spoke first.

'Of course, I could lift you up.'

'No, thanks.' she realised how foolishly she was acting, so tried to make a
joke of it.

'You'll probably break your back or something yourself.'

'What? Lifting a shrimp of a thing like you?'

'What?' she tutted and looked away. She knew his sort, all macho-look
at-my-muscles type. No thanks. They fell silent, she sitting on her sloping
bridge, he staring into the water.

The day was growing darker and rain threatened even stronger with a couple
of circles ever-increasing in the water. The lad looked up, he looked alright,
she supposed, blue eyes and brown hair ... he spoke carefully,

'You're not from round here are you?'

'Dudley.'

'Yow'm frum Dudley, am ye?' he attempted a thick Black Country accent and
somehow it irritated her.

'No-one in Dudley speaks like that!'

'You do.' he changed the line of questioning.

'I'm John... and you are...?'

'Gina Wood.' she eyed him like a cat. 'And where are you from?'

'Leamore.' He indicated behind him, where she presumed Leamore lay.

'Oh.'

'So what brings you from fair Dudley?'

'I'm tracing my family tree.' she challenged him in look and tone. He raised
his hands in defence.

'I'm just asking... Prickly in Dudley, aren't you?'

'No.'

'So you have a family in Walsall.' He meant the borough as a whole.

'Used to.'

'Whereabouts?'

The conversation never ceased from that moment on and when they finally parted, it was with each other's telephone numbers and a promise. She doubted she would ever see him again, but it was nice while it lasted.

He wandered off, past her, toward RaybThis something-or-other, he had said, where he worked. She glanced at her watch. Five minutes more, then she would make her way back into Walsall town centre for the bus back to Dudley.

She looked downwards, it was a long way. It would kill you now if you slipped, of that fact she didn't query, but in past days, when a train would whistle beneath her... what a way to go! She smiled at the thought, though she couldn't see anything to smile about...

Suddenly the heavens opened and the rain thundered down, she made to slip down onto the grass, but... there were hands! Strong hands which pulled and pushed at her... forcing her, where?...

She struggled against them, unseen... but then, in the split second before she fell into the valley below she saw him, hair slicked back, his brownish suit, and his eyes - with the intense jealously even in that briefest second... she knew who he was ...

As she fell, he fell beside, then beneath her, and she thought she heard him call to her,

'Sarah...'

Buffeting heavy skirts, which somehow had replaced her jeans to assail her ears and pull her downwards... and close below she heard a train whistle, then her own screams of terror. Then nothing.

The Wheel of Fortune

By

Irene Chambers

As a small boy Cecil Bazar resented the fact that he had been christened after his uncle. He felt it went oddly with his father's surname, which was peculiar anyway. He envied his brother William, who at least had one ordinary name with which to go through life.

But when at about the age of eight, Cecil discovered the joy which music brought to him, he no longer worried. Indeed he grew to like the sound of Cecil Bazar, feeling it might be a suitable name for a concert pianist, which he fully intended to become.

He was assiduous in practising, he became alive when he played the piano. Music filled his heart and soul to the exclusion of all else. Imagine then, how shattered he was when, after his business failed, his father committed suicide.

As head of the family William said that Cecil must now do something useful in life, and earn his living in a safe job.

William, himself, four years older than his brother, had already qualified in the legal field sufficiently to go into practice. Mrs Bazar, who favoured William, looked to her elder son for guidance, and agreed with him. So it was that Cecil entered the Civil Service and, after passing the entrance exam quite brilliantly, found himself signing the Official Secrets oath. Thus began what was for him, a soul-less occupation.

Fortune was to favour him though , through his uncle, whose namesake he was. Uncle Cecil also loved music, and he had been quite an accomplished pianist. However, in middle age he developed arthritis in his hands, and found himself no longer able to play. So he asked young Cecil, whose talent was becoming apparent, to play for him on his grand piano. This pleased them both, and the boy resolved to save up his money, so that he could buy a grand piano for himself.

However, Uncle Cecil died at a comparatively early age, and bequeathed his Victorian house, contents, and grand piano to his namesake, who at the time was in his twenties.

By this time William, now a partner in a well established firm of solicitors, was doing very well for himself. When their mother died, she left her home and possessions to him, her favourite son. So William, his wife, son and daughter were really quite wealthy. They loved money and were prodigal with it - to themselves, but not to others. However, William was not able to enjoy his affluence for long; he was killed in a car crash. His estate benefited by a huge sum paid out by the insurance company. His widow and children, Babette and Malcolm, became even richer.

Cecil like his uncle, never married. He had only met one female who appealed to his aesthetic tastes. She turned him down because she thought he was mean. He was. His loved his piano he kept in perfect condition, but he never spent money on house and home, unless it became vital to save things from falling to pieces. When carpets and curtains became threadbare, he regretfully had to buy new ones.

So all William's family lived in luxury in their beautiful home, and ran around in their fine cars, but when one Christmas they dutifully invited their Uncle Cecil for his annual visit, they expected him to provide his own transport, for they knew he had plenty of money.

Uncle Cecil didn't possess a car himself. he walked to most places, or used public transport. When he retired he didn't go out much, put on weight and tired easily.

He found he needed hep in his big old house, and he was lucky in finding Bella who, in two days a week, was willing to keep things in order. The garden was sadly neglected. Cecil had never done much to it, because he was afraid of spoiling his hands, and so being unable to play. He read an advertisement in a local newspaper, in which a student wanted a part-time job. And that was how James came to work for him. Such a nice young man, pleasant personality and hard worker. He loved to hear Cecil play the piano, and would ask whether he could stay and listen when it was too dark for him to work in the garden. This made them both happy. In gratitude for the hours of joy the music brought to him, James would often cook a meal for his employer. And so their friendship grew.

On the whole Cecil was a pleasant person to be with, it was only occasionally, as he grew older, that he lost his temper. This was when he misplaced something, and accused Bella or James of taking it. When the lost article was found, he would feel sorry and ashamed, and broadly hint that he was mentioning them in his Will. Bella and James held no grudges, and being nice people they didn't really count on being beneficiaries. They thought it a pity he didn't take the legendary advice of Ómar Khayyam 'Make the most of what we yet may spend, before we too into the dust descend.'

Cecil's neighbours, Alf and Mabel, had been friendly since he first moved into his Uncle's House. On his birthday he used to ask them in for a cup of tea. Mabel would often do a bit of shopping for him. Cecil would give them some apples from his trees - there were more than he could use anyway, so it didn't cost him anything.

Alf was much older than Mabel, and when he died, Mabel came to see Cecil more often, to shop, change his library books or take him to the Bank. He got the feeling that she was after his money, and became a bit worried. If she seemed in a coy mood, and ready to stay longer than necessary, he would make some excuse about being busy to get rid of her.

As time passed, Cecil grew more tetchy and more mean. At Christmas he asked Bella if her husband, Joe, would run him over to spend the day with his sister-in-law and family.

'But Mr Bazar, it's twenty miles away - forty the double journey.'

'I'll pay for the petrol.'

'My parents come on Christmas Day, can't you get a taxi?'

'They charge so much - double on Christmas Day,' answered Cecil pettishly.

One year Bella said

'No. Joe isn't very well, and I can't ask him.'

Cecil didn't like it at all. A burning lump of resentment grew inside him. He telephoned his sister-in-law, asking if they could fetch him. She told him very shortly that she would be cooking the dinner, and Babette and Malcolm had other plans, but Cecil would be very welcome to join them for the day. All he had to do was to hire a car. This made Cecil very annoyed, and he told her he wouldn't be coming this year.

A plan formed in his head, Bella could shop for a chicken, pudding, mince-pies and so on, and he would get James to spend Christmas Day with him and cook the meals.

James was astounded when the plan was revealed to him.

'I'm sorry, Cecil (he had been asked to call him that), but I can't leave my mother to spend the day alone.'

'I shall be alone,' Cecil pouted. Then looking at James' downcast face he added, 'I've told you boy, I'll see you're not left out of my Will.'

James told his mother.

'Invite him here,' she said.

'We'll get Horace next door to fetch and return him in his car, and we'll pay him. It's only ten minutes ride.'

Cecil was pleased. He enjoyed his day ... until he found that when he was ready to go home Horace didn't want to take him until later. So Cecil eventually retired to bed in a very upset state. He had been eating very heartily, and had violent indigestion.

James had promised to come early on Boxing Day and get Cecil's breakfast. He had a key to let himself in, and soon had a pot of tea made. When he knocked on the bedroom door, there was no reply, so he opened it.

Cecil, his face contorted, lay beside the bed, having evidently collapsed with a stroke. James, horrified, rang the doctor, who came within fifteen minutes, Cecil never recovered consciousness. James, who had served his employer so valiantly, was deeply distressed.

He and Bella attended the funeral, and were asked by the relatives to go back to the house.

Neither of them really expected to be mentioned in the Will, but they were. Cecil's grabbing family were shocked and wounded to learn that he had left half of his considerable estate to be divided between James and Bella. Mabel, his neighbour, had been remembered too. Cecil had bequeathed to her a photograph of himself and a small oil painting by an unknown artist. Mabel never had liked still life.

Making Connections

By

N Stone

Terry Carter, twenty four, with a four-years training and a brand-new Teaching Certificate, posted his seventh Job Application in Stoneford High Street. He bought the Friday Weekly and strolled back towards his mother's bungalow. Why hurry? All Junior teaching posts were filled by mid-October.

He paused at the railings of his old school. It was morning break. The din was thrilling and he wanted, desperately, to be part of it. 'Get down off that wall!', he yelled in his promising King Street Junior, Radio Four, voice. it worked, and Terry's chin rose an inch.

The woman in the adjacent garden stopped sweeping.

'They'm allus at it', she confided venomously.

'Still? I used to be one of them. And I climbed the wall.'

And like to go up another, he added to himself.

Back at home, his mother was ironing shirts as if any day now she expected him to pack. He opened the paper at the Posts Vacant page but felt scarcely equal to Glass-blowing, Caretaking or Delivering Leaflets. A small insert caught his eyes and he read it twice, reaching automatically into his top pocket for a red pen.

> Small toymaker qwality moddles,
> cart's van's boat's ect
> Odean Workshop's Nabberton

'How tall is a toymaker, Mother?'

She gathered this was not a how-long-is-a-piece-of-string question.

'Between five and six feet, give or take ...'

'So a *small* toymakers should be worth seeing. Why the illiteracy? Wonder if he would welcome some free advice?'

'Where is he?'

'It says Odean Workshops, Could that be the Nabberton Odeon?'

He went out through the kitchen door and she saw him wheel his cycle from the shed, checking its tyres.

'Not above twenty miles,' he called. 'See you tonight.'

Since his father had died, last year, his mother worked noon till six at the Cottage Hospital. Lately, it had begun to rile him, seeing her set off, while he still had no job. Half of his applications received a brief 'regrets' while his interviews had not been fruitful. He would soon begin to think there was something wrong with him.... He pedalled away, uphill and out of town, following the old Roman road towards the west, trying to be positive, hoping he could be useful to someone somewhere, if only to this, 'Small toymaker' with his 'moddles'. Moddles, doddles, boggles, goggles ... does it really matter? Today's is a world of sound, not of spelling. But that, he knew, was only his despair, griping...

At Nabberton, the long-boarded-up Odeon was now open as Enterprise Workshops, its precinct dotted with tatty vans and bikes. He locked his own, noting with a grin how it matched the scenery, then climbed the steps and drifted around the partitions.

'Sandy Loam!' At his exclamation, a redhead chap in frayed jeans jerked round from a workbench.

'Cor! Terry the Toff!' They exchanged punches, old pals from Stoneford Comprehensive and allied resorts.

'So what's brewing, Sandy?'

'Mekking moddles. Me and me Dad. E's redundant, so he's founded me. Got a six-month free werkshop, to see how I mek out...'

Terry, in jeans and anorak, no longer the 'Toff', whistled his admiration at the richly varnished farm-carts, hay-wains, gigs, and caravans ranged on a shelf above the bench. Sandy kicked a way through half-open cartons of bits and pieces, to lift down a red and yellow gipsy-caravan.

'Me latest. All to scale. Dad does me maths, but I mek it.'

Terry received the replica as reverently as it was offered, setting a spoked wheel spinning with his thumb. He lifted the curved roof and smiled with a boy's delight at the inside fittings - cooking stove with tin pan and kettle, the box-bed, the minute geranium pots on the window ledge. He took a deep breath.

'Sandy, it's incredible!. How I envied you those 3c Craft periods while I stewed over English Lit and History! Man, you've made it'

Terry didn't mean the caravan. He was thinking more of latching on to life, achieving a goal. The worn phrase, 'equal opportunities' drifted into his mind and he suddenly saw their old comprehensive as a genial uncle, encouraging all and sundry to have a go, connect with life in their own way...

Sandy took him literally, 'Ah, mate, I *made* it, but 'oo wants it?'

'See what you mean. I saw your advert, and it strikes me you are barking up the wrong tree, Stoneford folk, mostly unemployed, can't afford these. They aren't *toys*, they're collector's pieces!'

He grinned as he sized up Sandy's willowy five-foot-ten. Some small toy-maker! His mother had been right, she usually was.

'Your advert is all wrong, Sandy.'

'Oh ah? Me Dad said advertise. 'Ere he comes.'

Dad was a greying version of Sandy, with the same lively eyes, and hands that seemed all sinew. His grip hurt. Got to toughen up, Terry reminded himself. He proceeded to explain about the badly written advertisement giving the wrong image, aiming at the wrong market.

'Go for a Classy Mag'!, Mr Loam. Offer the models as Handcrafted Miniatures of Bygones,. Include a photo of, say, this gipsy-caravan alongside the Thomas Hardy hay waggon...'

'That what?' put in both Loams.

'... then send to, maybe, Country Life? Heritage? National Trust? How many are finished? Only Twelve? You'll need to treble that by Christmas. What are you asking, by the way?'

Sandy looked at his Dad. Dad said, 'We don't hardly know. Mind, it's best timber and ply. I do the metal bits on me lathe. The rest is time. It's Sandy has the vision.'

Vision, thought Terry. Splendid word. A craftsman's vision. The old man has something. If only faith! Dammit, I've got faith, too. Got to have ... He came back to their expectant faces.

'Name a figure,' he said, sliding a careful finger along the gleaming shafts and chains of the caravan, the swinging water-bucket and black stove-pipe chimney. Three weeks' work - apart from the visioning.

'Twenty-five quid?' ventured Sandy.

'You mean *hundred and twenty five*. Of course, a good advertisement costs, but you might recoup with your first sale.'

The Dad looked thoughtful, worried.

'Them mags are bit out of my line. Would you set it up, like?'

Terry nodded.

'Be glad to. And take a photo, if you'll lend me the caravan?' He began gesturing with his hands, demonstrating to his non-existent class.

'Back it up against Mother's potted fern - on a polished table - give a nice reflection ... I've got film in my camera. While I'm about it, I might do a painting. Okay?'

Other details settled, Terry cycled back with a large baked beans carton strapped firmly behind. Some old tag of a poem ...

'I wish I lived in a caravan, With a horse to drive, like a pedlar man...' took him back down the Roman Road. Had something, those Romans, knew where they were going, went straight for it, made the right connections with river and ford, town and market... Sandy needed the right connection ... Maybe everything should be connected ... somewhere.

For the next few days, with camera and typewriter, pencil and paint, he messed about whistling and hopeful. His Mother, noting signs, began dettol-ing his old College suitcase and duffel bag.

'Sandy Loam was looking in the wrong place,' he remarked .'It's all right having a product, the problem arises, where to market it.'

'Maybe that applies to you, Terry.'

It hit him with the 'blinding flash' of that other Roman Road, the one to Damascus, only this one was eye-opening. He gave her a hearty thwack on the shoulder and the dettol rag flew wide.

'Mother, you're a genius! Here I am, proffering *untested* goods in the *saturated* market of Junior teaching, when Comprehensives might kneel at my feet. The stress-turnover there is greater, they say, but what's stress to a willing horse? I'm rearing to go. - Of course, it would mean leaving home.'

'Not to worry. I've been a big girl now for many a year.'

The invoice for the advertisement came as a shock to them all. Sandy's Dad bore the brunt, but before Christmas, the cherished caravan, a Viking water-worthy ship and three hay-wains had lifted the Loams well into the black. The 'small toymakers' had more orders than was actually comfortable, even though Terry coped with mountains of correspondence, accounts and records. In early December, he said,: 'Sandy, you'll have to marry a typist, so she can act as unpaid secretary.'

Both Loams suspended absorption over the bench.

'You leavin' us?'

'Hope so. In one week, I've got three interviews, all for schools like our old one.'

The older man nodded. 'Good luck then! You've done us proud, put our foot right. It's your sort they want out there.'

'Thanks Mr Loam. But remember, it'll be hell if you don't get somebody to do the paperwork. You've got to keep records to a penny, all orders and receipts and what you pay for your stuff. I've left plenty of examples, 'moddles' you might call them, of how to answer, and spell, and keep figures. Get yourself a nice girl, Sandy, one from our old school, and if she can varnish, apart from her nails, she'll be hooked .. See you!'

Terry returned from his first interview - also hooked. He had accepted a post in a streamed school where Maths, English and Craft would be his requirement. Oiling his bike to take with him, he pondered, then rejected, the idea of an old banger for Easter. No, I'll keep basic for a bit. Might make for better connections...

His mother was asking, 'Which sweaters? All three?'

'Please. Plus a new one for Christmas?' He wiped oil on a rag.

'I wish I lived in a caravan, With a horse to drive like a pedlar man,
What's his mileage, nobody knows - but you can work it out from A to B,
along with his timing at 4 mph, with half-hour brew-up every two hours.

'How's that Mother? Eng Lit. Maths and Craft, all in one fell swoop. Who could ask for anything more?

He went off into a different sort of tune, then added,

'You'll send me news of the small toymakers? I'm worried to death they'll get in a mess with the accounts.'

Mrs Carter put on that wise look that all mothers do so well.

'Vision is all very fine, Terry, but folks do need to keep their feet on the ground. Maybe, when you're gone, I'll pop over. I used to be a dab hand at accountancy.'

He said nothing, finding it expedient to examine a worn brake-block. After all, work is the best time-filler.

No One Cares

by

Anita Pruden

The bus shuddered to a grinding halt before opening its doors wide to the on-slaught of pushing passengers eager to get out of the cold rain.

Meg Johnson, watched passively from across the aisle as the young girl, seated on the high seat by the door, rose and gave a helping hand to the old man, who, having been parted from his wife shuffled, unsteadily towards the seat.

'Can't you wait?' She retorted sharply to the men and women who jostled the old man in their efforts to be seated. 'Where are your manners' she mimicked in their faces. They stared back balefully, itching to slap that righteous look from her face before scurrying down the aisle like frightened sheep.

'Don't worry'. She sang out to the old man's wife, who had been showing their bus passes to the driver. 'Take your time'. The woman responded by giving her a grateful smile that softened the tired features before hurrying towards her husband.

Meg, turned towards the window dismissing the scene from her mind. She had other things to think about. She was still trying to thaw out and huddled deeper into her coat.

At least she didn't have to listen to idle chit-chat. Her fellow passengers were happy to slip into their own day dreams, oblivious to what was going on around them.

Shifting into a more comfortable position she enclosed herself in her own thoughts.

'I'm going Mother and you're not stopping me!' Meg tried to shut out the image of her young daughter's rebellious face.

'Honestly! You young ones. You couldn't care less about the consequences.' Meg had rounded on her, angry that she had been put in such a position. Visions of their name splashed all over the newspapers sent a wave of fear cascading over her. What would her friends think?

'And what about your generation Mother!' The harsh persistent voice of her daughter brought her back to reality. 'You don't give a damn what's happening outside as long as it doesn't penetrate your safe little world'. The young eyes were ablaze with a passion of defiance that made Meg uneasy.

'That's not true. Your father and I, always try to help the needy. There's not a day goes by without someone asking at the door for charity'. She defended herself.

'That's just to ease your conscience. What about giving some of your own time, but that would be too much to ask, wouldn't it?' The look of pity her daughter shot at her, made her squirm with guilt.

The bus jolted over the uneven road so that Meg was left with her own reflection, looking sadly back. She closed her eyes to make it disappear.

Meg, was on her way to town hoping she could speak to her daughter before the rally began and persuade her to see some sense. Her father would go mad if he found out she intended to march through the city centre protesting.

The slight sound of the querulous voice floating across the still air, brought Meg out of her deep thoughts. She glanced towards the old couple.

Something had upset the old man, but his wife moved closer, gently calming his agitation.

The young woman, on the high seat half rose, then hesitated, before sinking back.

Meg, gave a swift glance over her shoulder to see if the other passengers had observed the incident, but they were oblivious to anything but their own isolation.

'No, No! I don't want to go?' The harsh voice of the old man rose higher as his hands flayed the air at an imaginary enemy.

There were faint stirrings amongst the passengers, but after swift irritating glances they studiously ignored the commotion and sank further down in their seats.

Meg, also embarrassed by the incident glanced quickly away, avoiding the eye of the old woman who looked upset and was trying hard to keep some sense of dignity.

'It was all so distasteful. People shouldn't air their grievances in public' Meg, thought before settling uneasily in her seat.

'I'm getting off! Stop this bus. I told you I didn't want to come?'

The old man's harsh voice startled the passengers forcing them to be aware that something was amiss.

'We're nearly there now' the anxious voice of his wife tried to calm him, but it seemed to send him into a frenzy.

'Shut up woman, I want to get off, I'll find my own way home'. Each word was punctuated with a clench fist hitting the old woman around her shoulders and arms as she tried to ward off the attack.

'Hey! Stop that old man'. The bus driver dragged his gaze from his mirror where he had been watching the commotion, before slamming on his brakes. He wrenched open the cabin door and moved threateningly across the small distance that separated them.

'Keep those fists to yourself or else?' He towered over them.

'It's all right. He doesn't mean it. I'll calm him down'. The old woman gasped in fright, pinning the old man's hands down. Shielding him with her body.

The bus-driver hesitated. 'If he gives you anymore trouble I'll throw him off. The bus is late enough as it is'. He turned and made his way back.

People began to mutter amongst themselves, fidgeting uneasily in their seats as the old woman turned towards them 'I'm sorry, he'll be all right now'. The slight plea for understanding was ignored.

The young girl slid across her seat, before bending over the old man. Whatever she was murmuring seemed to have a calming effect. The bus passengers avoided each other's eyes.

'I'm getting off, I'm getting off. You made me come. Stop the bus'. The voice started again ending in a frightening crescendo.

The screeching of brakes could be heard over the noise as the bus came to a shuddering halt.

'That's it! I've had enough. You can stop Misses, but your husband is getting off. The old drunkard'. The driver moved determindly towards him.

The old woman collapsed in her seat. Her grief, like her tears, oozing out with every shudder of her frail body.

'He's ill! He can't remember things.' She wailed frantically. 'It makes him so frustrated. He was never like this. He's been a good man to me. I'm the only one he has'. The old woman babbled on to no one in particular, before drying the tears with the back of her hand, and with some resemblance of dignity, pulled herself up from the seat.

The high, wailing, childish voice of the old man still split the air. It's anger directed at the one who was helping him.

'Look! Stop covering up for him. He's had too much to drink'. The bus driver was agitated now. He couldn't afford, too long hold up. He was running late. The quicker he could get rid of this distraction the quicker he could be on his way.

'Here! Let me help him'. The young girl stooped down towards the old man who had now slumped inertly in the seat, feebly mouthing obscenities. 'We can get a taxi home once he's quietened'. And with the strength of youth, pulled him up, his arm slung round her shoulders for support, while she put one arm under his like a crutch.

'He is ill! I know, my grandfather went like this, but if it eases your conscience just keep pretending he's drunk'. The scorn in her words echoed round the bus as she stood there defiantly with her heavy load, before turning towards the door. No one moved to help!

The bus driver sprang into action, eagerly assisting her down the steps and helping the old man on to the hard seat that was situated by the bus-stop, before climbing thankfully back into his cab.

The old woman paused at the door turning to look back at the passengers sitting so stiffly in their seats.

'No one really listens, no one cares!' The resignation in her voice was all the more frightening because of its matter-of-factness.

The engine of the bus sprang into life and the doors closed, shutting out the disturbance making the occupants inside safe again in their own little world.

Meg, watched through the window, taking in the old man's bewildered face.

The old woman had been wrong. Someone cared, someone had listened. And as the bus drove away Meg caught the eye of the young girl as she sat patiently, beside the old man. They sent the same message as her daughter's, the same passionate defiance of wrong doing against humanity.

Shafts of guilt shuddered through Meg, awakening something deep inside, that she had almost forgotten. She would stand and watch the rally, and applaud her daughter, because someone had to care, someone had to listen!

Egg

by

Mark Woodward

When his wife had gone, Harry's thoughts first turned to food and then to Lydia. Both thoughts made him uneasy. Harry had no desire to cook nor any experience, having barely raised a saucepan since birth. His desire for Lydia, on the other hand, was constant, but its fulfilment seemed as remote as a decent meal. Cooking and adultery, Harry considered, had much in common. When the dish was set before him he could tuck in as well as the next man. His appetite was good, even voracious. But he loathed the tortuous preparation and the mess that was always left to be cleared up later. Ordinarily his wife took care of that. But his wife had gone, leaving Harry marooned between fear and desire.

He hovered in the kitchen, staring blankly at clean surfaces and shelves as if they were contours of an alien land. Though the dark units jutting from every wall oppressed him, the white and gleaming applicancies filled him with dread. They seemed to mock, to throw down a challenge they knew he would fail. Then Harry had an idea. 'Eggs!' he said aloud. 'That's it, there must be some eggs!'

Eggs had been Harry's favourite food since childhood. He loved their shape, their texture and their soothing uniformity. Each one felt the same, tasted the same and when cracked stared with the same yellow eye. Besides they were convenient, the only food, as Harry often said, that Mother Nature made ready-packed. He searched the kitchen cautiously until he found six, size three, in a cardboard box, which his wife had thoughtfully left him.

Having solved the problem of food he hurried from the kitchen. In the lounge he poured a stiff drink, gulped it down and poured another. His palms were sweating as he lifted the phone.

'Hello....Lydia?' He twisted the flex tight round his white, chubby fingers. 'It's Harry.. yes Harry, that's right. We met last week...' Lydia paused, uncertain what tone to adopt until the thin, almost anxious voice was matched to a face.

'We've discussed the interview, of course, but there are still one or two matters we'd like to clarify. I was wondering..over dinner, perhaps?' Finally Lydia placed him. He was that shy little man with glasses, who sat on the end

119

and hardly said a word. But wasn't it the quiet, inconspicuous ones who often had power? She decided that it was.

'Why Harry, I'd be delighted.'

He wanted to drown himself in her rich, soft voice, but instead spelt out his address.

Harry normally ate his eggs in pairs, either scrambled or fried with bacon for breakfast or soft-boiled for a suppertime snack. So on the following evening, when only two eggs remained, he planned to eat both. He spooned one gently into the boiling water then raised the other above the pan. But as the final egg was poised in the steam, he hesitated. Through the thick folds of his dressing-gown his free hand prodded the soft mound of his stomach. Did Lydia find plump men attractive? Unsure, but unwilling to take the risk, he put the egg back. It nestled in its carton, as smooth and dumb and faceless as all the eggs Harry had ever seen.

He ate his supper, slid another plate onto the pile in the sink and climbed the stairs. He was unsatisfied. There was a hollow somewhere in his stomach where that last egg should have been. He slid between cool sheets, switched out the light and fell into troubled sleep. The egg remained alone in the silent night, beneath the bedroom where Harry slobbered and tossed, surrounded by the dark warmth of the kitchen.

Harry paid it no attention next morning. There was nothing to see in any case, except the lid of the cardboard carton slightly raised. It might simply have been a mistake - a size two egg squeezed into a size three box, for instance - or some atmospheric effect of the kitchen.

Besides, Harry had more pressing problems. In a few short hours he would help Lydia from her cab, shifting his hand from arm to waist as he ushered her indoors. Yet there was not a single clean dinner plate in the house, nor had he any idea what Lydia might eat. He recalled the gleaming cabinet in the supermarket, stacked to the brim with frozen ready-meals. 'Yes,' he thought, 'one of those should do the trick'. So Harry bought something with chicken, a large bottle of wine and two perfect white plates.

He was lying in his scented bath that evening, feeling deliciously hot water lap against his chest, when he heard a faint crash. It seemed to have come from the kitchen. Harry listened intently, then rose from the steaming bath and wrapped his dressing-gown round his dripping skin. On his way downstairs he picked up a china ornament, which he brandished as he flung back the door.

On the tiles, the sugar-bowl lay smashed. Directly above it, in a shaft of moonlight that pierced the plastic blinds, the cupboard door was ajar. Harry switched on the light, then peered through the opening onto the shadowy shelf. The egg, now swollen to three times its former size, perched cuckoo-like on the crushed remains of its carton.

Having put down the china ornament Harry lifted the egg from the shelf to examine it. It was creamy-pale, like Lydia's skin, and as smooth and cool as her soft hand. Beneath the semi-translucent shell were blue veins, which beat with a distinct, faint pulse. Harry stared for a while, wondering what to do. Eventually he put it down on the draining-board while he cleared the cupboard shelf of everything breakable. Then he replaced the egg and locked the cupboard door. After sweeping up the glass and sugar he returned to his bath, which he topped up h fresh hot water before stepping in. As he subsided, small waves kissed his stomach.

Lydia's legs seemed longer than the remembered, even when folded beside her on the sofa. Her lips were redder, her eyes more bright, and the black dress clung more tightly to her skin. Harry stared at her as he stood to re-fill their glasses.

'Harry...'

Lydia turned to look over her shoulder, stretching her white neck like a swan.

'What is it Harry? What's that noise?'

Harry listened. A soft tapping came from the kitchen.

'Oh it's nothing.' he said, too quickly. 'Nothing at all. But let me play some music if it disturbs you.'

He chose what he hoped was some sensuous jazz and took the chance to dim the lights a fraction.

'There', he said, pulling his armchair a little closer to Lydia. 'That's better, isn't it?'

Lydia smiled and moved her legs on the sofa. He was so timid, she thought, it was almost too easy. Her long fingers curled around the wine-glass, stroking the stem as though it were precious, yet familiar. Harry, his mouth dry, gulped his drink.

Later he lay in darkness, remembering the black dress peeling from her hips like foil from their ready-meal. Her skin was pale as chicken flesh, her limbs had parted like dark meat leaving the bone. He remembered her lying motionless, face pressed into the sofa cushion, her white teeth biting her swollen lip. As he remembered he began to sweat, and a hand slid over the folds of his belly. He did not recall her tears.

Harry was barely awake next morning when the front door slammed. His wife set down her basket in the dining-room, where the remains of last night's meal still stained the carpet, while Harry pulled on his pyjamas and hurried downstairs.

'Hallo dear,' she said. 'I tried to phone but there was no reply. Come and see.'

She beckoned Harry towards the basket. He stepped cautiously forward, then glanced inside at the wrinkled monkey-face with narrow eyes and blotches on its skin.

'Beautiful.' he said. 'It's lovely.'

He felt sick and searched for a reason to leave the room.

'Why don't you sit down for a minute? I'll make some tea.'

In the kitchen the cupboard door was bulging. Ropes of clear fluid, thick and flecked with red, had seeped through the keyhole and the cracks. The tapping was much louder, and the door vibrated beneath Harry's outstretched palm. As he turned the key the wood splintered. Then the egg exploded, splattering blood and mucus in Harry's face as its monstrous contents slid to the kitchen floor. It engulfed him, cutting short his cries. They barely heard him in the dinning room, where Harry's wife bent over her basket and smiled.

A Bottle for Christmas

by

A Clarke

'So what have we got, Jim?'

The Superintendent looked up from the report on his desk.

'A man of forty-five, good job, happily married, no worries, receives a bottle of Scotch at Christmas through the post. As a buyer with a large company he receives many. When he drinks a glass from this bottle he is taken ill and dies on the way to the hospital. Poison is found in the whiskey.'

'A week of enquiries has revealed no suspect and no motive. The murder was carefully planned, so the killer had a motive.' He paused and stroked his greying hair thoughtfully. 'Damm it, Jim there must be a motive; we both know that, and I think the answer must lie there. I must take the rest of the team off the case, but I want you to investigate the victim's background thoroughly. There's something there we've missed.'

An hour later the inspector, Jim Peel, was talking to the manager of the engineering company where the dead man, Ted Evans, had worked. At the end of the interview he had learned very little. Evans had been with the company for fifteen years, the last ten as chief buyer. The manager described him as efficient, hardworking and popular with colleagues, and was certain that Evans had had no enemies in the company. Before joining the company he had served as an officer in an infantry regiment.

A phone call to Army Records revealed that he had served for ten years, three of them overseas, and the regiment had an ex-members' association. Jim spoke to the area secretary and obtained the name and address of a man who had served with Evans. He arranged a meeting that evening with Andrew Walters, ex-sergeant, in the comfortable lounge of a large pub.

He explained the purpose of the meeting and asked Walters if he had known Evans well.

'We only served together for six months in the Middle East, but were quite close during that time.'

Jim sensed a certain reluctance and dropped the subject. Some time and a few drinks later, Walters' initial reserve had melted and he was talking to the inspector like an old friend.

'I came out of hospital and was stuck in a transit camp at El Tahag, thirty miles from the Suez Canal. A few tents surrounded by desert; two weeks there and I was ready to do a runner. There was an appeal for volunteers to form a unit to help police Palestine, and I couldn't get my name down fast enough.

There were thirty of us; Captain Evans was in charge, and three days later our five vehicles rolled across the Sinai Desert and into Jerusalem. There were just five more months of the British mandate to run, and the military presence was being run down. The two main Jewish terrorist groups were coming into the open more every day. They had established areas where the police and army did not patrol; exploding bombs were a regular feature, and after dark snipers so persistent that sentries were protected by sandbagged shelters.

We were resented by both Jews and Arabs: stoned by kids during the day, and shot at by their fathers at night, but our only casualties were four slightly wounded. Police and servicemen with vehicles and equipment were withdrawn regularly over the next few months. Some drove to Egypt, but others were shipped to Malta or the U.K.

Ours was the last party to leave for Haifa, two days before the end of the mandate, and everyone was keyed up but happy to be going.

Before our convoy of five three-tonners and two fifteen-hundredweight trucks took to the road, a lieutenant on a motor bike went on ahead. His task was to ensure arrangements for our embarkation had been made. Things were chaotic, and if any military personnel were left in Palestine after the expiry date, the League of Nations would have a field day.

We had not travelled twenty miles before we caught up with him again, lying beside the road, dead. There was a bullet wound in his chest, and from the scratches and oil on the road it was obvious he had been ambushed as he rounded a bend. The bike had gone. All vehicles were scarce: a 500cc Norton was valuable and may have been the reason for shooting the rider.

I was driving a 15cwt with the captain as passenger and I had never seen him so angry. The lieutenant had been a good friend, and he probably felt guilty about sending him on alone. After ordering the convoy to proceed he rejoined me and told me of his plan.

'That bike will not be rideable, and I doubt if they had transport here. We will look for it and perhaps find the bastard who did the shooting.'

We left the road at the first junction, assuming that anyone with a stolen army bike would do that. A few hundred yards down the dusty track was a small orange grove: we parked the truck and entered the trees. Leaning against a tree trunk hidden from the lane we found the battered bike.

124

'If you will bring the truck round to the open ground on this side of the grove, we w ill load the bike', said the captain. 'I will stay here and take a look round.'

Just as I reached the truck I heard shots and made my way back cautiously. He was bending over one of two bodies that lay on the edge of the grove. A horse in the shafts of a cart was tethered to a tree. 'They came to collect the bike, and I got them both', he said. 'One of them is still alive; give me a hand to lift him on the cart.'

When we had lifted the unconscious man on to the cart, he took a rope, secured it to a branch, then made a noose in the other end. It was only then that I realised his intention and protested.

'Look, this man is probably dying. I am only speeding up the process and making a protest against murder. If you don't like it, sod off back to the truck.'

So I did that; he rejoined me later and the incident was not discussed again. The next day we sailed home, went on leave, and I never saw him again.'

The next day Jim repeated the story to the superintendent, who listened carefully. 'Well, Jim you have found a motive for somebody, but we don't know who and probably never will. Twenty-five years is a long time, but I think we will close the case with the postscript 'An eye for an eye, and a tooth for a tooth.'

Everyone said that Mrs Evans was very brave and dignified following the death of her husband. She wondered how long she should remain a grieving widow before leaving the area to become a merry one. No more pretending that her marriage to that cold, intolerant creep was a happy one. Putting poison in a bottle of his favourite brand of whiskey had been so simple. She should have done it years ago.

The Eye of the Tiger

by

Joanne Holden

Her mouth fixed in a hard, angry line, Edith emptied the overflowing ashtrays into the waste bin, brushing away the numerous piles of ash adorning the beige dralon suite. Arnold was doing his once-a-week hourly stint in the garden, the only proof that he had been there being the chaos that he left behind. If he mowed the lawn, clumps of loose grass decorated the borders for days unless Edith cleared them, and his weeding comprised of digging up tender bulbs and shoots, and leaving unsightly weeds to run riot. At least it gave her a respite from his constant moaning and griping, a chance to tidy the cottage, and spray away the ghastly cigarette smoke. A waste of time, for when he returned the place acquired the appearance of a pigsty again.

Wearily she sank onto the settee. How could a promising marriage become such a disaster? During Arnold's working days, with all his excessive overtime, she had seen little of him, and their home had been her pride and joy, bright as a new pin. But since his retirement, their relationship had deteriorated. He cared nothing for his personal appearance. Even a visit to Lacy's barbers five minutes down the road, took on the mountainous proportions of an African safari. How different her life might have been if ... ifs and dreams, all she had left now. She stretched her foot, running her toe caressingly over the rather shabby tiger-skin rug adorning the hearth.

She leaned down, gently stroking the silky gold and black fur, admiring the gleaming rows of teeth; the slitted eyes were sad, understandable with that stupid old man always walking all over it!

That was another bone of contention between them. Arnold was forever clumsily falling over the poor animal, threatening to set fire to it. Edith had even found the beautiful skin draped over the dustbin for the refuse men to collect. 'Like living in a morgue', Arnold grumbled. 'Dead animals should be buried.'

But to her it was alive, warm. Sometimes, sitting in the firelight while Arnold was propping up the bar at the Red Lion, she could swear that the animal was breathing, that the golden eyes were watching her. She talked to it, poured out her dreams, her fears, her loneliness. They understood each other. Poor crea-

126

ture. It should be roaming the land of its ancestors, not trapped, as she was, longing for freedom.

She removed a wad of cigarette ash from behind its left ear, just as Arnold appeared. Without washing his hands or removing his dirty boots, he trundled across the room, sinking into his armchair. Edith flung her duster at his head.

'You great filthy oaf! I've just cleaned this room.'

He glared back at her, blowing cigarette smoke into her face. 'Nag, nag! God knows how I've put up with your nagging for forty years.'

'Forty years! A life sentence! Murderers get less.' She moved the ashtray to catch the fall-out from his cigarette, but he deliberately flicked it onto the floor. 'Arnold!'

'Woman, shut your mouth! I'm going to the pub for some peace!' He headed for the door.

'Good.' she screamed. 'And don't bother to come back!'

He turned. 'You'd like that wouldn't you? You'd like me dead, so you'd have all my money.'

'And I deserve it, with what I have to live with.'

'Think I'd let you get your hands on it? Never! Tomorrow I'm over to Mearton, to the solicitors, to change my will!'

She sank to a chair as the slamming of the front door echoed through the house. She patted the tiger's head. 'Don't worry,' she reassured, 'it's all talk. He doesn't mean it.'

After lunch, the next day, her husband appeared in the kitchen, wearing his Sunday suit and hat. Edith stared open-mouthed. 'What you dressed up for, on a Tuesday?'

'I told you', he hissed, 'I'm off to the solicitors. Thought I was joking didn't you? When I'm dead and my money goes to the dog's home, you'll know that I wasn't!' She could still hear him laughing as he walked away up the street.

Panic seized her. If he changed his will, she would lose everything, the money, the cottage, be out on the streets. In the lounge, she sank to the hearth, fingers fearfully tangling in the tiger's fur. 'What are we going to do?' The gold eyes regarded her impassively. 'He must be stopped. If only you could help me.' She rose slowly to her feet. 'I'll go to the solicitors, persuade Arnold to change his mind. If I catch the bus, I'll be there first. He'll walk across the heath - too mean to pay the fare.'

The curve of the animal's mouth strongly resembled a smile. She patted his head. 'I know you'd help if you could. Wish me luck.' She grabbed her coat and purse, and hurried from the cottage.

Edith scurried up the village street towards her home. After ascertaining from the receptionist that Arnold had not yet arrived, she had waited all afternoon, in the doorway of the solicitors, sheltering from the bitter wind. When the office closed and he had still not appeared, she had gratefully caught the bus home. Stupid man had been teasing her. All a waste of time!

A dark figure stood outside the cottage, just in the act of ringing the bell. A police car was parked on the kerb. She quickened her step, and the officer turned as she reached him.

'Mrs Palfrey?'

'Yes, what ...?'

'Could we go inside? I need to talk to you.'

'Of course,' her cold fingers trembled as she turned the key and ushered him inside. 'Would you like a cup of tea?'

'No thank you. Mrs Palfrey, I think that you should sit down. I have bad news, I'm afraid.'

'Bad news?' She sank onto a kitchen chair.

'It's your husband. I'm sorry to have to tell you, he's dead. His body was found on the road over Mearton Heath at about 3 o'clock this afternoon. He had been knocked down by a car.'

'Dead,' she echoed the word. 'Dead?'

'Would you like a glass of water?'

'No,' she raised her head. 'No, thank you. A car, you say?'

'That was the obvious cause of death, yes. But,' he hesitated, 'we believe he ran blindly into the road. The motorist said that he could not avoid him. His face wore an expression of terror, as if he was running away from something.'

'He was being chased?'

'We think that he had been attacked, by an animal of some kind. His arms and back were covered with bites and scratches.'

'A dog?'

'Probably, although it must have been a huge beast. I'm sorry, Mrs Palfrey, this is so distressing. Is there someone that I could send, for, to be with you?'

Edith shook her head. 'No. I...I would rather be alone'. Her head was spinning. She needed to think. 'Really.'

He nodded. 'If you are sure. I'll call again tomorrow. If you need me call the station. There will be an inquest, of course, but without witnesses, it is doubtful if we shall ever know what attacked him. The animal could be anywhere on those moors. You have a hot drink, and an early night.'

Gratefully Edith closed the door behind him, removing her coat and scarf. Strangely, she felt no sorrow, no distress, just a calm relief. Arnold had not reached the solicitors!

She pushed the door open into the sitting room. In the flickering firelight, golden eyes sought and held her gaze. She sank to her knees, raising the proud head between her hands. Understanding flowed between them. Unbelievable, impossible, and yet, suddenly, she knew. Laughter rising in her throat, she settled herself more comfortably before the welcoming heat, drew a tissue from her pocket, and carefully began to wipe the bloodstains from the gleaming teeth and claws of the tiger ...

Easy Target

by

Stephen Jason Beresford

He crouched behind the tombstones at the end of the graveyard.

Waiting.

Another routine job. He had been shown the photograph. A clear head and shoulders shot. Youngish man, clean shaven, neat hair. Not distinctive to most people, but to Mikey very memorable. Mikey had no choice but to remember that face. His job depended on it.

His leathers creaked as he adjusted his position. He wiped the rain from his motorcycle helmet visor and stared at the church doors.

Should be any time now.

Pulling his cuff back, Mikey glanced down at his watch. Half past eleven. Any moment now.

Regular as clockwork, he had been told, the man always went to church every Sunday.

That was why Mikey was sitting in this particular graveyard. In five minutes his job would be complete and he would be on his way home. He was looking forward to a relaxing pint in the local with his mates.

Then the church doors opened.

Conversation and laughter spilled out and a few people started emerging.

Mikey concentrated as he scanned each face for a perfect match. He never carried the photograph of his target on him. Too dangerous if he was stopped. Every detail was committed to memory.

Glasses. Can't be him.

Moustache. Nor him.

Woman. Definitely not.

Hair too long. Too old.

A couple of people put up umbrellas against the rain. Others jogged the short distance back to their cars hoping to stay dry. It hardly mattered either way. The rain had all but stopped and had become nothing more than a fine mist hanging in the air.

Then a group of three people walked out of the church doors. A woman arm in arm with a bearded man. They were talking to another man. This man was average height and average build, but to Mikey there was nothing at all average about his face.

It was the face from the photograph.

Automatically Mikey started to rise from his crouched stance, but then stopped suddenly as he registered the scene before him.

The target was a vicar.

A vicar!

Mikey quickly crouched down again behind the gravestone. Could he really do it to a vicar? He wasn't particularly religious, but he had always thought that it was better to be safe than sorry.

He glanced back up, wiping his visor again. The three still stood together talking and laughing. There was no mistake. It was definitely him.

Don't panic, Mikey told himself. It's just another job. You have done this to lots of others. Underneath that robe he was just an ordinary man.

An ordinary man who had gambled with Mr Bartholomew and lost. Lost heavily in fact and was now refusing to pay his debts. A gambling vicar who now had a contract out on his life.

Mikey weighed the options for a moment. Incur the wrath of God or the wrath of Mr Bartholomew. No choice really when he looked at it like that.

He rose quickly and strode purposefully towards the church. The three were still chatting.

Mikey would never shoot long distance. Too risky. He wasn't that accurate and could easily miss. Up close was best. No escape for an easy target.

As he got within a few yards of the vicar, Mikey unzipped his leather jacket and pulled out his Magnum. He felt just like the cop in the movies.

The woman noticed him and screamed. The bearded man pushed her forcefully to one side and they fell to the floor.

The vicar raised his hands to protect his face.

'Oh dear God! No!'

Mikey fired once into the vicar's chest. Then again and then twice more. The roar echoed off the stone walls of the church and died away. The vicar fell back and slumped onto the stone pathway behind him. Then there was silence. No one spoke or moved for a few seconds.

'Bless you, my son,' said Mikey, his voice muffled by the large helmet. He turned to walk away. Some of the women started to scream.

'Hold it right there.'

What!

Mikey stopped in his tracks, startled. No one ever tried to stop him leaving. After all, not even he would stop a leatherclad gunman who had just shot an apparently innocent victim in cold blood.

Slowly he turned around.

'Says who?' asked Mikey.

'Says me,' shouted the bearded man. 'Now put the gun down. Slowly'.

The bearded man stood legs apart, both hands holding a gun that was pointed directly at him.

'Police! Put the gun down!'

Mikey hesitated for a moment and then saw the woman had also got up and also had a gun. There was no way he could get both of them before they got him.

Reluctantly, he bent over and gently laid the gun down on the path.

'That's good', said the bearded man. 'Now, lie face down and put your hands being your head'.

Mikey did so.

The bearded man ran over to Mikey and knelt over him with his knee pressed in his back.

'We'd like a word with you regarding your association with a certain Reginald Bartholomew', he said clicking the handcuffs into place. 'Think you can help us?'

Mikey just grunted as the handcuffs bit into his wrists.

'Are you okay, Steve? shouted the woman.

The vicar lifted his head slightly. 'Yeah, I'll be fine.' He sat up slowly and felt his chest. He winced as he fingered the four gaping holes in his robe that provided the evidence of the attack. 'I hate undercover work,' he added.

As he got to his feet the undercover vicar rubbed his chest and said, 'Thank God for bullet-proof vests.' He paused. 'It hurts like hell though.'

Then he glanced back at the church and then to the sky, 'Sorry'.

Freedom

by

R J Hulford

The lane was lined with gardens heavy with colour, they seemed like notes in a piece of music, each one different but in harmony with its neighbours. In spite of the beauty of the gardens this was the part of a walk which I disliked the most, tramping a hard unyielding metalled road before reaching the point where I would take to the footpaths and meadows. 'The open road' is not a phrase beloved by ramblers, and yet at the start, anticipation is at its zenith when the prospect of a fine day's walking stirs the most stoic of hearts.

My car had been left by the church from which this land and others stuck like spokes in a wheel. It had been forty minutes from Birmingham, forty minutes from a flat in a grey building standing in a grey road, forty minutes from another life.

There at last was the kissing gate set in a hedge where the houses finished. A green sign bearing the legend 'Public Footpath' pointed like a finger to the field beyond the hedge.

Scraping through with my haversack jammed into the vee and the gate jammed into me, I wondered why they are called kissing gates. Gut crushers would be more apt. Perhaps I ought to lose a few pounds. That's what Trish had said and maybe she was right. That was last week or was it month? No matter, it isn't important. Importance is relative. How true that is. How relatively bloody true that is.

The tall meadow grass was flecked with brown where the summer's sun had dried it, driving the life giving moisture deep into the red earth. Flattened grasses formed a soft path from the kissing gate to the far corner of the field where a stile presented me with a vista of a larger field in which cattle grazed and the grass was short.

The nearest cows raised their heads and watched uninterestedly. Cows scared Trish, scared her with their size. It was irrational, horses which could kick and were faster and more mobile held no terror for her, neither did fast cars.

The cows were left behind as I dropped into a narrow lane before following a green track to a small wood which tumbled like green foam to a stream. The trees were heavy with leaf, cutting the light from the path around which only wiry brambles and Enchanter's Nightshade grew.

In spite of telling myself to keep calm, I began to hurry to reach the sunlight which was only yards away. As I burst from the trees I wished that the world that now inhabited me could as easily be left behind.

By lunchtime I had reached a high meadow. The Wrekin was a few miles to my left, rising from the flat lands that surrounded it, a true landmark, marking the land as an island does an ocean. I felt hungry and this was a marvellous place to stop, where I could feast my eyes as well as my stomach.

Before leaving I had thrown into my haversack a few pieces of bread, some cheese, a tomato and an orange. It was all I had been able to find. Where is everything? But it would be enough. Self sufficiency is the buzz phrase. The food tasted good, I was hungry, the surroundings were perfect and I was self sufficient. I had need of no-one, least of all her. The thought tasted as good as the food.

The map showed that my way from the high meadow was across a stile and past the backs of a couple of cottages to a small track which led by a farm to a bridge. The farm, I estimated, would be the halfway point of my walk. After that I would be heading back, the end only six miles away. My finger traced the paths I would follow, the symbols and coloured lines would soon take forms, leaving me with memories upon which I would feed in the time ahead.

A woman was hanging washing in the garden of the first cottage. Her strong arms pegged the clothes to a line stretched across the garden. As I passed the end of her garden she smiled, then picking up her empty basket she returned to the kitchen door, shepherding a little girl before her. The girl looked as her mother must have done a few years ago, with cheeks the colour of rosy apples and hair like ripe corn.

I lengthened my stride when I reached the track, my boots cushioning my feet from the sharp stones which peppered its surface.

The farmhouse was a disappointment. Plastic windows, sham Georgian style with wide white straps making them look as if the packaging had not been removed, were stuck incongruously, on to a building which owed more to pig-sty design than architecture. I hurried on, helped by the yelping of a couple of farm dogs, hoping that the next farm would be memorable for the right reasons.

I had always wanted to be an architect. It must be very satisfying to point to a building and say, 'That's me over there'. To have transient thoughts and ideas transformed by concrete, brick and wood into permanency.

Being an accountant has given me no chance to fulfil my destiny, although it has given me a clinical mind. I'm careful, meticulous, precise, not qualities which spring to mind as the most desirable, but they have their uses.

Giles, my partner, had none of those qualities. He had flair and was intuitive, and he had a Ferrari, although I think his intuition let him down and as for his Ferrari, well it was fast, it had comfortable seats for two and it was a most potent sex symbol, but it could, under certain circumstances, also be a steel tomb.

I came upon the bridge suddenly. One moment I was striding along the track which was bordered by high hedges from which delicate faces of dog roses peeped and wild honeysuckle perfumed the air, the next moment there it was, the hedges giving way to buff blocked parapets worn by the winters and summers of a hundred years or more. The bridge's surface was covered with turf and stones, the same as the track, which was why I had not noticed it as I had approached.

I leaned over the parapet to look into the small river running beneath. The water was clear, long reeds moved beneath the surface like a field of wheat dancing in the wind.

I saw Trish's face, pale, her hair garlanded, staring from beneath the water. She rocked gently with the current, the reeds a green shroud enfolding her.

I thumped the parapet with both hands and twisted away, disgusted by my imaginings. Trish had played Ophelia when we had first met, she had belonged to the local dramatic society. She was not Ophelia. Ophelia had drowned, Ophelia had drowned.

The path which I was to follow left the tract by the side of the bridge, dropping by the river past alder and willow. Cattle stood in the mud between clawed roots lapping water with thick fleshy tongues whilst flies buzzed and settled by their eyes.

After half a mile the river swung away to the right and I kept to the path which cut by a hedged field to a small rocky outcrop from where I could again see the Wrekin when I turned, for it was now at my back. Clouds were forming around it, clouds which although white against the sky, were thickening as I watched, gathering before an assault on the Midland plain. I wondered if rain would come before I reached my car. Although I carried waterproofs in my haversack I would resent having to take them out and lose my freedom of movement.

The church tower looked dark against the scudding clouds, the trees which had partly obscured it, moved as the increasing wind shook them. Large spots of rain started to spatter the ground as I walked past the houses in the lane.

There was that smell of dust and dampness which sweetens the air at the end of a drought. The colours of the gardens were muted, their brightness sullied by the rain swollen clouds.

My car came into view. A police car was parked alongside, two uniformed officers stood watching me as I neared them. One of the policemen walked to meet me. He stopped a few yards from me as if unwilling to come closer, to invade my private space.

The rain was dampening his cap and the shoulders of his tunic. His eyes were weary, his face sad as if life could no longer hold happiness for him. His voice when he spoke was slow and mournful. He said that there had been an accident, my wife and partner, they were both dead.

I feigned surprise.

Seduction

by

Barry Maddocks

Tomorrow I am to be hanged, but I feel no remorse for my crime. Instead I am overjoyed at what I did. I believe that what I did was honourable; I believe that I should die a martyr and not a criminal, but isn't it a fact that saints are never recognised as such until their bones are rattling in the grave? I saved the world - not literally, of course, but I saved mankind as a whole from an influence so vile that it posed a menace to society. A menace I am proud to say I destroyed.

They do not realise what greatness I have achieved, how I saved their souls, how I protected their innocence. They do not see what a service I did unto them. What I did, I did for all men and women and children; I did it for my enemies, even. But most of all I did it for love, that strongest, most overpowering of emotions that soothes to tranquillity and enrages to anger. I did it for love.

My tale begins on one late autumn afternoon, not more than six months ago. I lived with my mother and sister. Mother was bedridden and had not very much longer to live, according to Dr. Goldermann. Jane, at two and twenty several years younger than I , was contrastingly more vital. In fact it appeared that the weaker Mother got the more life Jane appropriately gained. I rarely saw my sister; she would eat alone in her room, and she went out for most of the day. I on the other hand, never went out. I stayed at home, helped the maid attend Mother. At other times I was to be found in my chamber, writing. I was a man of letters, and had become a self-taught student of philosophy. I was a recluse, but often one's own company is preferable to that of others.

Upon the said afternoon I was familiarising myself with some of the more intricate studies of the German thinker Immanuel Kant. My concentration was interrupted by the sound of footfalls and hushed voices on the passage outside my door - Jane was back, along with a gentleman whose tones I did not recognise. The conversation I was able to distinguish suggested that they were very much in love; at this I started, for surely Jane would have mentioned any romantic involvement on her part to me. Then the door adjacent to mine closed.

A short while later I was disturbed again. I heard them making love; low guttural grunts from him, breathless ecstatic gasps from her and, of course, the complimentary squeaks of the mattress. This went on for several minutes, then it fell silent - obviously the couple had dropped off to sleep. I was anxious to see who had smitten my little sister so, who had grabbed hold of her heart with a grasp strong enough to make her desire to give up her virtue to him; I slipped into the next room. I now realise that this act of curiosity alone heralded my downfall, and once or twice during sad reflection I have even gone so far as to regret that I bothered to assume my long-neglected role of protective big brother, but even the most sincere regrets cannot alter the course of history.

Gently I twisted the door-handle and stealthily I crept into the chamber beyond. Immediately in front of me was the bed; two forms lay beneath the white coverlet. The one nearest to me was that of Jane - she lay on her back, the sheet was around her waist, her arms were stretched above her head. Her long wavy hair was loose and tumbled over her shoulders in a beautiful shower of deep bronze. Her skin was white and soft, only her cheeks possessed any pigmentation at all. She looked just like a child. Feeling somewhat guilty observing my sister in her nakedness, however, I averted my eyes.

The man sleeping next to her was quite unlike any man I have seen before or since; he haunts my dreams unto this very day. That gentleman I instantly knew to be the devil. No visible feature upon his person told me this, but I recognised him as soon as his form graced - disgraced - my vision. He was lean and muscular, swarthy skinned, black haired. There was about him an air of malevolence, which it was impossible to deny the existence of even in his unconscious form. He appeared to be in his late-twenties, but I knew that really he was older than it is possible to conceive. Fearing I was about to pass out with nausea, I quickly left the room.

I was unable to return to my philosophy studies that afternoon, indeed I never returned to them. For days and weeks afterwards all I could see in my mind was the image of the devil - waking, laughing at me, his eyes stripping my soul bare, seeking out the evil that constitutes a part of everybody's persona. Later he spoke to me, convinced me that he was my friend, that with his help I would make many new friends and destroy my enemies. And for a while I often willingly entertained his notions. I said nothing to Jane-if I had said to her that I had been tempted by the devil, then she wouldn't have needed much help in reaching the conclusion that I had been spying on her with her lover. As far as I know, she never met him again. At any rate she never brought him home. Every day though she went out, until around three months after the occasion of her ruin. Then, she stayed at home for days on end. Like me, she took to her room, and many times she relieved myself and the maid of the duty of waiting upon Mother.

Passing along the corridor that ran outside Mother's room one evening, I heard Jane murmuring in a low voice. She was speaking quietly, softly, tearfully. Mother did not interrupt. I stopped by the door, put my ear to the wooden panel and listened to Jane reveal the cause of her misery; she loved a man, who had said he loved her but didn't really...and she was expecting his baby.

Both shocked and angered I went into my own chamber. It being the usual hour of my retirement, I undressed and climbed into bed. Now my mind violently rejected the temptations of the devil. He had almost succeeded in seducing me; but alas, alas for Jane. She had not been so lucky-for he had tempted her and she had succumbed to his charms. Yes, I saw it all now; my little sister had been seduced by Satan, he had taken her to bed and made love to her. He had sown in her womb seeds of a future life, whilst simultaneously he had sown in her mind seeds of the future all life would one day inherit-a future of destruction, desolation, evil. I knew he had polluted her mind because of the way Jane spoke. It wasn't much to go on-a few absent mumblings to herself which I overheard but ignored-yet I knew. I knew that the devil had destroyed Jane's mind and replaced it with a simple capacity for the corruption and or depletion of all worldly things, a mere receptacle for the twisted teaching of Satan himself. I knew that soon my Jane would become one with the devil.

Later that night I awoke. I was going to deal with the enemy within-now. If Jane's child were allowed to be born, if Satan were permitted to regenerate here on earth, then there would be no stopping him. His power would grow, his influence would spread. At all costs I had to destroy that unborn baby.

In Jane's room, I stood at her bedside. Pulling the covers down from her chin-without a second's hesitation or doubt-I plunged my paper-knife into the flat of her stomach. Then I stood back, watching the dark blood spread and stain the white lace of her nightdress. The child was dead, good. I didn't want to harm Jane - with any luck I could save her. In the morning she would thank me for what I had done. How foolish I was.

In the morning I was arrested. The maid had found Jane dead. - Dead! That wasn't in my plan; and I was prime suspect. The officers said that I was the only one present that night in the house. The maid was still at home for the weekend, arriving early this morning to discover Jane. Mother had passed away; Dr Goldermann later told me, she had died sometime yesterday afternoon, before Jane's confession; and there were no signs of a break-in.

I was fairly tried, but sentenced to death. But ever since the day I was taken in I have maintained the story I tell now. During these long, lonely days before the execution I have had but one visitor-Dr Goldermann. He disbelieved my story. It had not been the devil who had seduced Jane, he said, but a young upstart from the next town who had panicked at the news of Jane's pregnancy and hastily emigrated to America. The scandal was hot gossip at the time; I would have heard of it had I gone out. And my temptations-the work of whom, if not the devil? The work of my own lonely mind, the wise doctor replied, a formulation of revenge upon the society that had once spurned me.

Still though I believe the devil tempted me. Maybe I'll re-encounter my tormentor in the afterlife, or-since I committed no crime-maybe I'll meet my maker. Whatever, I must now try to get some sleep...I have a long day tomorrow.

The Afternoon Recitals

by

Jonathan Hughes

It was the Summer of my twenty-first year. I was spending it at my parents house, situated upon a hill in the suburbs. I had come to a standstill after dropping out of polytechnic a few months earlier, the futility of that life and the miserable rain that seemed never to stop brought on a thick depression. I left without a trace of dignity. I had been referred by my doctor to a counsellor. I stopped attending in case people found out, although in my wretched state I confessed to various so-called friends.

I have always been something of a loner, and although I saw old friends I was also happy with my own company. From time to time I ended up in various bars, a solitary drinker at closing time. The time spent in my own company gave me no real chance to think, however. I felt as if a great weight had settled upon my mind leaving me unable to entertain a single thought of my own. My thoughts , or the nearest thing to having real thoughts, were the words of songs playing on the jukeboxes in various pubs. Like alcohol, however, these words gave me only a passing relief. I had only the faintest idea that I was crumpled like paper. I could do nothing to change the situation, or I had not the strength to.

Occasionally, a girl I once was seeing came round to see me. I always enjoyed her turning up at the door. I had sent her two depressing letters in an attempt to arouse her interest. She dutifully came, but I was in no state to talk with her. A great chasm had opened up between myself and other people. The friends who I had once trusted were gone; replaced by mocking parodies of their former selves. I thought people saw through my disguise, and so my disguise began to fall away. I tried to remedy the situation by becoming a 'selfless' person. Assertive enough to cope, yet also caring into the bargain. This mask soon fell away. It revealed itself to be a lie of the very worst kind. At every turn I was forced to witness the false promise of other peoples life. I boasted about my weakness. I displayed my miserable face and thought others would find it nice to look at. I acted like a fool putting my worst foot forward while stamping on my best. What disgusting display of ego! I was a drain on the energy of anyone who chanced to come near me. I played the part to the hilt, then I despised myself and others for the shameful roles that had been played out.

It was during these first Summer months that I realised that my relationships with other people were all an act. I realised that I had, in fact, been lying all along! It made conversation very difficult because when I began to express an opinion the words turned to ashes in my mouth. I knew that my words were completely false. I was sometimes forced to stop speaking in the middle of a sentence because I knew that if I carried on everyone would see that I really didn't believe a word I said! I tried to appear normal to others, because I was afraid that they would notice if I didn't. To be noticed, that was my greatest fear at the time.

Around that time I was left alone in the house for a week. The days when I saw no-one and no-one saw me were a great relief. I was aware that I was suffering from too much humanity, but had been unable to remedy the situation. Every morning I woke and was able to walk freely around the house without fear of any lumbering human being requiring anything from me. I depend upon solitude. Other people cause in me a vague dis-ease which grows if left unhindered. Every second spent in the company of people causes this great malignant toadstool to grow larger. I realized that this was a chance to pour a little weed-killer at the base of my own particular fungus.

The days were long and sunny and I was more than able to observe myself and habits. I saw all my ambitions and desires and that they had been implanted by malevolent strangers. Even my thoughts seemed to become strangers to me during those days. In the afternoons I was able to rest and speak to myself as I had never spoken before. I drank tea and smoked cigarette after cigarette. And in between all of this I listened to the chatter within my mind. My eyes were closed and I felt myself first an old man, croaking words of wisdom. Then a woman singing to herself. Then a child talking earnestly in a garden. Memories came back to me and tormented me. I groaned because I was forced to see what a fool I had been. Yes, what a fool not to have seen the trickery of the world. We all act out our parts thinking that we are important when really the world is, in fact, controlled by another race entirely. It is controlled by a race of super-intelligent beings from the next galaxy along from our own! I was given this information by the two agents appointed to our home: Chester and Cherry. I was amazed when these two sidled up to me in their sly way and then, ignoring all convention, began to tell me of Judgement Day. I was so amazed that I flung them both out into the garden because I was not used to the tone of their voices. I went to bed as usual that night but was unable to sleep. I kept thinking about what the cats had said to me. I even got up and went out to look for them, but there was no trace of them at all.

The next day I still found no evidence of either of them. But I was more concerned by the fact that three space craft had landed in the back garden! They were cleverly camouflaged as trees, but I knew they were spacecraft as I saw people moving behind the windscreens. I realized that I must be under observation for my actions with the cats. I decided to remain calm and explain the situation when the chance arose.

In the afternoon I sat, as usual, in the living room listening to records. The antenna had been tampered with, however, as instead of music, high pitched voices were broadcast. After a moments listening I was able to make out the diabolical message. It took the form of a poem of Judgement passed upon the human race. The aliens had grown tired of human beings and intended to replace them with a set of quadratic equations. At that moment I noticed one of the cats waving his ariel tail in the air. Quick as a flash I rushed after him to stop the signal, but he was much too fast! I spent the remainder of the day in a state of tension. I was very anxious in case I was kidnapped. Nothing out of the ordinary happened, however, and I enjoyed a very pleasant supper consisting of two fresh crabs that I managed to catch outside.

I woke next morning in a cheerful mood. Obviously I was not considered a threat. I felt hungry and strolled outdoors. As luck would have it I spied two large Herring basking in the sunlight. It was a difficult task to reel them both in, but my hunger gave me strength. As soon as I was back inside the house, however, I realised that I had made a great mistake. The Herring were larger than I had originally thought. They were also devilishly quick and had me cornered. One of them grabbed me from behind in an evil stranglehold. The other approached me with a large needle which he slowly inserted into my bare arm. I cried out in pain and fear and begged them to stop. They rolled their fishy eyes at me and waggled in the sunlight. The radio was switched on. My vision faded.

Fatal Warning

by

Chris E Hancock

Dave Norton drove steadily down the winding road in his Metro car. His wife, Barbara, sat next to him talking. Their conversation consisted of the events that had taken place that night.

'Well,' said Dave with a laugh. 'I'll say one thing for your brother he knows how to have a decent party. Last time I went to a party like that...oh, it's been a few years.'

'Was it your stag night Dave?' giggled Barbara

'It probably was you know, all those years ago.'

Ten years to be precise. Now in their thirties, Dave and Barbara Norton found that life was a precious, delicate thing. They very rarely argued with each other, and when they did, it was only over simple matters. They were both what you could call a perfect couple, and were often envied by their neighbours and friends alike. But it did not bother them. They felt a sense of pride in their marriage.

'I'll tell you what made me laugh tonight though,' said Barbara.

'What? Your brothers-'

When Dave failed to complete his sentence Barbara knew something was concerning her husband. She looked across at him, his eyes betrayed what his mind held. She followed his gaze through the windscreen and down the dark, spectre like lane to what his eyes were fixed on. Less than half a mile away there stood a curved, ball of light hanging just above the roads surface. The light had a bright, piercing effect.

As Dave pressed down hard on the brakes, Barbara caught a quick glimpse of the time on the car clock 12.35. She also saw a faint impression of a small figure by the ball of light, and then all was dark. The ball was gone and the winding dark lane continued to be seen. Dave drove the car straight through the space where a few seconds ago they had both seen what?

'What was that, an explosion?' said Dave.

'It was just there, and then it went...' Barbara's voice showed traces of fear 'God, I'm scared Dave.'

'Don't be, whatever it was, it's gone, we've nothing to fear now.'

'I'm not so sure, look at the clock.' said Barbara.

Dave gave the clock a quick glance,

'So? It's one o'clock, we're not missing anything are we?'

'No Dave, but you are, when I noticed the clock a few moments ago, it was half past twelve, now it's one o'clock.'

Dave considered this for a moment and then said

'The clock's faulty, there's something wrong with it.'

'The clock is fine!' She gave her husband a serious look. 'Dave we've just lost half an hour!'

'That's stupid!' We would have noticed something! Look, we just saw a -'

'Saw a what? A UFO, a space ship? Face it Dave, whatever we saw back there has got something to do with us loosing half an hour!'

For a moment, Dave Norton believed that his wife was saying the truth. The 'incident' however did not end there and then. The following morning they both woke up with terrible headaches. Barbara noticed a red mark on her shoulder that had not been there previously. They both thought that it was time to investigate what had actually happened to them that night. Two days later they visited a hypnotist at a local hospital.

Dr Conrad Spencer was a pleasant looking gentleman in his fifties. He welcomed the Nortons into his office and listened patiently to their story. He waited until they finished before he said anything to them.

'Interesting.' He commented.

'So you want me to try and locate an area of your mind that you believe to be blocked off?'

'Yes.' Dave replied.

'We'd also like you to tape record whatever we say onto this tape.' He handed Dr Spencer a small tape cassette.

'Well Mr Norton, I'm just as curious to find out what happened to you as much as you are, shall we begin?'

Within five minutes, Dr Spencer had the two Nortons in a trance as he talked to them subconsciously,

'Now Mr Norton, it is 12.35, what do you see in front of you?'

In a slow, slurred voice Dave replied,

'...light. A bright light. There I also see figures like children, the car stops, I can't start it and then -'

'Then what Mr Norton?'

'The figures all around me, we can't escape them...'

'What do these figures look like?' asked the hypnotist carefully,

145

'Their skin is black, very black...' said Dave

'They're small about four feet high, no face except for two large bright eyes, like headlights. They have two arms and two legs, and they have two flaps on each hand instead of fingers.'

'Now what are they doing to you?' said the doctor in a deep voice,

'They make us walk to the ball of light, we just walk into it...'

'Is it no longer hovering in the sky then?' asked Dr Spencer,

'It is hovering, but we are able to enter it, inside it is very large, there are more figures looking at us. The walls are covered in purple panels, but I can't see any controls or anything to make it fly, now the figures speak.'

'Are they talking in English, or in another language?'

'In another language but we can hear them in English. The leader alien introduces himself as Birochi and explains that they are from another star system far away from Earth. He says that they have been to Earth many times before, but they always avoid being seen by too many people...'

'Why have they never made contact with us then?' Asked Dr Spencer.

'Birochi say's that we are too primitive to understand their lifestyle at this point in our development, but they have spoken to many humans over the years...now Birochi tells us of a warning, we must be careful...'

'What of Mr Norton?'

'He tells us of another race of aliens, the Mondormen. They are here on Earth We can't see them because they are human like us, but their minds are superior to ours. They can control our minds and read our minds, they can do telekinesis, and practice ESP. All of the major accidents and disasters are caused by them. Birochi tells us the Mondormen live on many planets, including their own world. Birochi's people and the Mondormen are old enemies, so they have come to warn us of an invasion to be made by the Mondormen...'

The hypnotist looked at Dave Norton in surprise, a look of fright on his face,

'Mr Norton,' he gasped, 'When is this invasion?'

'Next Tuesday, but we can stop them...'

Dr Spencers next question was inevitable,

'How?'

'Two days before the invasion we must go to London and tell this news to the Prime Minister and the government, they will believe us because of the gift that we will bring...'

'What gift?'

'A trydonamedos, it is a device that will explain about the Mondormen and Birochi's people. The government will understand this, and they will be able to prevent the invasion by defeating the Mondormen. Before this day we will forget all about this meeting with Birochi, but we will remember in time why we must go to London. Birochi tell's us that we may suffer from headaches because of the radiation on board their spaceship, but nothing fatal will happen to us, as long as we tell nobody about this meeting until we go to London. Now the aliens send us out of their spaceship and put us back into the car. They return to their spaceship and take off. We see it go, and then...it is one o'clock. We remember nothing..'

Dr Spencer clicked his fingers,

'Wake up Mr and Mrs Norton.'

The couple did so, and returned to the world of the conscious. Barbara looked at the doctor,

'What happened to us Dr Spencer? Can you tell us?'

The hypnotist smiled

'Perhaps you can listen to your own evidence on this tape. You may believe yourselves rather then me, if you wait outside now while I duplicate this tape recording for my files you understand, I'll be with you in a moment.'

The two Nortons stood up and left the hypnotists office Dr Spencer removed the tape cassette from the recorder and looked at it carefully, as though he was studying it. If the Nortons had been in the office with him, they would have been surprised to see two red beams of light strike from his eyes and slash into the tape, burning it within seconds. With a smile, the hypnotist watched as the tape reformed in his hand perfect without any burn marks. He placed it into the tape recorder, and listened to the Nortons voices describing a completely different event. He moved to the phone and dialled a number. He waited for some time and then spoke to the voice on the other end of the line.

'It's Conscer here, there's no need to worry about the Nortons anymore, I'll see to them. Yes, they're the British ones, I'll convince them that what they saw was an explosion. They will believe me, that's right, they spoke with Birochi. He was assigned to inform two people in Britain about our invasion, the fool, if he really wanted to help this miserable planet he'd make contact with the people here, but because they're different, alien looking, they're scared that the humans will attack them rather then understand them. But we can walk amongst the humans un-noticed, we Mondormen are superior the humans, as our invasion next week will prove.....

Fifteen Minutes

by

Maggie Pinder

'Open that fire escape will you, it's boiling in here.' I pushed back my chair, stood up and pushed firmly on the strong metal bar across the fire escape door. Joan was right, it was hot in here. The door opened with a loud 'thunk'. I walked out onto the top step,
'That's better' I thought as I stepped into the fresh air.

I looked back into the office, it was a large office with glass on three sides, which accounted for us alternately freezing to death in winter and baking in the summer. A fading plaque on the outside door announced 'Sales Office Typists'. Oh how happy I had been to be promoted to this office. I had been at the steel-works for a year now, since leaving school, and had loved every minute of it.

Sales Office Typists was a misnomer, General Office would have been better. Down the right hand side three glass boxes were home to the two Sales Representatives (hardly ever at home), and the Sales Office Manager; a remote figurehead, who rarely addressed us personally, preferring to speak through his mouthpiece - the Sales Office Supervisor. From her desk at an angle across the far corner of the office, she ruled over the eight sales order typists, and would have ruled us too given half a chance. The order typists were grouped near the door. The next group were thy Buying Office typists, of which I was one. The final group comprised of Export typists.

From my position two floors up, I looked down at the railway track which runs past the offices. One of our little yellow and black engines was passing, pulling its trucks, all neatly covered in green tarpaulin. With a little smile to myself I thought of Bill. On a day such as this a couple of years back, so rumour has it, Bill, who worked in the office just down the corridor from ours, had opened the window, leaned back in his chair and watched mesmerised as a light breeze had carried the sales orders out of the window and onto a passing freight truck. Though the orders had been posted back from Doncaster three days later, it had been too late for Bill. He had already been moved sideways into the Purchase Accounts. Bill had worked in almost every department at the works, but had only ever moved sideways, never onward and upward. He remained in Purchase Accounts until one day, at the age of 35, he slumped forward over his desk and died. I had never actually met Bill, but was eternally grateful for his early demise, as it was I who had subsequently filled his vacant position.

I returned to my desk, put paper and carbon into the typewriter - Dear Sir...

'Tea Trolley! Be a love and fetch me a tea, I've just got to finish this letter'. I obliged.

Tea Breaks in 1963 were tea breaks, two ladies, long past retirement age, trundled the trolley up and down the corridors of the offices while we formed an orderly queue until it was our turn. We then had fifteen minutes to drink it and return the cups before resuming our work.

Joan had finished her letter and already had her knitting out when I returned with the tea. Joan is a professional 'Granny', her whole life revolved round her two grand-daughters and 'another one on the way'. She was a typical works employee, having been here most of her life 'since our Sheila started at the big school', her husband worked here, as did her two brothers. 'Our Sheila' had also worked here until she married and started producing grand-children for Joan to knit for.

'That's nice, what's happened to the white one?' I asked, noticing the pink wool she was working with today.

'I finished that one while 'He' was down the pub last night. I told our Sheila it'll be another girl you mark my words, so it's pink wool today'.

I pulled out my paper and resumed the crossword I'd been doing during the morning break.

'There's some American guy here' announced Sue, who sits next to me and is around my age. Sue always scans the papers and reads out the best bits to anyone who cares to listen.

'This American guy reckons everyone is famous for fifteen minutes of their life.'

'I've never been famous' Joan sighed 'but He has'. 'He' was Joan's husband, we never knew his name, he was always referred to as 'He'.

'He stopped that train that ran over Stan. If he hadn't done that Stan would have been dead for sure, as it was he only lost his leg.'
We had all heard this story many times, 'He' had had a bravery award and had been in all the local papers.

'I suppose Stan was famous too' she added.

'Bill was famous when he died at his desk' ventured Sue. We all giggled, any mention of Bill always had that effect.

'I'd like my moment of fame now', she continued,

149

'While I'm young enough to enjoy it.'

'Me too', I agreed.

'You going out tonight?' Sue always like to know what I was up to, she'd had the same boyfriend since she was thirteen, and they only ever stayed in and watched television - 'we're saving to get married' she'd say. I think she was a little envious of my single life, but she'd grown up where everyone was 'left on the shelf' if they weren't married at twenty.

'Yes, we're going to the fair'.

'I thought you weren't allowed, you said your dad wouldn't let you.'

'Dad won't know, he's not invited' With that the bell went, tea break over and cups returned, we resumed work till 5.00pm.

I was glad to leave, it had been so hot all day, and though the fire escape door had brought welcome relief for a few minutes, we soon realised the air outside was just as hot as that inside. I jumped on the crowded bus, and thirty minutes later was back in my home town. I walked the last twenty minutes home, cutting through the park and throwing the last of my lunchtime sandwiches to the ducks on the pond.

'Hi Mum, we're going down Carol's tonight' I greeted Mum,

'I'm going up to change, we're going out early'. I dashed upstairs, popped my head round Mary's door and nodded for her to follow me to the bathroom. Mary is my sister, she, Carol and Jaqui are my best friends. Inside the bathroom I turned on the taps, we always do this when we don't want anyone to hear us.

'We're going to the fair tonight' I whispered

'You know we can't do that, we're not allowed.' Mary was always cautious and besides she was looking forward to a date the following night and didn't want anything spoiling that.

'They needn't know, anyway Carol and I discussed it on the bus this morning'.

'It'll be ok they won't find out anyway.'

'We'll be grounded if they do.'

'Don't worry, I'll say we made you come with us.'

I pulled on my lemon linen dress with the brown stitching, the only short dress I had that my father vaguely approved of.

'It'd look quite smart if the hem were a couple of inches longer' he'd say. Shorter straight skirts were 'in'. My short brown hair slicked back behind my ears, and backcombed lightly on top, a touch of make up and I was ready.

'You look very dressed up for Carol's' Dad queried.

'Oh we're walking down to Jaqui's after, we can't walk down the road in any old thing. We might go into the park or the town' I ventured.

'Don't you be late back, girls' Dad was very, very strict, 10.30 deadline and not a minute later. Our parents had us quite late in life, I was never sure whether he was really strict, or just wanted us in so they could have an early night. By and large we stuck grudgingly to the hometime rule, it was no use arguing. If we tried to argue we were grounded anyway for backchat, so it was best to give in.

We picked Carol up at the end of the road. I was slightly in awe of Carol, though only a month older than I she had left school a year before me. As the youngest of six she had more freedom than Mary or I, perhaps her parents were past caring. Anyway her three older sisters had taught her all the tricks of picking your way through the parental minefield, which we were yet to learn.

We chatted happily walking down the main road to meet Jaqui.

'I got to open the fire escape today. It was great, you can hear the little engines going past all day long. Did I tell you about Bill's invoices going?'

'Yes, we've heard all about Bill's invoices' they chorused.

'Anyway, I'm going to be promoted to the other side of the building for the winter', the idea had just come to me,

'It's going to be cold by that fire escape then. If I get my exams at college I can get a secretary's job by the time the winter comes and have one of those nice little offices facing the works on the other side of the building.'

'There's Jacqui' cried Carol and we ran to meet her.

'Hi all, so it's the fair is it, I hope my Mum doesn't find out'.
Jacqui's parents were even stricter than ours.

Ten minutes later we were at the Fair. It came here every year, and every year we were banned. We couldn't see anyone likely to tell on us so we set about enjoying ourselves. Dodgems, waltzers, shooting, picking up fish - careful not to win, we don't want to be caught taking trophies home. Then we heard it -

'I want a young lady volunteer to ride with me on the Wall of Death'.

'I'll do that, I love motor-bikes', Carol was always game for anything.

'Like hell you will', I thought, and ran as fast as I could towards where the announcement had come from. Arriving seconds before Carol,

'I'd like to try the Wall of Death' I announced. A lean dark haired man, with a short beard, leaned against a bike outside the 'Wall'. He looked hard at me.

'Ever ridden a bike before?'

'Yes', I lied, 'loads of times.'

'Up you get then, on the rostrum. Stand here, get the crowds in. You'll be on the front of the bike you know. Not really dressed for it, are you' spotting my short, straight skirt.

Jacqui and Mary appeared at the bottom of the rostrum,

'You're not really doing it are you?'

'Yes, I am'.

'C'mon everybody see this young lady ride the Wall of Death' the tannoy boomed.

Carol, Mary and Jaqui wished me luck and joined the queue waiting to get in. Five minutes later we were all inside. It was just a round, wooden circular wall with a sawdust floor, two bikes propped precariously in the middle. I didn't mind. I'd beaten Carol to it. The engines were already running.

'Get up here in front of me. Don't panic, just sit still. It's only for ten minutes, we don't go fast'. I didn't need reassurance, nothing was going to stop me now. The engine revved louder, the sound magnified in the enclosed space. Then we were moving, slowly, steadily up the ramp, onto the wall. I looked up, high above I could see faces looking down, I could see Mary, waving madly, Carol and Jaqui, both shouting. Slowly round and round, getting faster, up and up, and all the faces looking down, it was becoming harder to pick out my friends. We were only inches now from the sea of faces. More and more smoke filled the arena. Round and round we went, I looked up again, the sea of faces turning to a blur now, a multitude of colours all screaming and shouting. A crescendo of sound, a whirl of colour, a smell of oil, smoke, and all at once knew - this was it. The whole world was looking at me. I no longer cared if I was grounded for a week, a month, a year, this was my moment. This was my fifteen minutes.

The Delivery

by

Simon Wright

The secret is to make the hand over as quick as possible, don't give them a chance to quibble or find fault. Just whisk them round the car to check it over, get them to sign the paperwork and then off home via the nearest railway station. Mind you, it's good delivery weather today, overcast and drizzly. With any luck Mr Payne won't even come outside to view his new vehicle, he won't want to get wet and that will make the whole thing even quicker.

Unlock the door and climb in. Don't touch the accelerator as it's an injection. Listen to the engine whirl into life and then gently purr. Select reverse and ease her out slowly. Hook her right, select drive and foot down, here we go.

I've got thirty-thousand pounds worth of brand new car to deliver. With only fifty-five miles on the clock it is untouched by human hands. She is mine to break in, whatever happens I'll have her virginity, I'll be her first...

The destination is Uxbridge, that's up to the M42, then the M40, M4 and I should pick up the signs from there.

Mark didn't stay in the pub long last night. He had two pints and didn't even bother to take his darts out. I just don't know what's wrong with him these days. It's ever since we came back off holiday. He's hardly said a word to me.

Mind you, what a holiday. Plenty of sun, sea and sand washed down with plenty of Spanish ale. A good time was had by all as they say. The holiday was a turning point for a few things. My bank balance for one. So what's a few hundred quid? Well spent I say. It isn't every holiday where things gel so well together.

Christ, that was close, that bend weren't half greasy. I felt the back end step well out of line. Not a problem. Caught it before it had chance to develop into anything serious.

I can't imagine most people knowing what was happening or even what to do. They'd be scratching their heads wondering why they were sliding to a halt in a ploughed field, after demolishing a hedge and half the car.

Mr Payne must have his new car in prime condition, so I think I had better slow down a touch. I might not have the time or the space to catch it next time.

It's dinner with Jenny and her parents tonight. It'll be roast beef with mixed vegetables, followed by fruit salad and coffee in the lounge. It has been the last three times I've been there.

Another long night of abstinence from the booze.

Funny bloke her old man, right out the 1950's. He wears them old-fashioned pin-stripe suits and has got a bowler hat. He still wears those ancient National Health glasses that poor kids used to have in school. The lenses make his eyes look beadier than they already are. I bet he's a sod to work for, the little Hitler. Her old dear ain't much better, they make a good pair him and her.

My face must have been a picture the first time I went round there. We had a cup of tea and one digestive biscuit because there were four on the plate - one each. As I got up to go and walked to the door Mrs Chalice, her mother, shot out of her chair and over to where I had been sitting. She shook the cushion and brushed the seat down with her hand where I had been sitting. Bloody cheek, I thought, as if I'm dirty. Jenny nudged me 'she's always like that', she said embarrassed, 'just ignore her.' It was that night Jenny said she loved me. Wow, I felt so good.

I think I'll go for a couple of pints first, I don't have to be there until half seven. Might give me a chance to have a word with Mark and see what's wrong with him.

The M42, it's all motorway from here on. It looks like the weather is breaking, I can see a bit of blue sky ahead.

What's this, a tape in my pocket. Just what I need a bit of heavy; Guns N' Roses. I'm fed up with Radio One. Slip it in the cassette feed, dolby on, up with the bass and up with the volume. Open my side window as the rain's stopped.

What did Phil say. Set the cruise control at 70 mph and put it into the cars memory, so whenever I hit the button the car will always return to 70 mph. Up the speed to just below 100 mph - as it's an automatic three month ban for being caught doing over the ton. Set the interior mirror slightly off centre, so you can see police cars up the slip roads you pass, and keep your eyes skinned. Phil said, if you see 'plod' hit the cruise control and the car will slow up really quick with no brake lights, because if he's behind you he'll spot them and know that you were speeding. Can't take no risks being a professional.

I love Jenny. I have never loved another girl so strongly before. She makes me feel so warm and secure inside. She lets me run my hands through her long red hair. It makes me feel so happy when she flashes her green eyes at me and I know what she's thinking.

I may be nothing to look at and inexperienced with girls but she understands. She was so sweet on holiday. On out first night together, she coaxed and guided me because I was afraid of doing something wrong. She wasn't angry when I got excited and finished too quick. 'Paul' she said, 'the first time is always the hardest, it's not important.' Then she kissed my forehead and held me close. Everything was alright then. The next night she said she wouldn't put pressure on me and that we'd try again when I was ready. Just sleeping next to her was enough.

I can't understand why Mark brought that floozy with him, though. She ain't the type of girl I'd take to Spain. That guy has had more girls than anyone I've ever known and out of all of them Dusty was the worst. When she wore that obscene dress to the disco and flirted with all the blokes it was so embarrassing. My Jenny ain't like that and she never went topless either. Dusty did, the slag.

Yeh, me and Jenny. I want to marry Jenny, we were made for each other.

Plod! Hit the cruise control. They're in a Senator, on the inside lane doing about 60mph. Wow, she slows down well. The two coppers are talking and don't even notice me. Just glide past. Up to 80 mph, keep them in the mirror. 85 mph, I think they're slowing. Yes, they're pulling on to the hard shoulder and stopping. 90 mph, 95 mph, 100 mph, 105 mph, there won't be another plod for a few miles and the outside lane is clear so I might as well make the most of it.

What's happening with Mark is really bothering me. It's not the first time he has dashed out the pub after a telephone call and leaving his pint. It ain't like him. I bet he's got a married woman in tow, or something like that. Her old man must bugger off down the pub and he goes straight round. It always happens just after I've phoned Jenny to wish her goodnight, so that must be about eight thirty. I wonder who it is?

Hold on, after I've phoned Jenny. Strange. No, he couldn't, not with Jenny, not Mark.

Come on pal, are you a driver or just a licence holder, get out the way, you're blocking up the lane. Up yours too and don't take so long next time!

Get a grip Paul, that's silly. They couldn't possibly. Why go to all that trouble to hide it? Why not tell me straight?

Jenny knows I won't phone again once I have called. That as good a time as any to see Mark. He could breeze round once he knows I'm out of the way. Sneaky sod. Wait until I see him. I'll break his neck.

What the hell's this idiot doing in front. Flash him. Typical, didn't even notice I was there. Some people shouldn't be allowed on the road.

That explains that night at the disco on holiday. She was away from me for about an hour, and I was worried sick as to where she'd got to. Then she comes in with Mark. Yeh, I remember now. Jenny says she saw a mate from Worcester and they were having a chat. Yeh, likely story. Mark said he'd had to go back to the hotel to get some more money. Likely story. Bloody having it away I bet. Having a good snigger over me. That's why Dusty didn't hang around long. She knew what the score was. Bastard, I'll bloody kill him.

Blue lights behind... Plod! Cruise control. Christ I'm doing 135 mph, sod that, it's too late now, shit, I'll have to try and lose him. My car is faster than his, they can't mess with an expert like me. I'll shoot off down the A40, they'll never know... *He sees her after I've phoned. They're afraid to hurt my feelings. See if I care...* I can't get through this traffic. A gap, I'll go for the hard shoulder, at least I might have a chance... *Oh Jenny I love you, forgive me, and I'll forgive you, don't leave me for that prat Mark...* Where did that lorry come from... horn... brakes...

Smash... *Jenny, please don't leave me...*

Cold

by

Ainsley D Rowley

The man waved Mark into the old farmhouse, shutting the door quickly behind him so as to let as little of the cold air inside as possible. The farmhouse was warm and inviting, the decor was what one might have expected in such a building, all oak beams and horse brasses - a lot more snug than Mark's draughty old cottage.

'Thank you. Thank you very much' said Mark as he stamped the snow off his wellington boots and removed his gloves.

'Well' began the man, 'I couldn't leave you outside in this weather could I?' He helped Mark off with his coat.

'Thanks. I'm sorry to trouble you but I didn't know what else to do. This weather sort of took me by surprise. I've just bought the old cottage up on the hill, and the heating's on the blink.'

'A young strong bloke like you shouldn't have much trouble with the weather' the man laughed, 'wait till you're fifty-seven like me. My name's Tom by the way. I wondered who'd moved in up there.'

Tom showed Mark into the lounge where a fire was blazing.

'Right, well my name's Mark. I'm sorry I haven't had the chance to meet you before but I only moved in there properly a couple of days ago.'

'Bad timing with the weather then.'

'You can say that again.'

Tom turned the fire on full.

'There. You just warm up a bit and I'll go and put the kettle on for a cuppa, eh?'

'That'd be very welcome indeed.'

Tom went into the kitchen, leaving the door to the lounge open.

'So, you say your heating's up the spout then?'

'Yes.' Mark began looking around the room, 'It must be the cold; I tried to call the repairman but the phone was out and there's no way I could drive anywhere with the roads like they are.'

There was a bookshelf set into the wall to the left of the fireplace. Mark turned his head sideways to read the spines. The books mostly seemed to be of

157

a macabre and misogynistic nature; amongst them was a study of Sade's 'Justine', a booking detailing the female anatomy and two studies of murders of girls and women.

'The lines must be down; my phone isn't working either', called Tom, 'anyway, the repairman probably can't come out here until some of the snow's cleared, it's just too deep.'

'You're probably right' said Mark as he walked into the doorway so that he could talk to Tom without having to shout. While waiting for the kettle to boil, Tom was scooping the contents of a tin of dog food into a huge silver dish. His back was turned to Mark whom he appeared not to have noticed as Tom opened a door to his right which Mark presumed to lead to the cellar. Taking up the dish, he walked through the door and appeared to go down some steps into the darkness.

'Dinnertime, Audrey', Mark heard him say. A few seconds later, he emerged from the cellar and jumped when he saw Mark standing in the kitchen.

'You got a dog then?' asked Mark.

Tom seemed slightly nervous and twitchy. He smiled. He was obviously trying to hide something. Perhaps he was ill-treating it?

'Er, yes... Audrey. It's a strange name for a dog I know, but...'

Whatever the situation with the dog, Mark wasn't bothered; it was none of his business. He decided to rescue Tom from his unease.

'Kettle's boiled' he said perkily.

'Right. I'll make the tea then. Sugar?'

'Two please.'

'Right. Well, you go and sit yourself back down in the lounge, I'll bring it in.'

Mark walked back into the warm room and sat down upon the sofa.

'How come you bought that place then?' Tom asked as he brought in the drinks.

'Well, I'm a writer and I thought it might be a bit more inspirational than being surrounded by traffic and city noise.'

'A writer eh? Are you famous?'

'Not really. I've written a few small things, but it doesn't earn me enough to buy anything like that cottage. That's come from an inheritance.'

'Well', said Tom as he sat back and took a sip of tea, 'I used to be a mechanic when I was younger. If you like, I'll throw a few tools in the back of the land rover and we'll try and get up there and have a look at your heating. We can probably fix it temporarily.'

'Thanks. I'd appreciate that.'

Tom knocked back the rest of his tea in one go and stood up.

'Right-o. Well, I'll just go out and get everything together then. Stay here 'till I see if I can get the land rover started - there's no sense in you getting all your kit on if we can't go anywhere.'

'Cheers.'

Tom wandered into the kitchen and Mark heard him rustling his jacket and putting on his boots. He heard the door open and the sound of the wind as it blew into the house and sent a draught of cold air as far as where Mark was sitting. Tom shut the door and the chill and the noise were gone. Mark wandered into the kitchen to look through the kitchen window, where there was a different view to that from the lounge. As he stood there, watching Tom load and unload the land rover, he heard a noise behind him, a noise like a chain dragging across a concrete floor. The noise was coming from behind the door that led to the cellar. Despite what he'd said to himself earlier about it being none of his business, curiosity was beginning to get the better of him. Just what *was* he doing to that dog down there? It wouldn't hurt to take a quick look. After all, the mystery would only get to him if he never knew...

Alright; just a quick look.

He turned the handle on the door and pushed it open. It was pitch dark. His hands felt for a light switch; found one. He took a quick look behind him out of the window to make sure that Tom was still occupied, and then switched on the light and looked into the cellar. He could scarcely believe what he saw. There was the silver food bowl, half empty on the floor and there *were* chains, one of which was attached at one end to the wall by a large padlock, the other attached not to a dog, but to a pale, scarecrow-thin girl. The girl, dressed in dirty rags and with long, filthy hair squinted in the light and cowered into a corner. Her hands were held by the second chain, about eighteen inches long, attached to her wrists by two more padlocks. Mark stumbled down the steps towards her. She opened her eyes and, realising it wasn't Tom, crawled towards Mark as far as her tether would allow her with her hands outstretched.

It was all Mark could think of to say: 'Who are you?'

'Please - you must help me. He keeps me prisoner down here. He's going to kill me - he has all these horrible books about hurting and killing girls.'

She was almost in tears; her voice was soft and trembling.

'Yes, I know... I...'

'He's done it before - with others' continued the girl, 'look in that freezer over there.'

She pointed to a large white chest freezer. Mark walked over to it and opened it. What he found inside almost made him throw up on the spot; there were human bodies mutilated beyond recognition; limbs and torsos and heads piled up on top of each other. He slammed the lid down. Reeling from the sight, he heard a voice behind him.

'Come away from there. You don't know what you're messing with here. You don't know what she is!'

Mark turned around. Standing there was Tom, pointing a double-barrelled shotgun at him. He advanced.

'I said come away.'

Suddenly, the girl leapt up behind Tom and flung the chain linking her hands around his neck and started to strangle him. Tom dropped the gun and grabbed at his throat. Before Mark could do anything to help, Tom slumped to the floor.

'He's only unconscious', said the girl, 'quick - you must release me before he comes round. The keys are hung on a nail by the door.'

Still in a daze, Mark searched for and found the keys. He undid the padlocks and the girl rubbed her wrists and leg where the chains had been attached.

'Those bodies' Mark began, turning to the freezer, 'they were so horribly mutilated. How could anyone cut up people like that?'

'They weren't cut up' replied the girl, her voice strangely low and relaxed, 'they were partially eaten.'

'What?'

Mark turned round. There stood the girl with an evil smile on her face, holding a large pick-axe high above Mark.

'Dinner-time, Audrey' she said.

Till Death do us Part

by

Stephen E Bennion

She gazed out across the deserted streets spread below, a look of sadness etched painfully across her features. It was ironic that it should end this way, overlooking the very town which had so promised a new beginning for her, the town where she had finally met someone to love. As a solitary tear appeared in the corner of her eyes, perhaps unavoidably the memories of a happier time came flooding back to her.

John was a local lad, she herself had moved to the Midlands from Leeds after being offered a job in the area. They had met at a party, during the whirlwind romance that followed she had felt as if all her childhood dreams were finally coming true, for once her life seemed complete.

However, though made in heaven, dreams were not always made to last. Their marriage of three years was over, she knew that much. What she couldn't understand was why.

The wind half-heartedly tousled the mass of dark brown hair she had hastily brushed that morning. Though naturally attractive, ever since he had walked out on her two weeks ago she didn't seem to want to put as much effort into her appearance as before, not that anyone would look their best at seven o'clock on a Sunday morning. This morning was the first time for days that she had actually bothered to wear any make-up, managing a quick smear of lipstick.

She looked down to the road far below once more. This time she spotted a lone car approaching around the ring road, turning off to make its way around the bottom of the multi-storey and disappearing through the entrance six storeys below where she stood. A large silvery grey saloon. His car.

The Mercedes pulled up next to her own ageing Mini. She waited for him to emerge, confused anger disrupting any sort of rational thinking that might have eased the situation. She wanted to scream at him, shout loudly so that the world could hear what he had done to her life. Just for a moment she hated him, wanted him to hate her, wanted him dead...

He climbed out of the car. Shutting the door carefully, he turned around slowly to face her.

161

Abruptly, the pent up anger and frustration vanished as if smoke on the breeze, leaving her mind empty and even more confused than before. Even her vocal chords seemed unwilling to provide anything more than a barely audible whisper.

'Hello John', she said at last.

He walked towards her, pausing a few feet away.

'Well, I came. What did you want?'

'What did I want?' She shook her head sadly. 'I wanted you. I've always wanted you.'

'Is this just going to be just another slanging match?' John asked, sounding emotionally weary. 'Caroline, I thought we said it all two weeks ago.'

'You walked out on me...'

'I know.'

'... after three years of marriage, you left me...' The woman sighed, pausing as if unable to admit the facts to herself. '... for your secretary!'

'I'm sorry.'

'Sorry!' Caroline almost spat at him. 'You're sorry?'

'Yes!' John said. 'Isn't that enough? I'm sorry it had to end this way, like I'm sorry I became unable to love you anymore. I'm sorry! Okay?'

Caroline took a step closer to him.

'Is that why you left?' she said, quietly. 'You no longer loved me?'

John nodded. 'That's the way it is. I am still very fond of you, nothing you do could ever make me hate you. And I was in love with you when we married, we both know that.'

'Then what changed?'

John sighed. 'People change. I changed. I met Claire, and I realised that what I felt for her was what I had once felt for you but had lost. That's the way it is.'

Caroline turned away. 'So what now?'

John shrugged. 'We get on with out lives, I guess.' Shaking his head sadly, he made his way back to where the Mercedes was parked.

'Don't you leave me!' Caroline screamed. 'You bastard! Don't you realise what this is doing to me? I love you! You can't leave me like this!'

John faced her once more, obviously taken aback by her outburst.

'But it can't go on. Our marriage is over!'

'Yes! But my life was our marriage. You have destroyed my life!' Caroline was on the verge of screaming. 'Forever! And like a man you leave me for dead, crawling back to that tart of a secretary!'

'Calm down!' he yelled. 'Get a grip on yourself! Yes, I'm going back to where I feel I'm wanted, and there is nothing you can do about it!'

Opening the door, he dropped wearily into the driver's seat.

'John...'

'No, it's no use. I cannot love you anymore.'

'But John, I still love you...'

He slammed the door shut. Starting the engine, he lowered the window. A picture of utter dejection looked back at him.

He faced her for what was to be the last time. 'Look after yourself, Caroline.'

Putting the Mercedes into gear, he moved slowly towards the exit ramp to start the long descent to ground level. In the heat of the moment, Caroline saw red. Convinced that she had been wronged, a wave of anger swept over her.

'Drop dead!' she yelled at the retreating car. Blind with grief and confusion, she sank to her knees.

'I want you, John...' she sobbed. 'I still love you...'

The wave of anger was replaced by one of self pity, which in turn was swept away by a cloud of depression. She wandered over to edge of the car-park, hardly seeing the six storey drop down to the street.

Her life was in ruins, she knew she couldn't possibly live without him. Her future looked empty and meaningless, she was at a total loss of what to do.

Suddenly an insane solution filtered into her mind. Before she had time to consider the possible consequences of her actions, she had clambered over the safety rail and onto the narrow ledge overlooking the road.

Out of the corner of her eye she spotted a car emerging from the multi-storey entrance far below. She smiled, then calmly stepped out into thin air.

As PC Davidson observed the scene in the street, the second ambulance pulled up. He hated this sort of work, any death was a tragedy but there was something especially sad about suicide incidents. As the ambulance crew got to work, the driver, finding he wasn't needed at the moment, walked over to join the police officer.

He lit a cigarette. 'What happened here, then?'

'A suicide attempt.' Davidson replied with a sigh. 'It must of been. No way could she of accidentally fallen over one of those parapets. We're not even sure who she is yet, although it shouldn't take long to find out.'

The ambulance man glanced back to where his colleagues were gingerly lifting the poor unfortunate onto a stretcher. The policeman shook his head sadly.

'What surprised me were the injuries sustained by the driver of the car. It was incredibly bad luck on his part to be passing underneath just when she decided to jump.' He paused, watching the stretcher being loaded onto the back of the ambulance.

'He's dead, you know', the driver said. 'As she fell through the screen his face was cut to ribbons. Choked to death on his own blood.'

The police officer shuddered. 'Is she alright? I'll have to visit her in hospital later on.'

'Miraculously, yes. Apart from concussion, just a few cuts and bruises. The man in the car cushioned her fall. Not that saving her life is any consolation to him, of course', he added.

Davidson sighed. 'The part I'm not looking forward to is breaking the news to his next of kin', he said. 'He probably has a wife or girlfriend somewhere, just how do you tell her that he was killed by a manically depressed woman's attempt on her own life?'

'How indeed', mused the ambulance driver. 'I don't envy you at all.'

The Prisoner

by

Derrick R Bickley

The arrest of Joseph Mankowitch stunned the whole village. Those who saw the two policemen march him at gunpoint down to the village police station in the early morning sunshine passed on their story in muted disbelief.

Three months had passed since that day. Sitting, propped up against the wall, I wondered, like many others, how he had managed to slip his guard and escape. Even more difficult to believe was that he had actually made it to the Channel Islands, this frail old man sitting opposite me on the floor in a crumpled heap, rumpled creaseless black trousers now soiled and frayed, a shabby fawn cardigan that once probably fitted him now appearing two sizes too big on a body withered with age. Had he really believed he could make it all the way to Britain?

How did you do it, Joseph?' The question had to be asked. 'How did you manage to get so far?'

A face looked up from the heap. 'The greatest motivator in the world, Gunther - fear.' He pointed a bony finger at me. 'You know what it is to be afraid, Gunther.'

'I was a boy then. Now I am grown up and a German. I do not know fear.'

Joseph laughed mockingly. 'You will, Gunther, before this war's over. You'll get so that you can smell it at thirty yards.'

'The war will be over in a few months', I assured him. 'Have you seen how the British fight their war? They send bombers to drop leaflets. They don't really want to fight. It's just a gesture. The British people will welcome our glorious Führer when he lands on their shores.'

Joseph grunted. 'Your glorious Führer is a madman.'

'You must not say such things', I said angrily. 'He has restored our pride, given us hope, given us a future. Once more we are a great power in the world.'

'He will be the ruination of Germany.'

'I thought you were a patriot, Joseph.'

'A German patriot. Not a patriot of the Nazi party.'

165

The two were inseparable now. Germany was the Nazi party. A new beginning.

'Why did you run, Joseph? Surely the charges would not stand up in court.'

'A child molester, they called me', he protested loudly. 'They said I enticed young girls on their way to school. At my time of life!'

The charges were impossible to believe. I had known Joseph for as long as I could remember. A kindly, caring man he had been like a second father to generations of kids in the village. He once saved my life. And had been prepared to sacrifice his own to do so.

'The charges were no more than an excuse to make the arrest', he went on. 'There was never going to be a trial. I'm a Jew, that's my real crime. A Jew in Hitler's Germany. For that there is no trial. I shall be sent to one of the camps.'

I had heard the rumours about the camps. Vicious propaganda put about by the Communists probably, or may be even by the Jews themselves. This was twentieth-century Germany. How could such places exist?

The boat had begun to pitch more noticeably, the weather up top obviously deteriorating. Thankfully, I had a strong stomach.

Tucked uncomfortably into a small alcove alongside the engine-room of an ageing, creaking cargo vessel taking us back to the French mainland, it became increasingly hot and clammy, so I was glad to loosen the top buttons of my uniform, the official dress of the Hitler Youth, the great national movement that had brought together Germany's young as a mighty power in itself. The rifle cradled in my lap was loaded with live ammunition. Bringing Joseph Mankowitch back was a big responsibility.

In a few weeks I would be old enough to wear a different uniform and the prospect of joining the German army excited me greatly. Perhaps I might even be in the invasion force, one of the first on British soil. Who knew what glory lay in store?

Joseph appeared to have fallen asleep, a victim of the stifling atmosphere and the soporific, rhythmic throbbing of the huge pistons. Poor Joseph, how had it come to this? There were such happy memories of him, my childhood and life in the village. I owed him a debt I could never hope to repay.

My mind wandered back, as if often did, to the day after my seventh birthday, when there seemed no escape from the quicksand tightening around my chest, sucking me down. Despite warnings about quicksand, the children of the village could never resist the lure of the quarry workings. To us it was an ideal playground.

Joseph was first to hear my screams. Unable to reach me from firm ground, without further hesitation, he plunged in beside me, somehow finding the strength to push me upwards and clear of the clinging, deadly mire.

But I could do nothing for Joseph. If the others hadn't arrived with a rope he would have died. That I should live.

The boat was rolling heavily, bringing me out of my waking dream. I couldn't believe my eyes. Joseph was gone.

Panic-striken, I raced up the steps into what was now a cold, storm-lashed night, my uniform soaking through to the skin instantly. He was making for the stern. My shouts drowned out by the howling wind, I threw aside the rifle and ran after him. Although slipping and stumbling on the wet, heaving deck, I could move much faster, but he had too much of a head start. Even his struggle to get over the rail failed to hold him up enough. I arrived at the very moment he jumped.

His weight and my momentum took me over with him as I grabbed his arm. For a moment we were in mid-air, hurtling downwards towards the storm-tossed sea, until my desperate grasping of the rail with my trailing hand brought our flight to a shuddering halt, Joseph wincing with pain as he crashed heavily against the hull.

The violent heaving of the boat, as I clung to Joseph's wrist, swung us crazily backward and forward, a giant pendulum skimming the tops of the huge waves as they reached up, trying desperately to pull us down.

'What are you trying to do, Joseph?' I had to yell to be heard through the roar of the wind, the sea and the unrelenting rain.

'Let me go, Gunther', he screamed back, 'let me die now.'

'How can I do that? I owe you my life.'

'If you value that debt, let me go now', he cried. 'Spare me the camps, Gunther. Spare me the camps.'

Joseph was proved right about fear. I came to see it, smell it, taste it, from the frozen hell of Stalingrad, through the battlefields of Italy, to the last desperate retreat to Berlin. Yet I saw nothing to match the terror in Joseph's eyes as he looked up at me that night. His was not the fear of dying, but the fear of survival.

I released my grasp, allowing Joseph's frail, old body to fall into the sea.

By the time I pulled myself back up onto the deck, he had disappeared from sight, swallowed up by the storm and the darkness. I had no idea how long I stood there. I knew only that I was grateful for the rain and spray that hammered against my face and hid the tears on my cheeks.

Father of the Bride

by

Joyce M Smith

'Will someone help me with this damned tie?' Jack shouted. No one came of course. A wife and two daughters in the house, all too busy dolling themselves up to bother about him. Wedding mania, that's what it was. Women everywhere in various stages of undress, bridesmaids in the bathroom, a hairdresser in the kitchen, the hall full of flowers and the doorbell ringing continuously. The living-room was overflowing with relations waiting to be served drinks and he, he was wrestling with this stupid tie and on one to help him. To hell with it. In desperation he stormed downstairs and demanded help from a woman in a large green hat who turned out to be his cousin Dorrie. She did his tie in no time and he managed to make drinks in spite of his trembling hands. A rather large whisky and soda made him feel a little better.

Dorrie spoke to him soothingly about the weddings of her two daughters. Jack should relax she said, everything would go off splendidly. It was all very well for her, he was of the opinion that he had every right to panic if he felt like it. He was going to try to explain that it was the strain of the last few months that had made him a nervous wreck, not the wedding itself but Gran was demanding another gin and there just wasn't time. It wasn't every bride-to-be who changed fiancées in mid-engagement as Amy had done - it had probably never happened before - and it had completely unnerved him at the time. However she had had the sense to realise her mistake and to put it right before it was too late. It had taken a lot of courage to do that Jack thought.

He had daughters to be proud of Jack reflected as the comforting warmth of the whisky rose from his chest to his head. Both beautiful and spirited, both a credit to Jane and himself. Amy, the older by two years lived life at a hectic pace, always seeming to be in some sort of a muddle but things usually turned out right for her in the end. Lindsey was hot-headed and determined to have her own way, but she was young, she would settle down given time. He felt more than happy about Mark the prospective bridegroom, how he would have felt if she had decided to marry Tex was a different matter. Tex! How could a chap be any good with a name like that?

168

He remembered the weekend Amy had arrived home with Tex in tow to announce that they were in love and intended to get married. No asking permission. Oh no, nothing as old fashioned as that. Perhaps Amy thought he would have refused for even in her love-besotted state she must have realised that she had chosen an odd-looking cove to say the least of it. Tex was over six foot tall with massive shoulders, a mane of red hair and a luxuriant growth of beard to match. Even by today's standards his clothes were outlandish, for together with the inevitable jeans he wore violently coloured shirts coupled with fancy silk waistcoats and sometimes a flowing scarf was added. He reminded Jack of a cowboy who had lost his horse except that cowboys did not usually wear earrings, and indeed this image seemed to match his name. Appearance was one thing, behaviour another for whenever Tex was in the house his huge presence seemed to take the place over. He seemed to be unable to sit on a chair in the normal manner but draped his body over it like a sack of potatoes and seemed to be so relaxed that he was liable to fall asleep at any moment and often did so. He made Jack extremely uncomfortable in fact he found him quite objectionable. Strangely Tex did not appear to notice the effect he had on his prospective father in law and seemed to think that they were the greatest of chums and had a habit of giving him a conspiratorial wink at every opportunity.

Jack suspected that Jane felt the same way about their prospective son in law even as she led the family into a whirl of wedding preparations. She was determined that the wedding would go off well and refused to enter into any discussion about Tex.

It was a mere six weeks before the wedding day when Jack had returned home one day to find the house in an even greater uproar than usual. Amy, red-eyed and defiant had informed him that it was all off between her and Tex. She now knew that she did not love him and was in fact in love with someone else and this time it was the real thing. It was an old friend of Tex's who had moved to Canada some years ago and had returned to England for a visit and to look up some of his old friends. One look was all that was needed Amy said, love at first sight she smiled. Tex she said had been just marvellous, had accepted the situation with good grace and the three of them remained friends, in fact he had even agreed to attend the wedding. Oh yes, they had decided to go ahead with the wedding she said and smiled that soppy smile again.

Jack could not believe his luck. The new love was produced and turned out to be a personable good-looking chap who's name was Mark. He appeared to be perfectly normal. He wore conventional clothes, his hair was well cut and his behaviour impeccable, moreover he did not wear earrings and he called Jack 'Sir'. He owned a booming business in Vancouver to which he had to return within two months, taking Amy of course. Jane was firm about the wedding. It was unusual perhaps she said but the obvious thing to do was to proceed as if nothing had happened, the only difference being the bridegroom - and thank heaven for that Jack thought privately.

The wedding day dawned bright and sunny and suddenly everything started to happen. The cars arrived and the guests left for the church. The bridesmaids assembled in the hall to await their car, two little nieces looking fit to explode with nervous giggles, and Lindsey endeavouring to maintain order, what a picture they made Jack thought, perhaps all that fussing had been worth while after all. How pretty Lindsey looked, dressed in pink which gave her a sort of glow, a real beauty she had turned out to be. Then they were whisked off and Amy drifted downstairs, a beautiful stranger in a cloud of white tulle and the sight of her made Jack catch his breath. Then he was in the car with the beautiful stranger by his side and she seemed so calm and happy that Jack began to relax.

After that things took on a lovely dream-like quality. Even escorting Amy down the aisle Jack felt himself to be in a sort of happy trance and the rest of the service merely a blur. He caught Jane's eye and she smiled at him and he thought how lovely she looked too - what a beautiful family he had, and now Amy was on Mark's arm walking towards him and they looked so right together that his heart was full of gratitude that things had turned out so well.

The whole thing seemed to last such a short time, then it was all over and they were outside the church and there was general kissing and congratulations and Jack felt his dream-like state begin to dissolve into a mood of relaxed goodwill towards all. Mark and Amy were well and truly married and it felt somehow right. He suppressed a shudder as he thought of what might have been - but things had turned out right after all.

All the fuss of the photographs was under way, the photographer concentrating his attentions on the bridal pair at the moment and Jack remembered his duty and began to circulate amongst the guests.

'Can we have the bridesmaids now please,' the photographer clapped his hands
imperiously.

The little ones were already in position.

'Give Lindsey a shout Jack, she's over there.'
She paid no attention when he called her name. He walked towards her, calling to her but still she did not hear him. Tex had draped his large body over a grave stone, he looked very relaxed. He appeared to be dressed as a lumberjack and had added a red cravat presumably to mark the occasion. The sun glinted on his ear ring. Lindsey was engaged in animated conversation with him, gazing, lost to all else. There was a look on her face that Jack knew well, he had seen it before, that look in the eye. Oh yes he knew it well, it was the look of love. Tex turned his head slowly, shook his red mane and looked Jack straight in the eye. He winked.

Psychopomp

by

Kate Masters

The woman walked slowly out of the Coronary Care Unit, feeling like a soldier temporarily withdrawn from the battle zone.

'There's nothing you can do at the moment, love', a nurse had told her with a tired, professional smile. 'You pop out for a breath of air - she's in the best hands.'

Outside the air was cold, metallic, heavy; it seemed unhealthy to breath. Three a.m. It was very quiet. She walked away from the hulking old hospital buildings towards the car parks, the only open space, picking her way through ruts and across pot holes. During the day the area was bedlam; H.G.V.'s, trucks and excavators vied with pneumatic drills and cement mixers to produce a furious cacophony. The hospital had been built as a workhouse; now it was being 'extensively modernised'. In the evil sulphurous glare of sodium lights, the machines lay silent, littering the area like huge armoured corpses.

Her steps leaden and slow, the woman walked towards the perimeter of the furthest car park. Even at this lonely hour there were a few cars, a reminder that others were keeping vigil. The thought of so much anguish was no comfort to her. Ahead were some stunted trees, beyond the remnant of a sagging metal fence like a broken rack of spears. She rested her hands on the top of the fence and gazed out across the valley. The ground dropped steeply under a coarse pelt of bleached rough grass, littered with torn newspaper, tattered polystyrene boxes and rusty cans. Below were mean narrow streets of back-to-back terraced houses, bathed in the evil yellow glare of street lights. Distant traffic murmured and groaned. The watcher wished she could cry or feel something, anything, apart from this emptiness and desolation.

To distract herself from her thoughts, she stared again at the regimented rows of houses. It was funny the way those houses hadn't seemed so cramped and grim when she had been a child. Trudging home from school, feet squelching in summer sandals through grey slush on a winter's afternoon, she'd look forward to reaching the cheery brightness of the little house - and Mam's warm welcome.

'Hallo Jean my love, give Mam a kiss then.'

172

The smell of baking had filled the tiny kitchen and the whole house. Smells could always bring her childhood back. Coal fires and real fog 'Yes, and real whooping cough and bronchitis to go with it', said Mam's voice in her head.

Diesel fumes reminded her of the fun of getting the bus into town to go shopping, her and Mam all excited, sitting on the top deck to see the world from a new angle, as Mam said. Peering into house windows from the bus to comment on other people's furniture and wallpaper - usually detrimentally - and looking at the gardens. Mam would have loved a garden full of roses, but 'They aren't for the likes of us, love' she always said.

The tiny flagged yard at the back of their house was too dark and high walled to grow plants, and local cats, desperate for open soil, even killed off window boxes.

The kids never cared if they had no gardens. In those days you could safely play in the streets, there were so few cars about. She remembered how they'd tie a piece of old clothes line to a lamp post, then one would 'turn up' and the others would skip, singing 'I had a little bubble car, number ninety eight,' or 'Under the moon, 'over the stars.' One summer's day Jean's Mam and Brenda's had come out and played with them, and couldn't they skip.

Jean remembered the two mothers taking a gang of kids from their street on a picnic to the local park - miles it had seemed, and the little ones had complained about the long walk - oh , but when they got there! The swings and the roundabout! The huge slide! and it was all so green and beautiful, there were flowers everywhere! They'd had their picnic in the rose garden, with 'pop' out of bottles, egg butties, home made cake, oranges and apples. By magic, Mam found a little purple-wrapped bar of chocolate in each child's ear, or hair, or pocket. Coming home worn out but happy in the evening to the immaculate little house, Jean and her Mam found Dad home early, furious because his wife and daughter had gone out behind his back.

Recognising the signs, Mam had packed the terrified child off to bed quick, with a jam buttie, while Dad fumed and muttered. But Jean crept down and crouched out of sight at the foot of the stairs, listening as he snarled at Mam while she quietly got on with making his tea. Finally he'd belted her one - or two - because the meal was not good enough for a man back from a hard day's work to find his missus making a show of herself in public.

Jean sighed. Dad had been gone for years now, walked out and never come back. It had been a relief to both of them.

'Now we'll get a bit of peace, just the two of us,' Mam had said, and got a job cleaning at the school where Jean was a pupil. And peace they had had, until

Jean passed the 'eleven-plus' and got herself a scholarship to the local grammar school. Her head-mistress was very keen that Jean should be given the best possible chance, but Mam was dead against it with her 'not for the likes of us' approach. Finally Jean and the head prevailed, despite Mam's complaint that Jean would not be taught shorthand and typing.

'How's she going to get a good secretarial job without them, eh?'

After that defeat their relationship lost some of its easy warmth; for the first time - but not the last- the accusation that Mam's ways were 'not good enough for Jean' was made. Once she realised that she was as clever as the others - cleverer Jean made new friends at her new school, girls from different backgrounds who widened her horizons. She began to see the little houses in a different light, and to long for better things as Mam had feared.

Remembering the battle over her university entrance, Jean sighed again, walked over to a large block of fallen masonry and sat down, with the bleak vista still in view. Mam couldn't see why Jean wanted to go.

'There's plenty of jobs round here for a smart girl like you, with all those O and A levels, why d'you have to go off to the other end of the country to pass more examinations?'

She didn't want to let Jean go, and the fact that only a legacy from her grandad, dad's dad - made it possible just made it a more bitter pill.

'Oh, he's got what he wants now, he's split you and me up, your Dad,' Mam said grimly, her back turned so Jean couldn't see the tears. 'You'll be off with your clever-clever pals, sneering at this place, you'll have no time for the likes of me.' But Jean went anyway.

Curiously enough, what Jean regarded as her biggest mistake was welcomed enthusiastically by Mam. When Jean brought Charles home, announcing their engagement almost before he and Mam had been introduced, the expected explosion never came. Mam approved, particularly since Jean, being pregnant, could not finish her degree.

'There's plenty of people round here who started married life with a babe on the way,' said Mam, 'And he's such a well-spoken young man, and doing so well in his father's firm.' Her smile had seemed triumphant to Jean. 'You'll be happier, more settled like, when you've your own home with a family to look after - you'll forget all this career nonsense.'

When Jean miscarried, two months after the wedding, Mam had stayed with them for a few weeks to look after her daughter. Charles had been so charming that he had won a friend for life - since Jean never repeated his disparaging remarks to her. In fact, when the marriage broke down three years later, Mam blamed Jean and her desire for a life of her own.

'He'd never've strayed if you 've made a decent home for him, Jean,' Mam said.

'The way you did for Dad, you mean?' Jean had retorted, hurt - and regretting the hurt the words caused immediately.

Thinking back it seemed to Jean that she and her mother fought the same battle over and over; there was always someone's life at stake, hers or Mam's. No-one ever seemed to win, but the wounds went deep: the scars still ached. Turning to look at the hospital Jean thought that no matter what had gone before, that was where Mam was fighting her last battle, and was time Jean went back and fought at her side, even if it only meant holding her hand.

She took a final look back across the ugly landscape. It seemed thoroughly despoiled, filthy, desolate. Suddenly, from the stunted twisted undergrowth close by, a blackbird began to sing. Jean was stunned by the beauty of the rivulet of sound. But it was three a.m.! It was winter! Why should the bird sing? To her amazement, across the valley another bird answered, seeming to call the first. Back and forth went the bright ribbon of sound, a duet of love and separation. Blackbirds - Mam's favourites.

Finally the chorus died away, and Jean walked slowly back towards the tall, dark building. She wanted to tell her mother about the loveliness of the birds' song; it seemed like a message of hope, a miracle, amidst all the ugliness and pain. She wanted to reassure her that she rejected all the ugliness, the drudgery, but treasured her mother's loving care. She could never reject Mam herself; Mam was the solid rock on which Jean's life rested.

Walking swiftly, purposefully down the long, glaring white corridor, she was suddenly overtaken by two green-robed figures, running flat out. At that moment the doors of the Coronary Care Unit opened and another figure appeared.

'OK,' he called. 'No rush - she's gone.'

The birds, Jean thought, I never told her about the birds.

French Onion Soup

by

J R Majer

It is a terrible thing to have a secret from your husband. I had always thought it otherwise, thinking of a warm conviviality between women from which males could be excluded, but now that the secret, with a primitive but insistent life of its own must soon be revealed..yes, must be revealed.. I am filled with a growing apprehension.

You cannot say that I have not made every effort to conceal it. On the very first day when he came home, and on crossing the threshold sniffed the air, I flew into the bedroom for my best perfume. I am still wearing it but the level in the bottle is getting dangerously low and to buy some more would arouse suspicion.

Then I managed to bury some of the evidence. There was just a small piece of open ground between the flower bed and the kitchen garden, and there I dug a shallow grave, filling it hurriedly, stamping down the earth, and then raking it to disguise the outline. I knew that it did not solve the main problem but it helped to have the feeling of doing something however futile and I continued to make absurdly small efforts to reduce the burden of guilt. It was that if only I could reduce the evidence to a reasonable size he would be more likely to forgive me, to understand.

As far as catering for the household is concerned I have conservative habits. The menu is always more or less predictable and I think he was happy with this state of affairs. When I began to change and serve up more stews and casseroles he did no more than raise his eyebrows, but when I started to make and serve soup before the meal he asked me if I was feeling alright. I have always hated onion soup and he probably suspected what he had continually dreaded, that I was pregnant.

I think I will have to explain it to you, as I will soon have to explain it to him, starting at the very beginning.

The morning was fine, the sky cloudless and I left the kitchen door ajar, so that as I worked I could glance from time to time across the garden and watch the birds coming and going. A single thrush was singing and this was the only sound to disturb my reflections, when I stopped work and prepared to make coffee.

The cottage is not isolated, it is part of a bustling little village not far from the coast but my neighbours have commitments which keep them absent until the early evening on most week-days. It was therefore with a sense of shock that I looked up from the table, and in the stillness of the morning, saw him standing in the half-open doorway, a slim figure in his early twenties. He was so completely the archetypal French youth that I stood and gaped at him. His heart-shaped face was swarthy and decorated with a jet black pencil line moustache. His eyes were dark and penetrating and his lips narrow and uncompromising. He wore a black and white striped jersey, black tapering trousers and a beret. I suppose he must have said to me

'Would you like to buy some onions mamselle?' but my brain refused to function and my reply when I heard it astonished me.

'Would you like a cup of coffee?' I said, indicating the coffee pot which I had just set down on the table.

'Yes, certainly mamselle,' he said

'That is very kind of you' and he slid into the chair opposite to me at the table. My hands shook as I poured out the coffee and milk and pushed the cup across to him.

'Do you mind if I smoke mamselle?' he asked, and I shook my head, quite unable to reply. In a few moments the bitter acrid smell of a Gaulois filled the kitchen and he was looking at me without speaking through a wreath of smoke. I struggled against a feeling of unreality: I am acting in a French film I thought, the kind I used to go to when I was a student. A young man arrives at the back door of a lonely farmhouse somewhere in Provence. The housewife invites him in, her husband is away on business. They talk together and then...

His voice broke in on my reflections as if he were well aware of their nature. Perhaps for him it was a familiar situation.

'Are you married?' he enquired politely, but although there was no trace of innuendo in his tone I blushed and stammered

'Yes, he usually comes in for coffee about this time,' and then I stopped short in what was quite obviously a transparent lie, there had only been one cup ready on the table.

'Your husband is a doctor possibly,' he said without interest.

'No...' I blurted out, and then stopped again feeling foolish. Men in my husband's profession do not return home to enjoy coffee with their wives.

'He's very late' I finished lamely. My companion regarded me gravely.

'Perhaps he will not come at all madame, and maybe it would be better if he did not.'

'Why?' I said as steadily as I could.

'Because I have drunk his coffee madame,' he replied and smiled at me encouragingly.

I wanted to turn my head and look through the inner door and the window opposite to see if there were any villagers lingering in the street but I dared not. His eyes might follow mine across the living room, past the stairs leading to the bedroom, and then if he looked at me enquiringly what would I do? Before I could pursue this speculation any further he rose from the table pushing his chair back with a harsh scraping sound:

This is it, I thought and closed my eyes, but nothing happened and when I opened them again he was stubbing out his cigarette in the sink. He turned and took a step towards me. I was completely at a loss.

'Do you live near here?' I asked quite absurdly, and he stopped surprised at the question.

'Why no madame,' he replied. ' I came across on the ferry for the day. My father has a little farm just across the water.' He was coming closer and I felt that this was the moment of crisis.

'How much are your onions?' I asked quickly as his hand reached across the table. He straightened up and made an obvious mental calculation. What was the highest price he could expect this silly woman to pay? He came to a conclusion.

'One-fifty a kilo,' he said at last.

'I'll take the lot,' I said desperately.

He looked at me with genuine surprise.

'But there are twenty kilos madame,' he protested.

'No matter,' I said 'I'll have them,' and I opened my purse. He came closer to collect the money and I began to shiver uncontrollably, but when I looked up he was counting it in his hand and moving away.

'Thank you madame,' he said. 'I can take the afternoon ferry back. Au revoir madame.'

As he went down the steps I closed the kitchen door and leaned on it, listening as I heard the rattle of his bicycle on the cobbles and his cheerful whistling as he rode away. The heap of string bags outside the door seemed mountainous and it was early afternoon before I had stowed them all away.

Most of them still remain hidden in the cupboard where my husband stores his tins of paint. There I hoped they could stay undetected until I had the chance to dispose of them a little at a time, but despite my best efforts to dissuade him my husband has decided that it is time to re-decorate the living room. Tomorrow he will open that cupboard to select his paint and there is nowhere else in this small cottage where I can conceal those piles of string bags. I will have to explain it all to him tonight.

Do you think he will understand?

The Fairy Godmother

by

Clarice Hackett

'And now two additional items.' The newscaster on the television said. 'Sir Francis Chawle, who is remembered for his controversial book on genetic engineering, died this morning.' He turned over a piece of paper and picked up another.

'A mystery women know to the staff of a big Midland Hospital as 'The Fairy Godmother' handed in a paper bag full of bank notes at lunch time today. This now brings the total of her yearly donations to £30,000. She usually arrives in a taxi and is heavily veiled. No one has any idea who she is, or why she brings the money...'

'That was interesting wasn't it James?' Anne reached out and switched off the television. Poor man she could see he was dreadfully bored. Doctors always made the worst patients. She had been a nursing Sister before she gave up her career to marry James, too late in life for them to have a family unfortunately, but regardless of this they were very happy.

'You knew Francis Chawle quite well didn't you?'

'We qualified together,' he answered. 'But I've had nothing to do with him for years. For one thing I didn't agree with his views.'

'Tell me what you mean.' She was determined to keep the conversation going.

'He was as fanatical as Hitler about breeding a perfect race,' James answered.

'I couldn't accept his obsession, especially in view of the fact he was so ugly and mis-shapen himself.

'Perhaps that was the very reason for it,' she replied.

'Maybe you're right,' James pondered for a while.

'I must admit he was very clever, that huge head of his housed a magnificent brain. Some people said he was a genius. We shared a great appreciation of music.'

'He never married did he?'

'No, he longed to have a wife and family but even plain girls passed him by, not so much because of his looks but because he was so dogmatic about his peculiar ideas.'

180

James shuffled in his chair in an effort to ease his leg in its plaster cast into a more comfortable position.

'With a bit of luck you'll be able to have that off next week,' comforted Anne.

'And in a couple of months you'll be able to play, golf again.

'Bones take longer to knit as one gets older,' James observed.

'But at least it makes me realise how lucky I've been. I've always been athletic and energetic, not like poor old Francis. Well he's gone now, God rest his soul.'

'I wonder who will get all his money,' Anne mused. 'He hasn't any family to leave it to has he?'

'It's very funny you should mention a family. I'll tell you something which I've never divulged to anyone before, and if I hadn't heard a few minutes ago that Francis was dead I very much doubt if I should be telling you now.'

'Don't tell me he had a lurid past after all.'

'Not lurid really, but very unusual. There was a girl and a child. I have a distinct feeling that the woman who has been taking the money to that children's' hospital all these years is the girl who Francis Chawle knew.'

He gazed pensively into the fire as though lost in thought.

'Is it a long story,' asked Anne, her curiosity aroused.

'Let me get you a large whisky to keep you going. I don't want any interesting bits left out.' He smiled as she went to fix the drinks. He was lucky, not many men came across a woman like Anne, especially old batchelor doctors. How good she was for him, she brought him so much comfort.

'Now tell me,' she ordered, handing him his glass.

'It's hard to know where to begin,' he said

'I shall leave out everything except the most relevant details, there will be plenty of time to fill those in later.'

He took a sip from his drink and began hesitantly as though searching for the words.

'I've told you how much Francis loved music,' he said

'I must also tell you that he had an aunt who had a great interest in singers, especially those who were training to be opera singers. She'd been one herself, not a well known one, but she'd married a man with a lot of money.'

'How lucky for her,' remarked Anne.

James ignored the interruption, by now he was getting into his stride.

'She gave lots of parties,' he went on. 'She loved to have young people and artistes around her, and it was at one of these parties that Francis and I met a most beautiful girl with a remarkable voice. It had a wonderful quality. Someone described it as being like honey poured through silk.'

'How very poetical,' Anne said.

'She would have made a poet out of anyone,' he said defensively and his tone confirmed to Anne that the remark had been his own.

'Her name was Melina, which actually means a canary, it was very apt. She came from somewhere in rural Worcestershire and she was completely unspoilt.'

'I bet you all fell in love with her,' his wife remarked.

'Of course we did, and old Francis was completely bowled over. Melina enjoyed her success with men, and because she was such a complete innocent at first, it was inevitable that she got carried away by all the attention. To my knowledge she had several romantic affairs.'

James gazed into the flames completely lost in his thoughts. He was remembering how she'd teased him, calling him Rufus because of his colouring. She said he reminded her of a pet fox cub her young brother had at home. Anne touched his hand.

'Tell me more about her, what happened to her then?'

'She was living on a shoestring, she only had a small grant from a scholarship, but everyone expected that she would eventually have a brilliant career. However she failed to make the grade. She hadn't enough stamina and her voice couldn't sustain power over long periods.'

'How tragic for her, poor girl.' Anne was sympathetic.

'We couldn't help her either,' James said. My friends and I were only housemen then and hadn't much money. All except Francis who was wealthy anyway. I know he asked her to marry him but she refused. Then he had one of his brilliant ideas. He asked Melina to bear him a child. He said that with her beauty and gift of singing and his genius they could produce a near perfect specimen.'

'He sounds mad to me,' Anne said.

'Madness and genius are very close together. She consented to accept a large sum of money and hand the baby over to his father when he was born. He sent her to live in a cottage he'd bought somewhere in Warwickshire and pretended he was her brother, while she wore a ring and said she was a widow. He could hardly wait for his son to be born.'

'And was it a beautiful gifted boy?'

'Unfortunately it was a girl, and spina bifida too. Francis was horrified and refused to have anything to do with her. He gave Melina the cottage and a good allowance for their expenses. I saw a lot of the baby as he was in hospital more than she was out. Melina really loved her and devoted her life to her, but the child died when it was about six years old.'

'Francis must have continued paying the money after the little girl had died.' Anne astutely put the pieces of the puzzle together. 'Now Melina denotes it to the hospital which looked after her.'

'Exactly, and he always paid it in old bank notes so that there would be no trace through his bank account. He didn't want his secret to come out.'

'Poor Melina, I wonder where she is now?'

'This may surprise you, she came out of hiding after her daughter died, changed her name and took up her singing career again. Although her voice wasn't strong enough for opera it was perfect for the microphone. She sings romantic ballads and is often on the radio.'

James broke off abruptly, and Anne went to refill his glass. For a few minutes while she was away from his side he allowed himself the brief luxury of remembering his first wild sweet love affair, just before Melina's life had changed so completely when she accepted Francis Chawle's offer. Something had nagged at the back of his mind for years. Both Melina and Francis had very dark hair and olive complexions. The baby had bright red hair, the colour of a fox cub's coat.

He smiled at Anne as she came back with their drinks. He'd be glad when he could get around again, sitting about made one morbid.

Todays Magic

by

Norton Cross

Lucy turned and looked wistfully at the Wrekin. How she would love to climb it once more. A sudden anger overcame her, damned Arthritis it spoiled all the fun, it wasn't only the pain and stiffness it was the terrible frustration. After all she felt quite well in herself, which made it all the worse. Her thoughts turned to her childhood, when she had climbed the Wrekin with her mother and grandfather. They had stopped at the half way house tea-rooms to order tea for when they returned. The view was breathtaking once one had reached the top. As a child she had thought it the roof of the world. On the return to the tea-rooms, the most scrumptious tea awaited them, fresh cream scones and strawberry jam followed by the most fanciest of cakes. Lucy turned away with tears in her eyes, partly tears of nostalgia, tears of anger and frustration, because she would never be able to climb the Wrekin again. Sadly she limped back to her car, getting her car key out of her pocket. She walked over to the bright blue car and put her key in the lock, for some reason the key wouldn't go in, she tried again still nothing.

'Excuse me madam but this happens to be my car' said an indignant voice. Lucy stood still with shock. She looked at the car and then to where the voice had come from. Suddenly she realised this wasn't her car, this was a foreign one and hers was a Ford.

'I'm so sorry' said Lucy apologetically 'I am trying to open the wrong car door.' She was getting flustered. She looked round to see where her car was, it was right behind this one, but it was almost the same shape and it certainly was the same colour.

'Oh, there's mine, I am so sorry, but I wasn't really paying attention' Lucy stumbled toward her car.

'I accept your apology, because I almost did the same thing.' the voice said with a smile

'Are you alright? Here let me do that for you' As Lucy was fumbling with her key. She turned round and had a good look at the voice, he was of medium height with darkish hair turning grey, his face was well sun-tanned with deep set eyes, which were looking at her a little puzzled.

184

'Er, thank you' Lucy said giving him the key to her car felling a little foolish.

'There you are' He said opening the car door and handing Lucy her key back. As Lucy was getting into the car awkwardly she cursed the Arthritis.

'Look I am driving to the hotel for coffee, would you join me? You look as if you need one. It is just a few yards down the road to the right. By the way my name is Ian Swain' he concluded holding out his hand.

'I would like a coffee, it is very nice of you to offer.' murmured Lucy still slightly flustered, my name is Lucy Foster.'

'Very well follow me' said Ian authoratively walking away.

Lucy sat in her car and pressed the starter, suddenly the enormity of the situation hit her, whatever would her daughter say? mind you she was always doing things that upset her daughter.

Lucy thought she would wait till he had pulled away and then she would drive off in the other direction. Yes, that's what she would do. At that moment Ian pipped his horn and waved as he drove off, she meekly followed him. What am I doing? thought Lucy nervously. Well a coffee in a busy hotel wouldn't matter, she thought, she could leave straight afterwards. They arrived at the hotel in a few minutes, Ian indicated the car park, which was oddly half empty so they could park side by side. So much for the busy hotel. The car door opened and Ian helped Lucy out of the car.

'Are you alright? queried Ian as Lucy struggled to get out.

'Oh, yes I always have this fight to get in and out,' she smiled, trying to hide the wretched pain in her leg. She locked the door and they walked to the hotel slowly.

The lounge was almost empty, Ian and Lucy sat down near the window with a view over beautiful gardens and on to the Wrekin beyond.

'What a lovely view' said Lucy nervously 'I wished my garden at home was like that' she sighed.

'I am afraid mine is sadly neglected' replied Ian. Just then a waitress came to take their order. Ian ordered coffee and cakes for them both.

'I love a garden, but mine is getting more impossible for me to keep up, so I tend to have small shrubs and conifers' Lucy volunteered, she felt as if she was talking to an old friend, which was ridiculous when she had just met this man. Ian looked around him feeling contented, the first time for a long while. He to felt it was ludicrous because he had only just met this woman. An awkward silence prevailed, broken by the waitress bringing their coffee and a plate of cakes.

'My they look delicious' laughed Ian relieved the silence had been broken.

185

'I hope you aren't on a diet? because I am sure these cakes will tempt you'

'I am on a diet but not the kind you mean. They certainly do look delicious' laughed Lucy. Ian handed her the plate of cakes, she chose a fresh cream eclair.

'Thank you' muttered Lucy taking a bite of eclair. Ian took a fresh cream strawberry tart. Once again silence reigned while they ate their cakes.

'Do you live near here?' asked Ian.

'No, no I live in Birmingham. I've brought my Mother down to stay with relatives. I am travelling back to-day, but I thought I would do some sight seeing.' said Lucy and went on drinking her coffee.

'I used to live near here when I was a child, so like you I am sight seeing before I go home.' reminisced Ian. 'I live alone, well it seems that way, I do have a son and daughter, my son is on an oil rig and my daughter is a secretary to an advertising agency. She is out more than in.'

'Yes I know what you mean. I have a married daughter and a son in the Military Band service and a daughter at home that teaches music,' sighed Lucy

'I always say our house is like a railway station.'

'You know that is a good description' laughed Ian putting his cup down. 'That was good. Would you like another coffee?'

'No thank you' rushed Lucy 'But do have one yourself, I am going to be reckless and have another cake.'

Ian called the waitress and asked for another coffee. Once more silence, each seemed deep in thought. The waitress brought the coffee and left.

'Er, the service is good here, don't you think?' stammered Ian trying to break the silence.

'Oh, yes, yes,' said Lucy who once more lapsed into silence. Ian tried once more.

'Are you travelling back to Birmingham now or are you having lunch first? startled Lucy didn't know what to say, she really hadn't planned anything.

'I don't know' she said vaguely 'I had made no plans as there is no one waiting for me, I just seem to drift.'

Ian looked thoughtfully at Lucy. She is like a lost sheep, he mused and so sad.

'I am driving back to Wolverhampton, perhaps you would like to follow and we could stop for lunch somewhere on the way.'

Lucy looked up, it had been so long since anyone had decided things for her, she smiled and said.

'That would be lovely' if only it could go for ever, no more drifting and no more decisions to make.

Once more the Wrekin had worked it's magic, just like it had all those years ago. Only then all she had wanted was a dog, which her grandfather had collected on the way home.

As they rose and left the coffee lounge Lucy found her leg wasn't as painful as usual after sitting so long. Ian paid the bill and they walked out to their cars they looked at each other as Ian took Lucy's key and opened the door for her.

'Drive carefully and I will see you for lunch.' Ian said feeling quite excited at the thought. Lucy sitting in her car smiled up at him.

'Thank you and drive carefully, I am afraid I usually go quite steady, so I hop I won't hold you up.'

'My dear we can crawl at 10mph and it won't matter, suddenly I feel as if we have all the time in the world.'

'I am not that slow and I don't think we would be very popular on the road if we did do you?' laughed Lucy light heartedly.

'See you later' with that Ian walked away feeling like a teenager again. Surely at 52 one didn't just fall in love at first sight or did one?. Lucy felt sure one did.

One in Seven

by

Stuart Roberts

The spacecraft, Triar, gently manoeuvered into its orbit around Mars. It had taken them three weeks longer than the mission profile had anticipated, due to problems with the new 'Pack-Horse' engine.

'Mars Base, this is Triar...come in!' demanded the radio operator of the console.

Almost at one a friendly voice replied;

'Hi, Triar, this is Mars Base Commander....what kept you folks?'

'Hey...come on this 'Pack Horse' engine gave us a few problems! But we are here now....and we do have that cream cake you wanted....'

'There are seven of us who are just dying to get at some cream cake, so if you don't mind we'll send you our Science pods. Ok?'

As soon as the Captain of the Triar had given them the go ahead, the two shuttles already attached to the Mars Bases Science pods, lifted off for the short flight from the Mars base up to the orbiting spacecraft.

As the first shuttle approached Triar, its pilot commented on the small size of the craft, which was due to the new, smaller 'Pack-Horse' engines. The second shuttle waited in orbit whilst the first shuttle docked with Triar. The pilot made use of the delay, by describing Triars elegant curves, to supplement the pictures that his colleagues in the bases control room were receiving from the small camera mounted on the shuttle. In the control room, everyone was crowded around the small screen that showed the picture of Triar, even though they knew they would be seeing it for themselves, shortly. Suddenly, the small screen, depicting Triar switched to an incandescent white glow....simultaneously, the reassuring chatter of the docked shuttle's pilot, became a mere background crackle. A split second later the shocked and shaky voice of the second shuttle's pilot, stammered a single word - 'Triar', before that radio link, too, became a background crackle.

A shocked silence descended on the control room, as everyone tried to come to terms with the fact that they were stranded on Mars, let alone the fact that they had insufficient air to last them the three months until another spacecraft could reach them from earth.

In a smart Board-Room, on Earth, a slightly overweight gentleman, dressed in an expensive suit, opened a bottle of Champagne to celebrate. Lifting his glass high in the air he announced;

'Gentlemen....to Triar and 'Pack-Horse'!'

'Triar and Pack-horse', responded everyone, jubilantly.

Meanwhile, a tense simulated normality had returned to the control room, as everyone grappled with the possibility that they might suffer the same fate as their colleagues. Suddenly the electronic door to the control-room opened and in charged Sam. Commander Riley looked up from his calculations and enquired;

'What is it, Sam?'

'Commander, I've been thinking....'

Sam went on to describe something that they had discovered whilst surveying a sector of the surface of Mars; namely a rock that gave breathable Oxygen when an electric current was passed through it. Unfortunately, this rock was found only in a very unstable area of the Martian surface and the team had lost all of their robot miners investigating it.

'Listen to me!', urged Sam, 'If Alan took me there in the Rover Unit, I could go and get some of it and we could hold out until a rescue craft from Earth arrives.' Commander Riley cut him off, saying it would not work, but Sam would not be put off. Eventually Commander Riley relented, conceding that they did not have any viable alternative.

The drive from the Base to the sector where the rock had been discovered, seemed to take an eternity, but eventually they arrived. Sam, in a bulky spacesuit, the design of which had hardly changed since the early years of space exploration, left the air lock. Striding across the surface, he soon reached the edge of the hardened Lava flow.

'This is Sam....I am going onto the Lava flow now....let's just hope we don't get a Volcanic Eruption!' came the familiar voice in Alan's headset.

A few minutes later Sam found some rock and in reporting it, he uttered his last words. Without any warning the core of the planet erupted, digesting Sam completely. Simultaneously, several tremendous earthquakes, which were common due to the unstable surface, rocked the planet. With tears in his eyes, Alan chokingly reported what had happened to Sam, before turning the Rover vehicle around to head back.

'Rover to Base, are you receiving?', announced a small speaker on the control panel.

'Yes, sure are, Alan', replied a tired and emotionally drained voice, which only yesterday had been the same one which had greeted the Triar so warmly.

'Minor problem....that tremor caused a crack in the crust and I am having to divert.'

The Rover vehicle turned to travel parallel to the gaping chasm....little did the driver know that there was no crossing point within the vehicles range and he was destined to die.

The Hyperspace communication console leapt into life showing the haggard face of a Mission Controller, who had earlier jubilantly drank Champagne;

'We have sent 'Fraiz' - Triar's sister ship to pick you five up' (the controllers did no yet know, due to the time delay inherent in hyperspace communication, of the latest two deaths), 'however, you will need to survive for a few months. One of our scientists, who has been working on Suspended Animation has designed something that might work....It's only been tried on rats and caused mild traumatism afterwards. If your rock idea fails we suggest you build it, because it is the only hope we can offer you! Sorry we can't do any more....the circuit diagrams will follow this message....'

The screen went blank before becoming a blur of diagrams and information. A wry smile broke out on the lips of the three sad faces surrounding the console;

'Mild traumatism!', they exclaimed almost together.

A short while later the three men gathered in the Control Room. Commander Riley cursed loudly as he realised that their limited materials would only allow them to build two units, before announcing himself as the person who must sacrifice the chance of life. The issue was not raised again as they all constructed the life-giving circuits. Upon finishing, they surveyed the units. As usual, 'Doc' summed up their thoughts by saying;

'They don't look much do they? I think we deserve a coffee after that!'

As the three sat sipping the hot drink, Commander Riley felt a sluggishness rapidly taking over his body. Suddenly realisation hit him, lurching forward he tried to grab Doc, but his limbs would not respond and he succeeded only in falling flat on his face next to Mike.

Doc stood in the control room, over the two bodies and laughed-he could not believe it had been so easy! Dragging them away to the corner of the room, he inserted the feed-drips and the oxygen lines. Then with a last glance at the still bodies of his two colleagues, he took a sleeping tablet.

'Don't worry, mate, you'll be alright....', came a dim voice from a swirling gloom.

Gradually his eyes focused....his limbs felt like lead and he had a pounding headache-but he was alive! However, the voice continued....

'It looks like you are the only one who survived....your Commander's unit failed and Lieutenant Poblitz died in his cabin-looks like he killed himself.'

Mike's brain swirled, but he suddenly realised who Poblitz was - 'Doc'! Intense anger surged through him as he remembered the dirty trick that Doc had played; then almost as quickly, he only had admiration for his colleague's courage in forsaking the chance of life.

'Anyhow....', the voice (which belonged to a young bearded man who was peering at Mike), continued,

'We bought you the cream cake that you wanted....'

Mike had an intense desire to be sick, yet somehow he managed to stammer;

'No cream cake for me....'

The Cost of Living

by

Debbie Rawlings

God he hated wine bars, full of their artificial furniture and artificial people, he looked around at all the black plastic and shiny crome, not a bit of wood in the place. Some hooray Henry was at the bar telling his friends about the hilarious happenings in the world of merchant banking. He sipped his glass of wine, the barmen had assured him that it was very nice, it wasn't bad but not as good as a pint of best bitter. He shifted uncomfortable in his seat, he wasn't happy in a suit he hadn't worn one since his wedding to Laura, Laura was the reason he was here today.

'Get yourself a job'. she said.

'How am I supposed to feed and clothe our children with no money coming in', she said the hundredth time.

And then as if by magic that letter arrived inviting him for an interview for a job as a computer operator for a company called Data Electronic Visual Information Limited. The interview was to take place the following night at seven thirty at the Flamingo wine bar. He'd never heard of the company and didn't remember writing to them for an interview, but as Laura said you can't look a gift horse in the mouth that was why he was sitting in a posy wine bar waiting for some stranger to come and listen to his past career and then tell him thanks but no thanks, he was so lost in his own self pity that he failed to notice the young lady standing in front of him.

'Mr Stevenson', she said.

He looked up to find himself staring into the most hypnotic blue eyes he had ever seen, she was blonde, tall and about twenty five he guessed and very beautiful.

'So glad you could make it at short notice', she said holding out her hand.

'No problem I need a job', then remembering the outstretched hand shook it.

She sat opposite him placing her briefcase on the floor, he suddenly realised he'd been staring at her and felt embarrassed.

'Can I get you anything to drink', hoping the low lighting had concealed his blushes.

192

'A white wine please' she reached into her handbag and brought out a packet of cigarettes,

'You don't mind if I smoke do say if you do I will not mind', she smiled

'No you go right ahead I'll go and get your drink', Lady with that smile you can do whatever you like, he thought as he pushed his way to the bar. he managed to get served quite quickly and away from the clutches of a rather amorous young woman who had had too much to drink.

'Thank you', she said taking the glass from him as she did their fingers touched, she was ice cold the last time he had touched anyone that cold was years ago when he went to visit his grandmother and had found her dead. But this person was alive, she must have bad circulation he thought, he then realised he didn't know her name.

'Please forgive me', she said 'I have not given you my name, it's Natas Fielding now Mr Stevenson you will no doubt want to know more about the company'.

'Please call me Jim', he liked her, should he mention that he was married, some women found that a challenge.

'Ok Jim basically we deal in computers video equipment, high security systems'.

She reached down to retrieve her briefcase from the floor.

'May I ask a question', he said wondering if she had any sandwiches in her case as he hadn't eaten anything since dinnertime.

'Please ask away and I will try and answer all your questions', she said smiling sweetly.

'It's your name it's rather unusual is it foreign?'.

'You could say that'.

'Well your not from around here', he said pressing 'Where were you born'.

'I was born at a place called Sedah, now Mr Stevenson can we get back to the business in hand, 'in other words my private life stays private.'

'As I said we deal with high security equipment installing them in banks, government buildings, we've just installed one in the Whitehouse', She said proudly.

'The Whitehouse, where the President lives', he could see himself now on Miami beach, surfboard under his arm surrounded by bikini clad women.

'Of course you would not be working in America, you would be employed to run our main branch', she said as if reading his thoughts.

'What would be my main line of work in your company', he enquired.

'Basically training new recruits , making sure that they are of the highest standard possible, now let's see of you are qualified', she paused to take a sip from her full glass of wine, he looked down to see that his previously empty glass was full, strange he didn't remember the waiter coming over with fresh drinks his mind must be going.

'Now you full name is James David Stevenson, do correct me if I get anything wrong you were born on the twenty seventh of September Nineteen Sixty Two at Wakefield Maternity Hospital, you were six pound three ounces born your mother was being treated on ward nine, ah yes you were born at seventeen ten on the afternoon'.

She paused long enough to make sure what she had said had registered, by the look on his face it had, she continued.

'Your mothers maiden name was Harris your father was a coalminer until he died, after his death you then had your mother put in a home for the elderly and is still there even though you never visited her', she paused again, yes she still had his attention.

'You're married to Laura who you only married because you thought you'd got her pregnant which turned out to be a false alarm you did become the proud father of two children, although they aren't yours. You have had several affairs with several different women including you sister in law and numerous baby-sitters'.

'How do you know all this', he said stunned.

'We are very thorough Jim we have to be there's a lot at stake we can't afford to take any chances, and I think you'll be perfect'.

'You mean I've got the job'.

'Subject to conditions of course'.

'Conditions, what conditions'.

'Every job has a price to be paid Jim',

She was talking but he wasn't listening he didn't remember leaving the wine bar and going to this strange place and why had it suddenly become very warm and where had the windows gone to, strange he thought if you read her name backwards it spelt Satan, but what did it matter at least he'd got a job, as he said to Laura as he was leaving. For a job he'd sell his soul to the Devil.

194

Sing For Your Daddy

By

Patricia Flannery

Looking out of the train's murky window a small round girl marvelled as the new land sped by. Their journey would have been an adventure had the eight old Anna not discerned her mammy's growing anxiety. Sure that would soon pass when reunited with the daddy, life would be made good again.

Last night on the boat from Belfast, buried, with the baby of the family under her brothers coats, Anna resented older siblings having the run of the ship while she was expected to sleep. Sleep, on hard, lumpy chairs on a boat forever rocking and in public too! Sleep was what she did not get, as the child roughly lurched by reeling seas watched her mammy's furrowed brow. Why so tense? Why worry? After all, the seven were making this journey of journeys in order to join the daddy and make new life in England. Anna could not wait, all would be conventional now, they would lead a predictable existence. The family together, just like everybody else... ' happy ever after'. The bullying of her boisterous brothers would be curbed as would their growing malevolence, her surly elder sister, daddy's 'wee pet' would laugh once more, even the baby would quit squealing... perhaps.

New Street Station, a murky, noisy, rumbustious bastion of confusion. Where was everyone rushing to, the child wondered? Never ever so many people in one place and all in such well matched hurry, the whole world must traverse through here in a day! What a thought for a wee small child tired, hungry and now perturbed by so much activity. Anna's mammy was agitated too, how she *grabbed at the fretful child, how she grumbled to the self conscious boys. When they caught the first glimpse of daddy everything would be fine, all their troubles over, Anna was convinced. For now though, the present, one fretful woman with six unruly children and way too much luggage to be manageable.

Birmingham, Anna did not stop to consider why there was no daddy there to meet them but accepted, as small children do the course of events, three bothersome brothers, one sulking sister and one smelly, very wet baby. She knew that when they reached their destination the daddy would be there with nice things to eat, a roaring fire and comforting words for mammy. The shy girl would sing for him, he was always wanting her to but wasn't she just too timorous back home! Now she knew that she would have the courage.

'Mammy I want a pee pee,' she announced. *Smack*

'You should have gone when I told you to,' her mother retorted looking lost and lonely as the small child felt. How come? Big people can not feel as insignificant as wee ones... can they? Misgivings were beginning to set in and it still daylight, when daddy appears it will be all ok. Anna comforted herself.

Into a gargantuan black cab they piled, things could only get better. 'I want my daddy' Anna wailed, tired she was and hungry too with a sore belly from suppressing the urge to wee. Oh no, they could not fit all into one cab, would she ever see the big brothers again? Things did not get better, she had lost her best dolly now. Giving way to her tears, she was swallowed whole into the formidable coal-black cavernous cab.

The city flashed by in a haze of tears and recriminations, multitudinous twists and turns, Salford Bridge minus Spaghetti Junction, more twists, further turns, then ... their house containing a daddy and who knows what other delights! She could not wait! But first, a shameful scene that the child would never forget, her mammy's horror at exorbitant taxi fares, plus, adding insult to injury 6d for each and every item of luggage and God knows, they had plenty! How the child felt for her poor distraught mammy. This might be the end of the world but daddy would be there. Very soon they should all be clasped in his mighty arms and enveloped by uproarious laughter.

Anna beheld the family's new house, it's white stucco walls, an enchanting garden with delightful winding path leading to a shimmering green door, surely the loveliest she had ever seen. She sensed everyones tension ease now they had reached journey's end. What a relief that uncertainty was a thing of the past, she could run into her daddy's arms wallowing in their surety (after she had visited the toilet that was).

Picture the child's horror and confusion when no familiar face answered their knocking, how they hammered at that still door while a distraught mother searched frantically for a key. Flustered, nervous, agitated children fought as the woman's patience finally broke. It was Sunday after all, why was there no answer from within? Bad enough that she traversed alone with six squealing brats and mountains of luggage... to struggle thus far only to find the silent house empty was too much to bear. Where the hell could her thoughtless husband be?

Inside the miserable hoard piled.

'Where's my daddy? Why's there no things in this house? Mammy I've wet my pants.', Anna lamented. No answer ... Stunned silence from all as they surveyed inapposite emptiness. The only sign of habitation was a miserable kitchen chair while upstairs lay a scruffy mattress bearing a letter from Ireland. Not a kettle, tea pot or cup as a sign of human existence, Anna's shattered dreams were worsened by the defeated, haunted look on the face of her poor mammy. She would recall this as the first time she had witnessed her mother cry, acerbic, woeful tears, oh how the child wished she could cuddle her better like she did back home. Oh, to be back home, daddy or no daddy.

It was a disconcerted, disillusioned woman who ushered those truculent, travel weary children out of the desolate house in search of a meal. Anna fretted about the absence of her poor father, what illness or malediction had befallen him? He was she knew, aware of the date and time of their arrival, she had seen the letter in her mother's hand. Panic set in, it was a long, weary walk to the greasy cafe where indigestion along with another unexpected bill awaited the sorry woman. Oh why had they left their home and family for this ... a missing husband and an empty house in this Sunday town?

The next priority was to search this godless place for that man. Anna saw that the baby had dropped into a deep slumber and how she wished to be carried too, cocooned from this harsh reality. Her brothers, aggressive now, spitefully taunted her while laughing at her tears.'Just you wait 'till my daddy hears about this, (She flung at their sneering faces). After much weary plodding, the elder sister stopped the bunch in their tracks. Laughter bellowed forth from a gloomy bar ... a cessation of movement as they took in the fetid aroma and the intimidating public house noises. Anna was aware of glares from colossal, ruddy men who moved incongruously about the murky doorway, she could not believe that inside stepped her brave mother and did not want to believe when that same mother returned moments later with an undeniably broken dream ... the sodden, unrecognisable excuse for a father. Oh the heartache and the bitter disappointment to discover him thus, after all the family had suffered together on that sorrowful day. The child's worries seemed absurd, now, embarrassing even as she surveyed the pathetic figure of a drunken adult tottering forth. This was not the way Anna had expected to be reunited with the man she had dreamed of, cried for, longed to stay beside. During those moments, his glory diminished along with the other titans and Anna knew that never ever would she sing for her daddy. How she longed to go back home.

In High Esteem

By

Emily Beard

Prayers were over at the Central girls school and the partition had been drawn separating the fifth form from the other classes.

'Who's going to read the lesson,' Miss Rowley said. A murmur went round the room 'Edna Cooper' Miss Rowley levelled her gaze in Ednas direction as if to say 'Well then' and Edna in reply took her shabby black bible out of her desk and flicked through it's gold edged pages. Then with it opened at the appropriate page, she stood out in the gangway.

'The first book of Corinthians and the thirteenth chapter,' she said in a soft clear voice.

If was her party piece and she had it word perfect. The message could, it seemed, have been all her own: so sincere did she sound. When she was halfway through the passage there was a slight disturbance: the door of the partition was pushed gingerly open and Florie Dean a habitual late comer crept in. Edna carried on reading, as if nothing had happened and the rest of the class continued to give her their undivided attention.

'Faith, hope and charity,' she wound up, 'these three but the greatest of these is charity.' Her words hung in the air as she closed the Bible and sat down.

The silence that followed was broken by a heavy thud. Florie Dean had fallen flat on her back, where she had been standing, alongside the end column of desks. The whole class stood up and would have closed in but Miss Rowley restrained them with an outward sweep of her hand; as she came down from her desk. For a few tense moments, Florie Deans fragile body shook vigourously from head to foot and her eyes rolled rapidly from side to side. Immediately consciousness returned so did Miss Rowleys presence of mind.

'Will someone get a coat,' she said. No offers were forthcoming. Florie Dean was the last person with whom any of them wanted to have contact.

It was common knowledge that whenever the District nurse came round for hair inspection: she was given a note to take home.

'I'll get mine,' Edna said at length and dashed off to the cloakroom. Miss Rowley folded the blue nap coat over to form a pillow, and told Edna to hold up Florie Deans head, while she slipped it under. Then she told her to fetch a

198

drink of water. At first Florie seemed reluctant to drink from the cold metal cup but after a while she leaned forward and gulped at the water. Then she sat still in the back row as Miss Rowley suggested.

In the playground at breaktime a group of classmates gathered round Edna discussing what had happened.

'I couldn't have done that,' one of them said, and a number of others chimed in 'nor me'.

Edna saw no reason for such a fuss.

She was the only daughter of a lay preacher and lived in a atmosphere which radiated nothing bur goodwill. On this occasion however, her behaviour was not entirely exemplary. When the end of the morning session came round there was the usual rush to be out of the building. By the time Edna had weaved her way through to the outside door Lucy Dawson, her best friend, was waiting with skipping rope poised.

'Race you', she said and they covered the stretch of main road to the fork none stop. Edna turned right along the short dirt road. She kept her eyes averted as she rounded the corner. Her mother would, she was well aware be in the shop and she was anxious to steer clear of any hindrance.

When she opened the kitchen door, Dinky her Jack Russel terrier, came fussing around her but she had no time for him; so he retired to his basket and looked on mournfully at what she was doing. First of all she spread her coat out onto the tiled floor. Then she went feverishly rummaging through the cupboards. When she had sorted out the necessary equipment: she tackled the task in hand.

The disinfectant gave off a nice healthy smell as it desolved in the hot water. With a stiff scrubbing brush dampened from time to time in it, she attacked the coat. When every inch had been cleased inside and out she shook it out and pegged it on the outside clothes line to dry in the fresh breeze.

Then she turned her attention to less important matters. The exertion had whipped up a good appetite. She hastily consumed the prepared meal and totally unaware of the hurt she had caused Dinky she fed him some scraps and returned the affection he was eager to lavish. Then finally put on her coat and with head held high sailed forth ready for the afternoon session.

School Boy

by

Edward Johnsen

He sat perfectly still, stunned by the brutality of this sudden interruption to his inner world of thoughts and dreams.

As an infant he had always felt a similar kind of shock when, lost in imagination he fell over. He would lie face down, briefly silent in the heat of confusion, before moments later lifting his red, contorted face and dissolving into screams and tears of hurt and rage.

Again the bedroom door shuddered under the now heavier and more deliberate blows of Mr Steven's knuckles.

'It's time to get up Richard. Are you awake?'

The seventeen year old paused, fearful of betraying the anger and exasperation surging through him. After all how could his father, of all people, have any inkling or understanding of what he had to do this day? He closed his eyes in concentration and assumed a forced calmness.

'It's alright Dad, I'm already up. I'll be through in a minute.' He listened as his father responded with a tired sigh. Floorboards groaned under his heavy tread as he headed back to the kitchen.

Richard Stevens stood up and tensely drew in a couple of slow, deep breaths. Of course he was up, hadn't he been up and dressed for over an hour? He had woken up as alert and as alive as the cat he had watched, minutes later, hunting a shrew on the dew-soaked lawn. For most of that hour he had sat by the window, gazing upon the first gentle beginnings of what looked like being another brilliant June day. But how utterly had the easy composure of that summer dawn failed to enter a young mind turned in upon it's own fears and doubts and longings.

'In one-and-a-half hours I'll have done it. For better or for worse I'll have bloody well done it.' He spoke quietly, and with a nervousness that made it seem as though he was frightened by the words that came out. Thrusting his watch with it's frayed and broken strap back into his trouser pocket, he looked uneasily into the mirror once more before pulling on his blazer and stalking out of the room.

When he left the house about half an hour later, he found the country morning awaiting him in all her radiant loveliness, eager to share her joy. With swift ease her sensuality made sure of his attention, no longer could he remain untouched by the freshness of her sights and sounds and smells; butterflies dancing on Mrs Burbage's fragrant lilac bushes; twittering finches skipping across the hawthorn hedges; the rich greenness of distant woods. Keenly he felt their beauty, and it pained him. Each manifestation of nature's full-blooded wholeness was to him another taunt which only served to alienate him from her.

'Morning Richard. You're a bit early today aren't you? But what a gorgeous day to be out!' Folding his ticket he acknowledged the truth of the station master's observations and looked around the waiting-room. Two neighbours were sitting under the window, relaxed and cheerfully chatting. It was unreal, their's was not his world, not today, he felt trapped and on edge. Escaping through the open door onto the platform he moved from the cool shadow cast by the ticket office to stand in the sun. He squinted into the distance. Perhaps the train would be late, it often was, and then he'd have to forget the whole thing and hurry through town to get to school on time. Perhaps she wouldn't even be there anyway. Torn between impatience and dread, he was aware of a tight and queasy sensation in his stomach. The blue and yellow diesel slid slowly into view from behind the trees.

He sat at the rear of the train and now he had found his place he was able to relax slightly. Inside this familiar, grimy carriage the development of proceedings required no effort on his part. He watched the adjacent track dashing by in a blur as they picked up speed. A window seat was always his preference, he was more interested in what he could see outside and anyway, it was embarrassing if someone sat facing him and there was no where else to look. That was what had happened that evening when, on the train home, she had herself sat opposite him. Within minutes he'd found his eyes fixed on her, and before he knew it she was looking straight back at him. Confused, he'd stared at the floor for the rest of the journey. Occasionally it happened again over the following weeks, sometimes as she got on at the next station, or as they queued with their tickets at the other end. They never talked, he knew almost nothing about her, but week by week she became an increasingly frequent inhabitant of his mind.

She got on as usual at the next stop. He felt hot as he watched her glancing into the carriage looking for her college friends, her blonde hair shining in the sun. Her eyes skimmed straight across him, she moved down the platform and then smiled as she recognised faces in the next compartment. The doors slammed, the train squealed, jerked and moved off.

He realised he was going to go through with it and he panicked. Suddenly all
the little flirtations, all the insubstantial suggestions of mutual attraction were
nothing. She had never betrayed any feelings, never given the slightest encour-
agement or hint of interest. In the last few weeks she hadn't even noticed him.
The train bent round the hill and the sun hit him full in the face. Sweat began
to dampen his shirt. His mind raced with doubt and hope. Could he really just
have imagined it all?

He was one of the last to leave the station and as he stepped into the street he
concentrated on a group about fifty yards ahead. She was the one on the right
hand side wearing the tight jeans and a white shirt. The blue padded jacket
under her arm was the same one that had helped him recognise her the only
time he'd seen her in a different situation: an afternoon last winter when she'd
ridden a lively-looking horse past him during one of his long reflective walks.
That was nearly six months ago.

It was the custom of the foursome to split at the traffic lights, everyone but
her turning right while she continued straight on to a newsagents in the square.
This then was the moment of truth: if she went on alone as usual he would go
through with it; but if she turned right with the rest, as she did on occasion,
then it would all be over.

She crossed straight over at the lights and headed towards the square.

The newsagents did good business at this time in the morning so he had to
wait outside for a few minutes. He peered timorously through the glass, frantically working over the words he would use. Now, having paid for her sandwiches, she was turning towards the door. He felt sick.

As she came out her face wore a blank expression. Her blue eyes glanced
quickly up at him and then, looking past him, she began to march away briskly.
He moved towards her. His voice felt shaky.

'Er hi.'

She continued along the street. He had to catch up and walk beside her.

'I was just er, just wondering if you were doing anything at lunchtime today.'

Had she heard him? She was still looking straight ahead, but her expression
was hardening into a frown. He didn't know what to do. Then her eyes nar-
rowed. Suddenly she looked impatient and severe. She stopped. Her voice was
scornful.

'I don't go out with school boys.'

Richard Stevens stood perfectly still. She strutted away down the street and
disappeared around a corner, but he remained rooted to the spot. For the second
time that morning he was stunned.

Tightly clutching his bag he started to walk hurriedly towards the school, his gait stiff and mechanical, his eyes staring ahead but seeing nothing around him. After tripping and staggering into an indignant traffic warden, he crossed over to the display window of the second-hand bookshop. His red and flustered face gazed back at him from the reflection. As he ran his eyes cursorily over the rows of ageing hard-backs his posture gradually relaxed. His face began to resume it's normal colour. When he looked above his own reflection he could see the bright clouds easing their way across the tranquil summer sky behind him. After a minute or so he turned to walk slowly down the side street, and noticing a stone, he kicked it with gusto along the pavement. As it clattered into the gutter a smile flickered across his face. After all, it was still such a beautiful day. And now he was free.